PERSUASION

TALLY HALL PRESS CLASSICS

PERSUASION

Jane Austen

TALLY HALL PRESS

Ann Arbor 1997

Published by Tally Hall Press, an imprint of Borders, Inc.
311 Maynard, Ann Arbor, MI 48104
All rights reserved.

Tally Hall Press and the lamp-post colophon
are trademarks of Borders Properties, Inc.

ISBN 0-681-22057-0

10 9 8 7 6 5 4 3 2 1

Printed and bound in the United States of America

PERSUASION

1

SIR WALTER ELLIOT, of Kellynch Hall, in Somersetshire, was a man who, for his own amusement, never took up any book but the Baronetage; there he found occupation for an idle hour, and consolation in a distressed one; there his faculties were roused into admiration and respect by contemplating the limited remnant of the earliest patents; there any unwelcome sensations arising from domestic affairs changed naturally into pity and contempt as he turned over the almost endless creations of the last century; and there, if every other leaf were powerless, he could read his own history with an interest which never failed. This was the page at which the favourite volume always opened:—

ELLIOT OF KELLYNCH HALL

Walter Elliot, born March 1, 1760, married July 15, 1784, Elizabeth, daughter of James Stevenson, Esq., of South Park, in the county of Gloucester; by which lady (who died 1800) he has issue, Elizabeth, born June 1, 1785; Anne, born August 9, 1787; a still-born son, November 5, 1789; Mary, born November 20, 1791.

Precisely such had the paragraph originally stood from the printer's hands; but Sir Walter had improved it by adding, for the information of himself and his family, these words, after the date of Mary's birth:—"Married, December 16, 1810, Charles, son and heir of Charles Musgrove, Esq., of Uppercross, in the county of Somerset," and by inserting most accurately the day of the month on which he had lost his wife.

Then followed the history and rise of the ancient and respectable family in the usual terms; how it had been first settled in Cheshire, how mentioned in Dugdale, serving the office of high sheriff, representing a borough in three successive parliaments, exertions of loyalty, and dignity of baronet, in the first year of Charles II with all the Marys and Elizabeths they had married; forming altogether two handsome quarto pages, and concluding with the arms and motto:—"Principal seat, Kellynch Hall, in the county of Somerset," and Sir Walter's handwriting again in this finale:—

Heir presumptive, William Walter Elliot, Esq., great-grandson of the second Sir Walter.

Vanity was the beginning and end of Sir Walter Elliot's character: vanity of person and of situation. He had been remarkably handsome in his youth, and at fifty-four was still a very fine man. Few women could think more of their personal appearance than he did, nor could the valet of any new-made lord be more delighted with the place he held in society. He considered the blessing of beauty as inferior only to the blessing of a baronetcy; and the Sir Walter Elliot, who united these gifts, was the constant object of his warmest respect and devotion.

His good looks and his rank had one fair claim on his attachment, since to them he must have owed a wife of very superior character to anything deserved by his own. Lady Elliot had been an excellent woman, sensible and amiable, whose judgment and conduct, if they might be pardoned the youthful infatuation which made her Lady Elliot, had never required indulgence afterwards. She had humoured, or softened, or concealed his failings, and promoted his real respectability for seventeen years; and though not the very happiest being in the world herself, had found enough in her duties, her friends, and her children, to attach her to life, and make it no matter of indifference to her when she was called on to quit them. Three girls, the two eldest sixteen and fourteen, was an awful legacy for a mother to bequeath, an awful charge rather, to confide to the authority and guidance of a conceited, silly father. She had, however, one very intimate friend, a sensible, deserving woman, who had been brought, by strong attachment to herself, to settle close by her, in the village of Kellynch; and on her kindness and advice Lady Elliot mainly relied for the best help and maintenance of the good principles and instruction which she had been anxiously giving her daughters.

This friend and Sir Walter did *not* marry, whatever might have been anticipated on that head by their acquaintance. Thirteen years had passed away since Lady Elliot's death, and they were still near neighbours and intimate friends, and one remained a widower, the other a widow.

That Lady Russell, of steady age and character, and extremely well provided for, should have no thought of a second marriage, needs no apology to the public, which is rather apt to be unreasonably discontented when a woman *does* marry again, than when she does *not;* but Sir Walter's continuing in singleness requires explanation. Be it known, then, that Sir Walter, like a good father (having met with one or two private disappointments in very unreasonable applications), prided himself on remaining single for his dear daughter's sake. For one daughter, his eldest, he would really have given up anything, which he had not been very much tempted to do. Elizabeth had succeeded at sixteen to all that was possible of her mother's rights and consequence; and being very handsome, and very like himself, her influence had always been great, and they had gone on together most happily. His two other children were of very inferior value. Mary had acquired a little artificial importance by becoming Mrs. Charles Musgrove; but Anne, with an elegance of mind and sweetness of character, which must have placed her high with any people of real understanding, was nobody with either father or sister; her word had no weight, her convenience was always to give way—she was only Anne.

To Lady Russell, indeed, she was a most dear and highly valued goddaughter, favourite, and friend. Lady Russell loved them all, but it was only in Anne that she could fancy the mother to revive again.

A few years before Anne Elliot had been a very pretty girl, but her bloom had vanished early; and as, even in its height, her father had found little to admire in her (so totally different were her delicate features and mild dark eyes from his own), there could be nothing in them, now that she was faded and thin, to excite his esteem. He had never indulged much hope, he had now none, of ever reading her name in any other page of his favourite work. All equality of alliance must rest with Elizabeth, for Mary had merely connected herself with an old country family of respectability and large

fortune, and had, therefore, *given* all the honour and received none: Elizabeth would, one day or other, marry suit-
ably.

It sometimes happens that a woman is handsomer at
twenty-nine than she was ten years before; and, generally
speaking, if there has been neither ill-health nor anxiety, it
is a time of life at which scarcely any charm is lost. It was so
with Elizabeth, still the same handsome Miss Elliot that she
had begun to be thirteen years ago, and Sir Walter might
be excused, therefore, in forgetting her age, or, at least, be
deemed only half a fool, for thinking himself and Elizabeth
as blooming as ever, amidst the wreck of the good looks of
everybody else; for he could plainly see how old all the rest
of his family and acquaintance were growing. Anne haggard,
Mary coarse, every face in the neighbourhood worsting, and
the rapid increase of the crow's foot about Lady Russell's
temples had long been a distress to him.

Elizabeth did not quite equal her father in personal con-
tentment. Thirteen years had seen her mistress of Kellynch
Hall, presiding and directing with a self-possession and decision which could never have given the idea of her being
younger than she was. For thirteen years had she been doing
the honours, and laying down the domestic law at home,
and leading the way to the chaise and four, and walking
immediately after Lady Russell out of all the drawing-rooms
and dining-rooms in the country. Thirteen winters' revolving frosts had seen her opening every ball of credit which
a scanty neighbourhood afforded, and thirteen springs
shown their blossoms, as she travelled up to London with
her father, for a few weeks' annual enjoyment of the great
world. She had the remembrance of all this, she had the
consciousness of being nine-and-twenty to give her some
regrets and some apprehensions; she was fully satisfied of

being still quite as handsome as ever, but she felt her approach to the years of danger, and would have rejoiced to be certain of being properly solicited by baronet-blood within the next twelvemonth or two. Then might she again take up the book of books with as much enjoyment as in her early youth, but now she liked it not. Always to be presented with the date of her own birth and see no marriage follow but that of a youngest sister, made the book an evil; and more than once, when her father had left it open on the table near her, had she closed it, with averted eyes, and pushed it away.

She had had a disappointment, moreover, which that book and especially the history of her own family, must ever present the remembrance of. The heir presumptive, the very William Walter Elliot, Esq., whose rights had been so generally supported by her father, had disappointed her.

She had, while a very young girl, as soon as she had known him to be, in the event of her having no brother, the future baronet, meant to marry him, and her father had always meant that she should. He had not been known to them as a boy; but soon after Lady Elliot's death, Sir Walter had sought the acquaintance, and though his overtures had not been met with any warmth, he had persevered in seeking it, making allowance for the modest drawing-back of youth; and, in one of their spring excursions to London, when Elizabeth was in her first bloom, Mr. Elliot had been forced into the introduction.

He was at that time a very young man, just engaged in the study of the law; and Elizabeth found him extremely agreeable, and every plan in his favour was confirmed. He was invited to Kellynch Hall; he was talked of and expected all the rest of the year; but he never came. The following spring he was seen again in town, found equally agreeable, again encouraged, invited, and expected, and again he did not come; and the next tidings were that he was married. Instead of pushing his fortune in the line marked out for the heir of the house of Elliot, he had purchased independence by uniting himself to a rich woman of inferior birth.

Sir Walter had resented it. As the head of the house, he felt that he ought to have been consulted, especially after taking the young man so publicly by the hand; "For they must have been seen together," he observed, "once at Tattersalls, and twice in the lobby of the House of Commons." His disapprobation was expressed, but apparently very little regarded. Mr. Elliot had attempted no apology, and shown himself as unsolicitous of being longer noticed by the family, as Sir Walter considered him unworthy of it: all acquaintance between them had ceased.

This very awkward history of Mr. Elliot was still, after an interval of several years, felt with anger by Elizabeth, who had liked the man for himself, and still more for being her father's heir, and whose strong family pride could see only in *him* a proper match for Sir Walter Elliot's eldest daughter. There was not a baronet from A to Z whom her feelings could have so willingly acknowledged as an equal. Yet so miserably had he conducted himself, that though she was at this present time (the summer of 1814) wearing black ribbons for his wife, she could not admit him to be worth thinking of again. The disgrace of his first marriage might, perhaps, as there was no reason to suppose it perpetuated by offspring, have been got over, had he not done worse; but he had, as by the accustomary intervention of kind friends they had been informed, spoken most disrespectfully of them all, most slightingly and contemptuously of the very blood he belonged to, and the honours which were hereafter to be his own. This could not be pardoned.

Such were Elizabeth Elliot's sentiments and sensations; such the cares to alloy, the agitations to vary, the sameness and the elegance, the prosperity and the nothingness of her scene of life; such the feelings to give interest to a long, uneventful residence in one country circle, to fill the vacancies which there were no habits of utility abroad, no talents or accomplishments for home, to occupy.

But now, another occupation and solicitude of mind was beginning to be added to these. Her father was growing distressed for money. She knew, that when he now took up the Baronetage, it was to drive the heavy bills of his tradespeople, and the unwelcome hints of Mr. Shepherd, his agent, from his thoughts. The Kellynch property was good, but not equal to Sir Walter's apprehension of the state required in its possessor. While Lady Elliot lived, there had been method, moderation, and economy, which had just kept him within his income; but with her had died all such rightmindedness, and from that period he had been constantly exceeding it. It had not been possible for him to spend less: he had done nothing but what Sir Walter Elliot was imperiously called on to do; but blameless as he was, he was not only growing dreadfully in debt, but was hearing of it so often, that it became vain to attempt concealing it longer, even partially, from his daughter. He had given her some hints of it the last spring in town; he had gone so far even as to say, "Can we retrench? Does it occur to you that there is any one article in which we can retrench?" and Elizabeth, to do her justice, had, in the first ardour of female alarm, set seriously to think what could be done, and had finally proposed these two branches of economy, to cut off some unnecessary charities, and to refrain from new furnishing the drawing-room; to which expedients she afterwards added the happy thought of their taking no present down to Anne, as had been the usual yearly custom. But these measures, however good in themselves, were insufficient for the real extent of the evil, the whole of which Sir Walter found himself obliged to confess to her soon afterwards. Elizabeth had nothing to propose of deeper efficacy. She felt herself ill-used and unfortunate, as did her father; and they were neither of them able to devise any means of lessening their expenses without compromising their dignity, or relinquishing their comforts in a way not to be borne.

There was only a small part of his estate that Sir Walter could dispose of, but had every acre been alienable, it would have made no difference. He had condescended to mortgage as far as he had the power, but he would never condescend to sell. No; he would never disgrace his name so far. The Kellynch estate should be transmitted whole and entire, as he had received it.

Their two confidential friends, Mr. Shepherd who lived in the neighbouring market town, and Lady Russell, were called on to advise them; and both father and daughter seemed to expect that something should be struck out by one or the other to remove their embarrassments and reduce their expenditure, without involving the loss of any indulgence of taste or pride.

2

MR. SHEPHERD, a civil, cautious lawyer, who, whatever might
be his hold or his views on Sir Walter, would rather have
the *disagreeable* prompted by anybody else, excused himself
from offering the slightest hint, and only begged leave to
recommend an implicit reference to the excellent judgment
of Lady Russell, from whose known good sense he fully
expected to have just such resolute measures advised as he
meant to see finally adopted.

Lady Russell was most anxiously zealous on the subject,
and gave it much serious consideration. She was a woman
rather of sound than of quick abilities, whose difficulties in
coming to any decision in this instance were great, from the
opposition of two leading principles. She was of strict in-
tegrity herself, with a delicate sense of honour; but she was
as desirous of saving Sir Walter's feelings, as solicitous for
the credit of the family, as aristocratic in her ideas of what
was due to them, as anybody of sense and honesty could
well be. She was a benevolent, charitable, good woman, and

capable of strong attachments, most correct in her conduct, strict in her notions of decorum, and with manners that were held a standard of good-breeding. She had a cultivated mind, and was, generally speaking, rational and consistent; but she had prejudices on the side of ancestry; she had a value for rank and consequence, which blinded her a little to the faults of those who possessed them. Herself the widow of only a knight, she gave the dignity of a baronet all its due: and Sir Walter, independent of his claims as an old acquaintance, an attentive neighbour, an obliging land-lord, the husband of her very dear friend, the father of Anne and her sisters, was, as being Sir Walter in her apprehension, entitled to a great deal of compassion and consideration under his present difficulties.

They must retrench; that did not admit of a doubt. But she was very anxious to have it done with the least possible pain to him and Elizabeth. She drew up plans of economy, she made exact calculations, and she did what nobody else thought of doing: she consulted Anne, who never seemed considered by the others as having any interest in the question. She consulted, and in a degree was influenced by her in marking out the scheme of retrenchment which was at last submitted to Sir Walter. Every emendation of Anne's had been on the side of honesty against importance. She wanted more vigorous measures, a more complete refor-mation, a quicker release from debt, a much higher tone of indifference for everything but justice and equity.

"If we can persuade your father to all this," said Lady Russell, looking over her paper, "much may be done. If he will adopt these regulations, in seven years he will be clear; and I hope we may be able to convince him and Elizabeth that Kellynch Hall has a respectability in itself which cannot be affected by these reductions; and that the true dignity of

Sir Walter Elliot will be very far from lessened in the eyes of sensible people, by his acting like a man of principle. What will he be doing, in fact, but what very many of our first families have done, or ought to do? There will be nothing singular in his case; and it is singularity which often makes the worst part of our suffering, as it always does of our conduct. I have great hope of our prevailing. We must be serious and decided; for after all, the person who has contracted debts must pay them; and though a great deal is due to the feelings of the gentleman, and the head of a house, like your father, there is still more due to the character of an honest man."

This was the principle on which Anne wanted her father to be proceeding, his friends to be urging him. She considered it as an act of indispensable duty to clear away the claims of creditors with all the expedition which the most comprehensive retrenchments could secure, and saw no dignity in anything short of it. She wanted it to be prescribed and felt as a duty. She rated Lady Russell's influence highly; and as to the severe degree of self-denial which her own conscience prompted, she believed there might be little more difficulty in persuading them to a complete, than to half a reformation. Her knowledge of her father and Elizabeth inclined her to think that the sacrifice of one pair of horses would be hardly less painful than of both, and so on, through the whole list of Lady Russell's too gentle reductions.

How Anne's more rigid requisitions might have been taken is of little consequence. Lady Russell's had no success at all: could not be put up with, were not to be borne. "What! every comfort of life knocked off! Journeys, London, servants, horses, table—contractions and restrictions everywhere! To live no longer with the decencies even of a private gentleman! No, he would sooner quit Kellynch Hall at once, than remain in it on such disgraceful terms."

"Quit Kellynch Hall!" The hint was immediately taken up by Mr. Shepherd, whose interest was involved in the reality of Sir Walter's retrenching, and who was perfectly persuaded that nothing would be done without a change of abode. "Since the idea had been started in the very quarter which ought to dictate, he had no scruple," he said, "in confessing his judgment to be entirely on that side. It did not appear to him that Sir Walter could materially alter his style of living in a house which had such a character of hospitality and ancient dignity to support. In any other place Sir Walter might judge for himself; and would be looked up to, as regulating the modes of life in whatever way he might choose to model his household."

Sir Walter would quit Kellynch Hall; and after a very few days more of doubt and indecision, the great question of whither he should go was settled, and the first outline of this important change made out.

There had been three alternatives, London, Bath, or another house in the country. All Anne's wishes had been for the latter. A small house in their own neighbourhood, where they might still have Lady Russell's society, still be near Mary, and still have the pleasure of sometimes seeing the lawns and groves of Kellynch, was the object of her ambition. But the usual fate of Anne attended her, in having something very opposite from her inclination fixed on. She disliked Bath, and did not think it agreed with her; and Bath was to be her home.

Sir Walter had at first thought more of London; but Mr. Shepherd felt that he could not be trusted in London, and had been skilful enough to dissuade him from it, and make Bath preferred. It was a much safer place for a gentleman in his predicament: he might there be important at comparatively little expense. Two material advantages of Bath over London had of course been given all their weight: its more convenient distance from Kellynch, only fifty miles, and Lady Russell's spending some part of every winter there; and to the very great satisfaction of Lady Russell, whose first views on the projected change had been for Bath, Sir Walter and Elizabeth were induced to believe that they should lose neither consequence nor enjoyment by settling there.

Lady Russell felt obliged to oppose her dear Anne's known wishes. It would be too much to expect Sir Walter to descend into a small house in his own neighbourhood. Anne herself would have found the mortifications of it more than she foresaw, and to Sir Walter's feelings they must have been dreadful. And with regard to Anne's dislike of Bath, she considered it as a prejudice and mistake arising, first from the circumstance of her having been three years at school there, after her mother's death; and secondly, from her happening to be not in perfectly good spirits the only winter which she had afterwards spent there with herself.

Lady Russell was fond of Bath, in short, and disposed to think it must suit them all; and as to her young friend's health, by passing all the warm months with her at Kellynch Lodge, every danger would be avoided; and it was, in fact, a change which must do both health and spirits good. Anne had been too little from home, too little seen. Her spirits were not high. A larger society would improve them. She wanted her to be more known.

The undesirableness of any other house in the same neighbourhood for Sir Walter was certainly much strengthened by one part, and a very material part of the scheme, which had been happily engrafted on the beginning. He was not only to quit his home, but to see it in the hands of others: a trial of fortitude which stronger heads than Sir Walter's have found too much. Kellynch Hall was to be let. This, however, was a profound secret, not to be breathed beyond their own circle.

Sir Walter could not have borne the degradation of being known to design letting his house. Mr. Shepherd had once mentioned the word "advertise," but never dared approach it again. Sir Walter spurned the idea of its being offered in any manner; forbade the slightest hint being dropped of his having such an intention; and it was only on the supposition of his being spontaneously solicited by some most unexceptionable applicant, on his own terms, and as a great favour, that he would let it at all.

How quick come the reasons for approving what we like! Lady Russell had another excellent one at hand, for being extremely glad that Sir Walter and his family were to remove from the country. Elizabeth had been lately forming an intimacy, which she wished to see interrupted. It was with a daughter of Mr. Shepherd, who had returned, after an unprosperous marriage, to her father's house, with the additional burden of two children. She was a clever young woman, who understood the art of pleasing—the art of pleasing, at least, at Kellynch Hall; who had made herself so acceptable to Miss Elliot, as to have been already staying there more than once, in spite of all that Lady Russell, who thought it a friendship quite out of place, could hint of caution and reserve.

Lady Russell, indeed, had scarcely any influence with Elizabeth, and seemed to love her, rather because she would love her, than because Elizabeth deserved it. She had never received from her more than outward attention, nothing beyond the observances of complaisance; had never suc-

ceeded in any point which she wanted to carry, against previous inclination. She had been repeatedly very earnest in
trying to get Anne included in the visit to London, sensibly
open to all the injustice and all the discredit of the selfish
arrangements which shut her out, and on many lesser occasions had endeavoured to give Elizabeth the advantage
of her own better judgment and experience; but always in
vain: Elizabeth would go her own way; and never had she
pursued it in more decided opposition to Lady Russell than
in this selection of Mrs. Clay; turning from the society of so
deserving a sister, to bestow her affection and confidence
on one who ought to have been nothing to her but the
object of distant civility.

From situation, Mrs. Clay was, in Lady Russell's estimate,
a very unequal, and in her character, she believed, a very
dangerous companion; and a removal that would leave Mrs.
Clay behind, and bring a choice of more suitable intimates
within Miss Elliot's reach, was therefore an object of first-
rate importance.

3

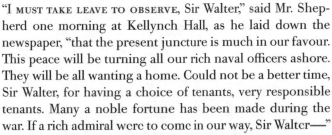

"I MUST TAKE LEAVE TO OBSERVE, Sir Walter," said Mr. Shepherd one morning at Kellynch Hall, as he laid down the newspaper, "that the present juncture is much in our favour. This peace will be turning all our rich naval officers ashore. They will be all wanting a home. Could not be a better time, Sir Walter, for having a choice of tenants, very responsible tenants. Many a noble fortune has been made during the war. If a rich admiral were to come in our way, Sir Walter—"

"He would be a very lucky man, Shepherd," replied Sir Walter; "that's all I have to remark. A prize, indeed, would Kellynch Hall be to him; rather the greatest prize of all, let him have taken ever so many before; hey, Shepherd?"

Mr. Shepherd laughed, as he knew he must, at this wit, and then added:

"I presume to observe, Sir Walter, that, in the way of business, gentlemen of the navy are well to deal with. I have had a little knowledge of their methods of doing business; and I am free to confess that they have very liberal notions, and are as likely to make desirable tenants as any set of people one should meet with. Therefore, Sir Walter, what I would take leave to suggest is, that if in consequence of any rumours getting abroad of your intention; which must be contemplated as a possible thing, because we know how difficult it is to keep the actions and designs of one part of the world from the notice and curiosity of the other; consequence has its tax; I, John Shepherd, might conceal any family-matters that I chose, for nobody would think it worth their while to observe me; but Sir Walter Elliot has eyes upon him which it may be very difficult to elude; and, therefore, thus much I venture upon, that it will not greatly surprise me if, with all our caution, some rumour of the truth should get abroad; in the supposition of which, as I was going to observe, since applications will unquestionably follow, I should think any from our wealthy naval commanders particularly worth attending to; and beg leave to add, that two hours will bring me over at any time, to save you the trouble of replying."

Sir Walter only nodded. But soon afterwards, rising and pacing the room, he observed sarcastically:

"There are few among the gentlemen of the navy, I imagine, who would not be surprised to find themselves in a house of this description."

"They would look around them, no doubt, and bless their good fortune," said Mrs. Clay, for Mrs. Clay was present: her father had driven her over, nothing being of so much use to Mrs. Clay's health as a drive to Kellynch: "but I quite agree with my father in thinking a sailor might be a very desirable tenant. I have known a good deal of the profession; and besides their liberality, they are so neat and careful in all their ways! These valuable pictures of yours, Sir Walter, if you choose to leave them, would be perfectly safe. Everything in and about the house would be taken such excellent care of! The gardens and shrubberies would be kept in almost as high order as they are now. You need not be afraid, Miss Elliot, of your own sweet flower gardens being neglected."

"As to all that," rejoined Sir Walter coolly, "supposing I were induced to let my house, I have by no means made up my mind as to the privileges to be annexed to it. I am not particularly disposed to favour a tenant. The park would be open to him of course, and few navy officers, or men of any other description, can have had such a range; but what restrictions I might impose on the use of the pleasure-grounds is another thing. I am not fond of the idea of my shrubberies being always approachable; and I should recommend Miss Elliot to be on her guard with respect to her flower garden. I am very little disposed to grant a tenant of Kellynch Hall any extraordinary favour, I assure you, be he sailor or soldier."

After a short pause, Mr. Shepherd presumed to say:

"In all these cases there are established usages which make everything plain and easy between landlord and tenant. Your interest, Sir Walter, is in pretty safe hands. Depend upon me for taking care that no tenant has more than his just rights. I venture to hint, that Sir Walter Elliot cannot be half so jealous for his own, as John Shepherd will be for him."

Here Anne spoke:

"The navy, I think, who have done so much for us, have at least an equal claim with any other set of men, for all the comforts and all the privileges which any home can give. Sailors work hard enough for their comforts, we must all allow."

"Very true, very true. What Miss Anne says is very true,"

was Mr. Shepherd's rejoinder, and "Oh! certainly," was his daughter's; but Sir Walter's remark was, soon afterwards:

"The profession has its utility, but I should be sorry to see any friend of mine belonging to it."

"Indeed!" was the reply, and with a look of surprise.

"Yes; it is in two points offensive to me; I have two strong grounds of objection to it. First, as being the means of bringing persons of obscure birth into undue distinction, and raising men to honours which their fathers and grandfathers never dreamt of; and, secondly, as it cuts up a man's youth and vigour most horribly; a sailor grows old sooner than any other man. I have observed it all my life. A man is in greater danger in the navy of being insulted by the rise of one whose father his father might have disdained to speak to, and of becoming prematurely an object of disgust himself, than in any other line. One day last spring, in town, I was in company with two men, striking instances of what I am talking of: Lord St. Ives, whose father we all know to have been a country curate, without bread to eat: I was to give place to Lord St. Ives, and a certain Admiral Baldwin, the most deplorable-looking personage you can imagine; his face the colour of mahogany, rough and rugged to the last degree; all lines and wrinkles, nine grey hairs of a side, and nothing but a dab of powder at top. 'In the name of heaven, who is that old fellow?' said I to a friend of mine who was standing near (Sir Basil Morley). 'Old fellow!' cried Sir Basil, 'it is Admiral Baldwin. What do you take his age to be?' 'Sixty,' said I, 'or perhaps sixty-two.' 'Forty,' replied Sir Basil, 'forty, and no more.' Picture to yourselves my amazement: I shall not easily forget Admiral Baldwin. I never saw quite so wretched an example of what a sea-faring life can do; but to a degree. I know it is the same with them all: they are all knocked about, and exposed to every climate, and every weather, till they are not fit to be seen. It is a pity they are not knocked on the head at once, before they reach Admiral Baldwin's age."

"Nay, Sir Walter," cried Mrs. Clay, "this is being severe indeed. Have a little mercy on the poor men. We are not all born to be handsome. The sea is no beautifier, certainly; sailors do grow old betimes; I have often observed it; they soon lose the look of youth. But then, is not it the same with many other professions, perhaps most others? Soldiers, in active service, are not at all better off; and even in the quieter professions, there is a toil and a labour of the mind, if not of the body, which seldom leaves a man's looks to the natural effect of time. The lawyer plods, quite care-worn: the physician is up at all hours, and travelling in all weather; and even the clergyman—" she stopped a moment to consider what might do for the clergyman—"and even the clergyman, you know, is obliged to go into infected rooms, and expose his health and looks to all the injury of a poisonous atmosphere. In fact, as I have long been convinced, though every profession is necessary and honourable in its turn, it is only the lot of those who are not obliged to follow any, who can live in a regular way, in the country, choosing their own hours, following their own pursuits, and living on their own property, without the torment of trying for more; it is only *their* lot, I say, to hold the blessings of health and a good appearance to the utmost: I know no other set of men but what lose something of their personableness when they cease to be quite young."

It seemed as if Mr. Shepherd, in his anxiety to bespeak Sir Walter's good will towards a naval officer as tenant, had been gifted with foresight; for the very first application for the house was from an Admiral Croft, with whom he shortly afterwards fell into company in attending the quarter sessions at Taunton; and, indeed, he had received a hint of the Admiral from a London correspondent. By the report which he hastened over to Kellynch to make, Admiral Croft was a native of Somersetshire, who having acquired a very handsome fortune, was wishing to settle in his own country, and had come down to Taunton in order to look at some advertised places in that immediate neighbourhood, which, however, had not suited him; that accidentally hearing—(it was just as he had foretold, Mr. Shepherd observed, Sir Walter's concerns could not be kept a secret)—accidentally hearing of the possibility of Kellynch Hall being to let, and understanding his (Mr. Shepherd's) connection with the owner, he had introduced himself to him in order to make particular inquiries, and had in the course of a pretty long conference, expressed as strong an inclination for the place as a man who knew it only by description could feel; and given Mr. Shepherd, in his explicit account of himself, every proof of his being a most responsible, eligible tenant.

"And who is Admiral Croft?" was Sir Walter's cold, suspicious inquiry.

Mr. Shepherd answered for his being of a gentleman's family, and mentioned a place; and Anne, after the little pause which followed, added:

"He is rear-admiral of the white. He was in the Trafalgar action, and has been in the East Indies since; he has been stationed there, I believe, several years."

"Then I take it for granted," observed Sir Walter, "that his face is about as orange as the cuffs and capes of my livery."

Mr. Shepherd hastened to assure him, that Admiral Croft was a very hale, hearty, well-looking man, a little weather-beaten, to be sure, but not much, and quite the gentleman in all his notions and behaviour; not likely to make the smallest difficulty about terms, only wanted a comfortable home, and to get into it as soon as possible; knew he must pay for his convenience; knew what rent a ready-furnished house of that consequence might fetch; should not have been surprised if Sir Walter had asked more; had inquired about the manor; would be glad of the deputation certainly, but made no great point of it; said he sometimes took out a gun but never killed; quite the gentleman.

Mr. Shepherd was eloquent on the subject, pointing out all the circumstances of the Admiral's family, which made him peculiarly desirable as a tenant. He was a married man, and without children; the very state to be wished for. A house was never taken good care of, Mr. Shepherd observed, without a lady: he did not know whether furniture might not be in danger of suffering as much where there was no lady, as where there were many children. A lady without a family was the very best preserver of furniture in the world. He had seen Mrs. Croft too; she was at Taunton with the Admiral, and had been present almost all the time they were talking the matter over.

"And a very well-spoken, genteel, shrewd lady, she seemed to be," continued he; "asked more questions about the house, and terms, and taxes, than the Admiral himself, and seemed more conversant with business; and moreover, Sir Walter, I found she was not quite unconnected in this country, any more than her husband; that is to say, she is sister to a gentleman who did live amongst us once; she told me so herself; sister to the gentleman who lived a few years back at Monkford. Bless me! what was his name? At this moment I cannot recollect his name, though I have heard it so lately. Penelope, my dear, can you help me to the name of the gentleman who lived at Monkford: Mrs. Croft's brother?"

But Mrs. Clay was talking so eagerly with Miss Elliot that she did not hear the appeal.

"I have no conception whom you can mean, Shepherd; I remember no gentleman resident at Monkford since the time of old Governor Trent."

"Bless me! how very odd! I shall forget my own name soon, I suppose. A name that I am so very well acquainted with; knew the gentleman so well by sight; seen him a hundred times; came to consult me once, I remember, about a trespass of one of his neighbours; farmer's man breaking into his orchard; wall torn down; apples stolen; caught in the fact; and afterwards, contrary to my judgment, submitted to an amicable compromise. Very odd, indeed!"

After waiting another moment:

"You mean Mr. Wentworth, I suppose?" said Anne.

Mr. Shepherd was all gratitude.

"Wentworth was the very name! Mr. Wentworth was the very man. He had the curacy of Monkford, you know, Sir Walter, some time back, for two or three years. Came there about the year —5, I take it. You remember him, I am sure."

"Wentworth? Oh ay! Mr. Wentworth, the curate of Monkford. You misled me by the term *gentleman*. I thought you were speaking of some man of property: Mr. Wentworth was nobody, I remember; quite unconnected; nothing to do with the Strafford family. One wonders how the names of many of our nobility become so common."

As Mr. Shepherd perceived that this connection of the Crofts did them no service with Sir Walter, he mentioned it no more; returning, with all his zeal, to dwell on the circumstances more indisputably in their favour; their age, and number, and fortune; the high idea they had formed of Kellynch Hall, and extreme solicitude for the advantage of renting it; making it appear as if they ranked nothing beyond the happiness of being the tenants of Sir Walter Elliot: an extraordinary taste, certainly, could they have been sup-

fearlessness of mind, operated very differently on her. She saw in it but an aggravation of the evil. It only added a dangerous character to himself. He was brilliant, he was headstrong. Lady Russell had little taste for wit, and of anything approaching to imprudence a horror. She deprecated the connection in every light.

Such opposition as these feelings produced was more than Anne could combat. Young and gentle as she was, it might yet have been possible to withstand her father's ill-will, though unsoftened by one kind word or look on the part of her sister; but Lady Russell, whom she had always loved and relied on, could not, with such steadiness of opinion, and such tenderness of manner, be continually advising her in vain. She was persuaded to believe the engagement a wrong thing: indiscreet, improper, hardly capable of success, and not deserving it. But it was not a merely selfish caution under which she acted, in putting an end to it. Had she not imagined herself consulting his good, even more than her own, she could hardly have given him up. The belief of being prudent and self-denying, principally for *his* advantage, was her chief consolation under the misery of a parting, a final parting; and every consolation was required, for she had to encounter all the additional pain of opinions, on his side, totally unconvinced and unbending, and of his feeling himself ill-used by so forced a relinquishment. He had left the country in consequence.

A few months had seen the beginning and the end of their acquaintance; but not with a few months ended Anne's share of suffering from it. Her attachment and regrets had, for a long time, clouded every enjoyment of youth, and an early loss of bloom and spirits had been their lasting effect.

More than seven years were gone since this little history

posed in the secret of Sir Walter's estimate of the dues of a tenant.

It succeeded, however; and though Sir Walter must ever look with an evil eye on any one intending to inhabit that house, and think them infinitely too well off in being permitted to rent it on the highest terms, he was talked into allowing Mr. Shepherd to proceed in the treaty, and authorizing him to wait on Admiral Croft, who still remained at Taunton, and fix a day for the house being seen.

Sir Walter was not very wise; but still he had experience enough of the world to feel, that a more unobjectionable tenant, in all essentials, than Admiral Croft bid fair to be, could hardly offer. So far went his understanding; and his vanity supplied a little additional soothing, in the Admiral's situation in life, which was just high enough, and not too high. "I have let my house to Admiral Croft," would sound extremely well; very much better than to any mere *Mr.* —; a *Mr.* (save, perhaps, some half dozen in the nation) always needs a note of explanation. An admiral speaks his own consequence, and, at the same time, can never make a baronet look small. In all their dealings and intercourse, Sir Walter Elliot must ever have the precedence.

Nothing could be done without a reference to Elizabeth: but her inclination was growing so strong for a removal, that she was happy to have it fixed and expedited by a tenant at hand; and not a word to suspend decision was uttered by her.

Mr. Shepherd was completely empowered to act; and no sooner had such an end been reached, than Anne, who had been a most attentive listener to the whole, left the room, to seek the comfort of cool air for her flushed cheeks; and as she walked along a favourite grove, said, with a gentle sigh, "A few months more, and *he*, perhaps, may be walking here."

4

HE WAS NOT MR. WENTWORTH, the former curate of Monkford, however suspicious appearances may be, but a Captain Frederick Wentworth, his brother, who being made commander in consequence of the action off St. Domingo, and not immediately employed, had come into Somersetshire, in the summer of 1806; and having no parent living, found a home for half a year at Monkford. He was, at that time, a remarkably fine young man, with a great deal of intelligence, spirit, and brilliancy; and Anne an extremely pretty girl, with gentleness, modesty, taste, and feeling. Half the sum of attraction, on either side, might have been enough, for he had nothing to do, and she had hardly anybody to love; but the encounter of such lavish recommendations could not fail. They were gradually acquainted, and when acquainted, rapidly and deeply in love. It would be difficult to say which had seen highest perfection in the other, or which had been the happiest: she, in receiving his declarations and proposals, or he in having them accepted.

A short period of exquisite felicity followed, and but a short one. Troubles soon arose. Sir Walter, on being applied to, without actually withholding his consent, or saying it should never be, gave it all the negative of great astonishment, great coldness, great silence, and a professed resolution of doing nothing for his daughter. He thought it a very degrading alliance; and Lady Russell, though with more tempered and pardonable pride, received it as a most unfortunate one.

Anne Elliot, with all her claims of birth, beauty and mind, to throw herself away at nineteen; involve herself, at nineteen, in an engagement with a young man who had nothing but himself to recommend him, and no hopes of attaining affluence, but in the chances of a most uncertain profession, and no connections to secure even his further rise in that profession, would be, indeed, a throwing away, which she grieved to think of! Anne Elliot, so young; known to so few, to be snatched off by a stranger without alliance or fortune; or rather sunk by him into a state of most wearing, anxious, youth-killing dependence! It must not be, if by any fair interference of friendship, any representations from one who had almost a mother's love and mother's rights, it could be prevented.

Captain Wentworth had no fortune. He had been lucky in his profession; but spending freely what had come freely, had realised nothing. But he was confident that he should soon be rich: full of life and ardour, he knew that he should soon have a ship, and soon be on a station that would lead to everything he wanted. He had always been lucky; he knew he should be so still. Such confidence, powerful in its own warmth, and bewitching in the wit which often expressed it, must have been enough for Anne; but Lady Russell saw it very differently. His sanguine temper, and

of sorrowful interest had reached its close; and time had softened down much, perhaps nearly all of peculiar attachment to him, but she had been too dependent on time alone; no aid had been given in change of place (except in one visit to Bath soon after the rupture), or in any novelty or enlargement of society. No one had ever come within the Kellynch circle, who could bear a comparison with Frederick Wentworth, as he stood in her memory. No second attachment, the only thoroughly natural, happy, and sufficient cure at her time of life, had been possible to the nice tone of her mind, the fastidiousness of her taste, in the small limits of the society around them. She had been solicited, when about two-and-twenty, to change her name by the young man who not long afterwards found a more willing mind in her younger sister: and Lady Russell had lamented her refusal: for Charles Musgrove was the eldest son of a man whose landed property and general importance were second in that country only to Sir Walter's, and of good character and appearance; and however Lady Russell might have asked yet for something more while Anne was nineteen, she would have rejoiced to see her at twenty-two so respectably removed from the partialities and injustice of her father's house, and settled so permanently near herself. But in this case Anne had left nothing for advice to do; and though Lady Russell, as satisfied as ever with her own discretion, never wished the past undone, she began now to have the anxiety which borders on hopelessness for Anne's being tempted, by some man of talents and independence, to enter a state for which she held her to be peculiarly fitted by her warm affections and domestic habits.

They knew not each other's opinion, either its constancy or its change, on the one leading point of Anne's conduct, for the subject was never alluded to; but Anne, at seven-and-twenty, thought very differently from what she had been made to think at nineteen. She did not blame Lady Russell, she did not blame herself for having been guided by her; but she felt that were any young person in similar circumstances to apply to her for counsel, they would never receive any of such certain immediate wretchedness, such uncertain future good. She was persuaded that under every disadvantage of disapprobation at home, and every anxiety attending his profession, all their probable fears, delays, and disappointments, she should yet have been a happier woman in maintaining the engagement, than she had been in the sacrifice of it; and this, she fully believed, had the usual share, had even more than a usual share of all such solicitudes and suspense been theirs, without reference to the actual results of their case, which, as it happened, would have bestowed earlier prosperity than could be reasonably calculated on. All his sanguine expectations, all his confidence, had been justified. His genius and ardour had seemed to foresee and to command his prosperous path. He had, very soon after their engagement ceased, got employ; and all that he had told her would follow had taken place. He had distinguished himself, and early gained the other step in rank, and must now, by successive captures, have made a handsome fortune. She had only navy lists and newspapers for her authority, but she could not doubt his being rich; and, in favour of his constancy, she had no reason to believe him married.

How eloquent could Anne Elliot have been! how eloquent, at least, were her wishes on the side of early warm attachment, and a cheerful confidence in futurity, against that over-anxious caution which seems to insult exertion and distrust Providence! She had been forced into prudence in her youth, she learned romance as she grew older: the natural sequel of an unnatural beginning.

With all these circumstances, recollections, and feelings, she could not hear that Captain Wentworth's sister was likely to live at Kellynch without a revival of former pain; and many a stroll, and many a sigh, were necessary to dispel the agitation of the idea. She often told herself it was folly, before she could harden her nerves sufficiently to feel the continual discussion of the Crofts and their business no evil. She was assisted, however, by that perfect indifference and apparent unconsciousness, among the only three of her own friends in the secret of the past, which seemed almost to deny any recollection of it. She could do justice to the superiority of Lady Russell's motives in this, over those of her father and Elizabeth; she could honour all the better feelings of her calmness; but the general air of oblivion among them was highly important from whatever it sprung; and in the event of Admiral Croft's really taking Kellynch Hall, she rejoiced anew over the conviction which had always been most grateful to her, of the past being known to those three only among her connections, by whom no syllable, she believed, would ever be whispered, and in the trust that among his, the brother only with whom he had been residing had received any information of their short-lived engagement. That brother had been long removed from the country, and being a sensible man, and, moreover, a single man at the time, she had a fond dependence on no human creature's having heard of it from him.

The sister, Mrs. Croft, had then been out of England, accompanying her husband on a foreign station, and her own sister, Mary, had been at school while it all occurred;

and never admitted by the pride of some, and the delicacy of others, to the smallest knowledge of it afterwards.

With these supports, she hoped that the acquaintance between herself and the Crofts, which, with Lady Russell still resident in Kellynch, and Mary fixed only three miles off, must be anticipated, need not involve any particular awkwardness.

5

ON THE MORNING APPOINTED for Admiral and Mrs. Croft's seeing Kellynch Hall, Anne found it most natural to take her almost daily walk to Lady Russell's, and keep out of the way till all was over; when she found it most natural to be sorry that she had missed the opportunity of seeing them.

This meeting of the two parties proved highly satisfactory, and decided the whole business at once. Each lady was previously well disposed for an agreement, and saw nothing, therefore, but good manners in the other; and with regard to the gentlemen, there was such a hearty good humour, such an open, trusting liberality on the Admiral's side, as could not but influence Sir Walter, who had besides been flattered into his very best and most polished behaviour by Mr. Shepherd's assurances of his being known, by report, to the Admiral, as a model of good breeding.

The house, and grounds, and furniture, were approved, the Crofts were approved, terms, time, everything, and everybody, was right; and Mr. Shepherd's clerks were set to work, without there having been a single preliminary difference to modify of all that "This indenture showeth."

Sir Walter without hesitation, declared the Admiral to be the best-looking sailor he had ever met with, and went so far as to say, that if his own man might have had the arranging of his hair, he should not be ashamed of being seen with him anywhere; and the Admiral, with sympathetic cordiality, observed to his wife as they drove back through the park, "I thought we should soon come to a deal, my dear, in spite of what they told us at Taunton. The Baronet will never set the Thames on fire, but there seems no harm in him:" reciprocal compliments which would have been esteemed about equal.

The Crofts were to have possession at Michaelmas; and as Sir Walter proposed removing to Bath in the course of the preceding month, there was no time to be lost in making every dependent arrangement.

Lady Russell, convinced that Anne would not be allowed to be of any use, or any importance, in the choice of the house which they were going to secure, was very unwilling to have her hurried away so soon, and wanted to make it possible for her to stay behind till she might convey her to Bath herself after Christmas; but having engagements of her own which must take her from Kellynch for several weeks, she was unable to give the full invitation she wished, and Anne, though dreading the possible heats of September in all the white glare of Bath, and grieving to forego all the influence so sweet and so sad of the autumnal months in the country, did not think that, everything considered, she wished to remain. It would be most right, and most wise, and therefore must involve least suffering to go with the others.

Something occurred, however, to give her a different

duty. Mary, often a little unwell, and always thinking a great deal of her own complaints, and always in the habit of claiming Anne when anything was the matter, was indisposed; and foreseeing that she should not have a day's health all the autumn, entreated, or rather required her, for it was hardly entreaty, to come to Uppercross Cottage, and bear her company as long as she could want her, instead of going to Bath.

"I cannot possibly do without Anne," was Mary's reasoning; and Elizabeth's reply was, "Then I am sure Anne had better stay, for nobody will want her in Bath."

To be claimed as a good, though in an improper style, is at least better than being rejected as no good at all; and Anne, glad to be thought of some use, glad to have anything marked out as a duty, and certainly not sorry to have the scene of it in the country, and her own dear country, readily agreed to stay.

This invitation of Mary's removed all Lady Russell's difficulties, and it was consequently soon settled that Anne should not go to Bath till Lady Russell took her, and that all the intervening time should be divided between Uppercross Cottage and Kellynch Lodge.

So far all was perfectly right; but Lady Russell was almost startled by the wrong of one part of the Kellynch Hall plan, when it burst on her, which was, Mrs. Clay's being engaged to go to Bath with Sir Walter and Elizabeth, as a most important and valuable assistant to the latter in all the business before her. Lady Russell was extremely sorry that such a measure should have been resorted to at all, wondered, grieved, and feared; and the affront it contained to Anne, in Mrs. Clay's being of so much use, while Anne could be of none, was a very sore aggravation.

Anne herself was become hardened to such affronts, but

she felt the imprudence of the arrangement quite as keenly as Lady Russell. With a great deal of quiet observation, and a knowledge, which she often wished less, of her father's character, she was sensible that results the most serious to his family from the intimacy were more than possible. She did not imagine that her father had at present an idea of the kind. Mrs. Clay had freckles, and a projecting tooth, and a clumsy wrist, which he was continually making severe remarks upon her in absence, but she was young, and certainly altogether well-looking, and possessed, in an acute mind and assiduous pleasing manners, infinitely more dangerous attractions than any merely personal might have been. Anne was so impressed by the degree of their danger, that she could not excuse herself from trying to make it perceptible to her sister. She had little hope of success, but Elizabeth, who in the event of such a reverse would be so much more to be pitied than herself, should never, she thought, have reason to reproach her for giving no warning.

She spoke, and seemed only to offend. Elizabeth could not conceive how such an absurd suspicion should occur to her, and indignantly answered for each party's perfection, knowing their situation.

"Mrs. Clay," said she, warmly, "never forgets who she is; and as I am rather better acquainted with her sentiments than you can be, I can assure you, that upon the subject of marriage they are particularly nice, and that she reprobates all inequality of condition and rank more strongly than most people. And as to my father, I really should not have thought that he who has kept himself single so long for our sakes need be suspected now. If Mrs. Clay were a very beautiful woman, I grant you it might be wrong to have her so much with me; not that anything in the world, I am sure, would induce my father to make a degrading match, but he might be rendered unhappy. But poor Mrs. Clay, who with all her merits, can never have been reckoned tolerably pretty, I really think poor Mrs. Clay may be staying here in perfect safety. One would imagine you had never heard my father speak of her personal misfortunes, though I know you must fifty times. That tooth of hers and those freckles. Freckles do not disgust me so very much as they do him. I have known a face not materially disfigured by a few, but he abominates them. You must have heard him notice Mrs. Clay's freckles."

"There is hardly any personal defect," replied Anne, "which an agreeable manner might not gradually reconcile one to."

"I think very differently," answered Elizabeth, shortly; "an agreeable manner may set off handsome features, but can never alter plain ones. However, at any rate, as I have a great deal more at stake on this point than anybody else can have, I think it rather unnecessary in you to be advising me."

Anne had done; glad that it was over, and not absolutely hopeless of doing good. Elizabeth, though resenting the suspicion, might yet be made observant by it.

The last office of the four carriage-horses was to draw Sir Walter, Miss Elliot, and Mrs. Clay to Bath. The party drove off in very good spirits; Sir Walter prepared with condescending bows for all the afflicted tenantry and cottagers who might have had a hint to show themselves, and Anne walked up at the same time in a sort of desolate tranquillity to the Lodge, where she was to spend the first week.

Her friend was not in better spirits than herself. Lady Russell felt this break-up of the family exceedingly. Their respectability was as dear to her as her own, and a daily intercourse had become precious by habit. It was painful to look upon their deserted grounds, and still worse to antic-

ipate the new hands they were to fall into; and to escape
the solitariness and the melancholy of so altered a village,
and be out of the way when Admiral and Mrs. Croft first
arrived, she had determined to make her own absence from
home begin when she must give up Anne. Accordingly their
removal was made together, and Anne was set down at Uppercross Cottage, in the first stage of Lady Russell's journey.

Uppercross was a moderate-sized village, which a few
years back had been completely in the old English style,
containing only two houses superior in appearance to those
of the yeomen and labourers; the mansion of the squire,
with its high walls, great gates, and old trees, substantial
and unmodernized, and the compact, tight parsonage, enclosed in its own neat garden, with a vine and a pear-tree
trained round its casements; but upon the marriage of the
young squire, it had received the improvement of a farmhouse, elevated into a cottage, for his residence, and Uppercross Cottage, with its verandah, French windows, and
other prettinesses, was quite as likely to catch the traveller's
eye as the more consistent and considerable aspect and
premises of the Great House, about a quarter of a mile further on.

Here Anne had often been staying. She knew the ways
of Uppercross as well as those of Kellynch. The two families
were so continually meeting, so much in the habit of running in and out of each other's house at all hours, that it
was rather a surprise to her to find Mary alone; but being
alone, her being unwell and out of spirits was almost a matter of course. Though better endowed than the elder sister,
Mary had not Anne's understanding nor temper. While well,
and happy, and properly attended to, she had great good
humour and excellent spirits; but any indisposition sunk her
completely. She had no resources for solitude; and, inher-

iting a considerable share of the Elliot self-importance, was very prone to add to every other distress that of fancying herself neglected and ill-used. In person, she was inferior to both sisters, and had, even in her bloom, only reached the dignity of being "a fine girl." She was now lying on the faded sofa of the pretty little drawing-room, the once elegant furniture of which had been gradually growing shabby under the influence of four summers and two children; and, on Anne's appearing, greeted her with:

"So you are come at last! I began to think I should never see you. I am so ill I can hardly speak. I have not seen a creature the whole morning!"

"I am sorry to find you unwell," replied Anne. "You sent me such a good account of yourself on Thursday."

"Yes, I made the best of it; I always do: but I was very far from well at the time; and I do not think I ever was so ill in my life as I have been all this morning: very unfit to be left alone, I am sure. Suppose I were to be seized of a sudden in some dreadful way, and not able to ring the bell! So Lady Russell would not get out. I do not think she has been in this house three times this summer."

Anne said what was proper, and enquired after her husband. "Oh! Charles is out shooting. I have not seen him since seven o'clock. He would go, though I told him how ill I was. He said he should not stay out long; but he has never come back, and now it is almost one. I assure you I have not seen a soul this whole long morning."

"You have had your little boys with you?"

"Yes, as long as I could bear their noise; but they are so unmanageable that they do me more harm than good. Little Charles does not mind a word I say, and Walter is growing quite as bad."

"Well, you will soon be better now," replied Anne, cheerfully. "You know I always cure you when I come. How are your neighbours at the Great House?"

"I can give you no account of them. I have not seen one of them to-day, except Mr. Musgrove, who just stopped and spoke through the window, but without getting off his horse; and though I told him how ill I was, not one of them have been near me. It did not happen to suit the Miss Musgroves, I suppose, and they never put themselves out of their way."

"You will see them yet, perhaps, before the morning is gone. It is early."

"I never want them, I assure you. They talk and laugh a great deal too much for me. Oh! Anne, I am so very unwell! It was quite unkind of you not to come on Thursday."

"My dear Mary, recollect what a comfortable account you sent me of yourself! You wrote in the cheerfullest manner, and said you were perfectly well, and in no hurry for me; and that being the case, you must be aware that my wish would be to remain with Lady Russell to the last: and besides what I felt on her account, I have really been so busy, have had so much to do, that I could not very conveniently have left Kellynch sooner."

"Dear me! what can *you* possibly have to do?"

"A great many things, I assure you. More than I can recollect in a moment; but I can tell you some. I have been making a duplicate of the catalogue of my father's books and pictures. I have been several times in the garden with Mackenzie, trying to understand, and make him understand, which of Elizabeth's plants are for Lady Russell. I have had all my own little concerns to arrange, books and music to divide, and all my trunks to repack, from not having understood in time what was intended as to the waggons: and one thing I have had to do, Mary, of a more trying nature:

going to almost every house in the parish, as a sort of take-leave. I was told that they wished it; but all these things took up a great deal of time."

"Oh, well!" and after a moment's pause, "but you have never asked me one word about our dinner at the Pooles yesterday."

"Did you go, then? I have made no enquiries, because I concluded you must have been obliged to give up the party."

"Oh, yes! I went. I was very well yesterday; nothing at all the matter with me till this morning. It would have been strange if I had not gone."

"I am very glad you were well enough and I hope you had a pleasant party."

"Nothing remarkable. One always knows beforehand what the dinner will be, and who will be there; and it is so very uncomfortable not having a carriage of one's own. Mr. and Mrs. Musgrove took me, and we were so crowded! They are both so very large, and take up so much room; and Mr. Musgrove always sits forward. So there was I crowded into the back seat with Henrietta and Louisa; and I think it very likely that my illness to-day may be owing to it."

A little further perseverance in patience and forced cheerfulness on Anne's side produced nearly a cure on Mary's. She could soon sit upright on the sofa, and began to hope she might be able to leave it by dinner-time. Then, forgetting to think of it, she was at the other end of the room, beautifying a nosegay; then she ate her cold meat; and then she was well enough to propose a little walk.

"Where shall we go?" said she, when they were ready. "I suppose you will not like to call at the Great House before they have been to see you?"

"I have not the smallest objection on that account," replied Anne. "I should never think of standing on such ceremony with people I know so well as Mrs. and the Miss Musgroves."

"Oh! but they ought to call upon you as soon as possible. They ought to feel what is due to you as *my* sister. However, we may as well go and sit with them a little while, and when we have got that over, we can enjoy our walk."

Anne had always thought such a style of intercourse highly imprudent; but she had ceased to endeavour to check it, from believing that, though there were on each side continual subjects of offence, neither family could now do without it. To the Great House accordingly they went, to sit the full half hour in the old-fashioned square parlour, with a small carpet and shining floor, to which the present daughters of the house were gradually giving the proper air of confusion by a grand pianoforte and a harp, flowerstands, and little tables placed in every direction. Oh! could the originals of the portraits against the wainscot, could the gentlemen in brown velvet and the ladies in blue satin have seen what was going on, have been conscious of such an overthrow of all order and neatness! The portraits themselves seemed to be staring in astonishment.

The Musgroves, like their houses, were in a state of alteration, perhaps of improvement. The father and mother were in the old English style, and the young people in the new. Mr. and Mrs. Musgrove were a very good sort of people; friendly and hospitable, not much educated, and not at all elegant. Their children had more modern minds and manners. There was a numerous family; but the only two grown up, excepting Charles, were Henrietta and Louisa, young ladies of nineteen and twenty, who had brought from a school at Exeter all the usual stock of accomplishments, and were now, like thousands of other young ladies, living to be fashionable, happy, and merry. Their dress had every

posed in the secret of Sir Walter's estimate of the dues of a tenant.

It succeeded, however; and though Sir Walter must ever look with an evil eye on any one intending to inhabit that house, and think them infinitely too well off in being permitted to rent it on the highest terms, he was talked into allowing Mr. Shepherd to proceed in the treaty, and authorizing him to wait on Admiral Croft, who still remained at Taunton, and fix a day for the house being seen.

Sir Walter was not very wise; but still he had experience enough of the world to feel, that a more unobjectionable tenant, in all essentials, than Admiral Croft bid fair to be, could hardly offer. So far went his understanding; and his vanity supplied a little additional soothing, in the Admiral's situation in life, which was just high enough, and not too high. "I have let my house to Admiral Croft," would sound extremely well; very much better than to any mere *Mr.* —; a *Mr.* (save, perhaps, some half dozen in the nation) always needs a note of explanation. An admiral speaks his own consequence, and, at the same time, can never make a baronet look small. In all their dealings and intercourse, Sir Walter Elliot must ever have the precedence.

Nothing could be done without a reference to Elizabeth: but her inclination was growing so strong for a removal, that she was happy to have it fixed and expedited by a tenant at hand; and not a word to suspend decision was uttered by her.

Mr. Shepherd was completely empowered to act; and no sooner had such an end been reached, than Anne, who had been a most attentive listener to the whole, left the room, to seek the comfort of cool air for her flushed cheeks; and as she walked along a favourite grove, said, with a gentle sigh, "A few months more, and *he,* perhaps, may be walking here."

4

HE WAS NOT MR. WENTWORTH, the former curate of Monkford, however suspicious appearances may be, but a Captain Frederick Wentworth, his brother, who being made commander in consequence of the action off St. Domingo, and not immediately employed, had come into Somersetshire, in the summer of 1806; and having no parent living, found a home for half a year at Monkford. He was, at that time, a remarkably fine young man, with a great deal of intelligence, spirit, and brilliancy; and Anne an extremely pretty girl, with gentleness, modesty, taste, and feeling. Half the sum of attraction, on either side, might have been enough, for he had nothing to do, and she had hardly anybody to love; but the encounter of such lavish recommendations could not fail. They were gradually acquainted, and when acquainted, rapidly and deeply in love. It would be difficult to say which had seen highest perfection in the other, or which had been the happiest: she, in receiving his declarations and proposals, or he in having them accepted.

A short period of exquisite felicity followed, and but a short one. Troubles soon arose. Sir Walter, on being applied to, without actually withholding his consent, or saying it should never be, gave it all the negative of great astonishment, great coldness, great silence, and a professed resolution of doing nothing for his daughter. He thought it a very degrading alliance; and Lady Russell, though with more tempered and pardonable pride, received it as a most unfortunate one.

Anne Elliot, with all her claims of birth, beauty and mind, to throw herself away at nineteen; involve herself, at nineteen, in an engagement with a young man who had nothing but himself to recommend him, and no hopes of attaining affluence, but in the chances of a most uncertain profession, and no connections to secure even his further rise in that profession, would be, indeed, a throwing away, which she grieved to think of! Anne Elliot, so young; known to so few, to be snatched off by a stranger without alliance or fortune; or rather sunk by him into a state of most wearing, anxious, youth-killing dependence! It must not be, if by any fair interference of friendship, any representations from one who had almost a mother's love and mother's rights, it could be prevented.

Captain Wentworth had no fortune. He had been lucky in his profession; but spending freely what had come freely, had realised nothing. But he was confident that he should soon be rich: full of life and ardour, he knew that he should soon have a ship, and soon be on a station that would lead to everything he wanted. He had always been lucky; he knew he should be so still. Such confidence, powerful in its own warmth, and bewitching in the wit which often expressed it, must have been enough for Anne; but Lady Russell saw it very differently. His sanguine temper, and fearlessness of mind, operated very differently on her. She saw in it but an aggravation of the evil. It only added a dangerous character to himself. He was brilliant, he was headstrong. Lady Russell had little taste for wit, and of anything approaching to imprudence a horror. She deprecated the connection in every light.

Such opposition as these feelings produced was more than Anne could combat. Young and gentle as she was, it might yet have been possible to withstand her father's ill-will, though unsoftened by one kind word or look on the part of her sister; but Lady Russell, whom she had always loved and relied on, could not, with such steadiness of opinion, and such tenderness of manner, be continually advising her in vain. She was persuaded to believe the engagement a wrong thing: indiscreet, improper, hardly capable of success, and not deserving it. But it was not a merely selfish caution under which she acted, in putting an end to it. Had she not imagined herself consulting his good, even more than her own, she could hardly have given him up. The belief of being prudent and self-denying, principally for *his* advantage, was her chief consolation under the misery of a parting, a final parting; and every consolation was required, for she had to encounter all the additional pain of opinions, on his side, totally unconvinced and unbending, and of his feeling himself ill-used by so forced a relinquishment. He had left the country in consequence.

A few months had seen the beginning and the end of their acquaintance; but not with a few months ended Anne's share of suffering from it. Her attachment and regrets had, for a long time, clouded every enjoyment of youth, and an early loss of bloom and spirits had been their lasting effect.

More than seven years were gone since this little history

of sorrowful interest had reached its close; and time had softened down much, perhaps nearly all of peculiar attachment to him, but she had been too dependent on time alone; no aid had been given in change of place (except in one visit to Bath soon after the rupture), or in any novelty or enlargement of society. No one had ever come within the Kellynch circle, who could bear a comparison with Frederick Wentworth, as he stood in her memory. No second attachment, the only thoroughly natural, happy, and sufficient cure at her time of life, had been possible to the nice tone of her mind, the fastidiousness of her taste, in the small limits of the society around them. She had been solicited, when about two-and-twenty, to change her name by the young man who not long afterwards found a more willing mind in her younger sister: and Lady Russell had lamented her refusal: for Charles Musgrove was the eldest son of a man whose landed property and general importance were second in that country only to Sir Walter's, and of good character and appearance; and however Lady Russell might have asked yet for something more while Anne was nineteen, she would have rejoiced to see her at twenty-two so respectably removed from the partialities and injustice of her father's house, and settled so permanently near herself. But in this case Anne had left nothing for advice to do; and though Lady Russell, as satisfied as ever with her own discretion, never wished the past undone, she began now to have the anxiety which borders on hopelessness for Anne's being tempted, by some man of talents and independence, to enter a state for which she held her to be peculiarly fitted by her warm affections and domestic habits.

They knew not each other's opinion, either its constancy or its change, on the one leading point of Anne's conduct, for the subject was never alluded to; but Anne, at seven-and-twenty, thought very differently from what she had been made to think at nineteen. She did not blame Lady Russell, she did not blame herself for having been guided by her; but she felt that were any young person in similar circumstances to apply to her for counsel, they would never receive any of such certain immediate wretchedness, such uncertain future good. She was persuaded that under every disadvantage of disapprobation at home, and every anxiety attending his profession, all their probable fears, delays, and disappointments, she should yet have been a happier woman in maintaining the engagement, than she had been in the sacrifice of it; and this, she fully believed, had the usual share, had even more than a usual share of all such solicitudes and suspense been theirs, without reference to the actual results of their case, which, as it happened, would have bestowed earlier prosperity than could be reasonably calculated on. All his sanguine expectations, all his confidence, had been justified. His genius and ardour had seemed to foresee and to command his prosperous path. He had, very soon after their engagement ceased, got employ; and all that he had told her would follow had taken place. He had distinguished himself, and early gained the other step in rank, and must now, by successive captures, have made a handsome fortune. She had only navy lists and newspapers for her authority, but she could not doubt his being rich; and, in favour of his constancy, she had no reason to believe him married.

How eloquent could Anne Elliot have been! how eloquent, at least, were her wishes on the side of early warm attachment, and a cheerful confidence in futurity, against that over-anxious caution which seems to insult exertion and distrust Providence! She had been forced into prudence in her youth, she learned romance as she grew older: the natural sequel of an unnatural beginning.

With all these circumstances, recollections, and feelings, she could not hear that Captain Wentworth's sister was likely to live at Kellynch without a revival of former pain; and many a stroll, and many a sigh, were necessary to dispel the agitation of the idea. She often told herself it was folly, before she could harden her nerves sufficiently to feel the continual discussion of the Crofts and their business no evil. She was assisted, however, by that perfect indifference and apparent unconsciousness, among the only three of her own friends in the secret of the past, which seemed almost to deny any recollection of it. She could do justice to the superiority of Lady Russell's motives in this, over those of her father and Elizabeth; she could honour all the better feelings of her calmness; but the general air of oblivion among them was highly important from whatever it sprung; and in the event of Admiral Croft's really taking Kellynch Hall, she rejoiced anew over the conviction which had always been most grateful to her, of the past being known to those three only among her connections, by whom no syllable, she believed, would ever be whispered, and in the trust that among his, the brother only with whom he had been residing had received any information of their short-lived engagement. That brother had been long removed from the country, and being a sensible man, and, moreover, a single man at the time, she had a fond dependence on no human creature's having heard of it from him.

The sister, Mrs. Croft, had then been out of England, accompanying her husband on a foreign station, and her own sister, Mary, had been at school while it all occurred;

and never admitted by the pride of some, and the delicacy of others, to the smallest knowledge of it afterwards.

With these supports, she hoped that the acquaintance between herself and the Crofts, which, with Lady Russell still resident in Kellynch, and Mary fixed only three miles off, must be anticipated, need not involve any particular awkwardness.

5

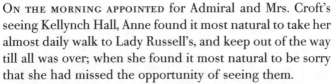

ON THE MORNING APPOINTED for Admiral and Mrs. Croft's seeing Kellynch Hall, Anne found it most natural to take her almost daily walk to Lady Russell's, and keep out of the way till all was over; when she found it most natural to be sorry that she had missed the opportunity of seeing them.

This meeting of the two parties proved highly satisfactory, and decided the whole business at once. Each lady was previously well disposed for an agreement, and saw nothing, therefore, but good manners in the other; and with regard to the gentlemen, there was such a hearty good humour, such an open, trusting liberality on the Admiral's side, as could not but influence Sir Walter, who had besides been flattered into his very best and most polished behaviour by Mr. Shepherd's assurances of his being known, by report, to the Admiral, as a model of good breeding.

The house, and grounds, and furniture, were approved, the Crofts were approved, terms, time, everything, and everybody, was right; and Mr. Shepherd's clerks were set to work, without there having been a single preliminary difference to modify of all that "This indenture showeth."

Sir Walter without hesitation, declared the Admiral to be the best-looking sailor he had ever met with, and went so far as to say, that if his own man might have had the arranging of his hair, he should not be ashamed of being seen with him anywhere; and the Admiral, with sympathetic cordiality, observed to his wife as they drove back through the park, "I thought we should soon come to a deal, my dear, in spite of what they told us at Taunton. The Baronet will never set the Thames on fire, but there seems no harm in him:" reciprocal compliments which would have been esteemed about equal.

The Crofts were to have possession at Michaelmas; and as Sir Walter proposed removing to Bath in the course of the preceding month, there was no time to be lost in making every dependent arrangement.

Lady Russell, convinced that Anne would not be allowed to be of any use, or any importance, in the choice of the house which they were going to secure, was very unwilling to have her hurried away so soon, and wanted to make it possible for her to stay behind till she might convey her to Bath herself after Christmas; but having engagements of her own which must take her from Kellynch for several weeks, she was unable to give the full invitation she wished, and Anne, though dreading the possible heats of September in all the white glare of Bath, and grieving to forego all the influence so sweet and so sad of the autumnal months in the country, did not think that, everything considered, she wished to remain. It would be most right, and most wise, and therefore must involve least suffering to go with the others.

Something occurred, however, to give her a different

duty. Mary, often a little unwell, and always thinking a great deal of her own complaints, and always in the habit of claiming Anne when anything was the matter, was indisposed; and foreseeing that she should not have a day's health all the autumn, entreated, or rather required her, for it was hardly entreaty, to come to Uppercross Cottage, and bear her company as long as she could want her, instead of going to Bath.

"I cannot possibly do without Anne," was Mary's reasoning; and Elizabeth's reply was, "Then I am sure Anne had better stay, for nobody will want her in Bath."

To be claimed as a good, though in an improper style, is at least better than being rejected as no good at all; and Anne, glad to be thought of some use, glad to have anything marked out as a duty, and certainly not sorry to have the scene of it in the country, and her own dear country, readily agreed to stay.

This invitation of Mary's removed all Lady Russell's difficulties, and it was consequently soon settled that Anne should not go to Bath till Lady Russell took her, and that all the intervening time should be divided between Uppercross Cottage and Kellynch Lodge.

So far all was perfectly right; but Lady Russell was almost startled by the wrong of one part of the Kellynch Hall plan, when it burst on her, which was, Mrs. Clay's being engaged to go to Bath with Sir Walter and Elizabeth, as a most important and valuable assistant to the latter in all the business before her. Lady Russell was extremely sorry that such a measure should have been resorted to at all, wondered, grieved, and feared; and the affront it contained to Anne, in Mrs. Clay's being of so much use, while Anne could be of none, was a very sore aggravation.

Anne herself was become hardened to such affronts, but

she felt the imprudence of the arrangement quite as keenly as Lady Russell. With a great deal of quiet observation, and a knowledge, which she often wished less, of her father's character, she was sensible that results the most serious to his family from the intimacy were more than possible. She did not imagine that her father had at present an idea of the kind. Mrs. Clay had freckles, and a projecting tooth, and a clumsy wrist, which he was continually making severe remarks upon her in absence, but she was young, and certainly altogether well-looking, and possessed, in an acute mind and assiduous pleasing manners, infinitely more dangerous attractions than any merely personal might have been. Anne was so impressed by the degree of their danger, that she could not excuse herself from trying to make it perceptible to her sister. She had little hope of success, but Elizabeth, who in the event of such a reverse would be so much more to be pitied than herself, should never, she thought, have reason to reproach her for giving no warning.

She spoke, and seemed only to offend. Elizabeth could not conceive how such an absurd suspicion should occur to her, and indignantly answered for each party's perfection, knowing their situation.

"Mrs. Clay," said she, warmly, "never forgets who she is; and as I am rather better acquainted with her sentiments than you can be, I can assure you, that upon the subject of marriage they are particularly nice, and that she reprobates all inequality of condition and rank more strongly than most people. And as to my father, I really should not have thought that he who has kept himself single so long for our sakes need be suspected now. If Mrs. Clay were a very beautiful woman, I grant you it might be wrong to have her so much with me; not that anything in the world, I am sure, would induce my father to make a degrading match, but he might be rendered unhappy. But poor Mrs. Clay, who with all her merits, can never have been reckoned tolerably pretty, I really think poor Mrs. Clay may be staying here in perfect safety. One would imagine you had never heard my father speak of her personal misfortunes, though I know you must fifty times. That tooth of hers and those freckles. Freckles do not disgust me so very much as they do him. I have known a face not materially disfigured by a few, but he abominates them. You must have heard him notice Mrs. Clay's freckles."

"There is hardly any personal defect," replied Anne, "which an agreeable manner might not gradually reconcile one to."

"I think very differently," answered Elizabeth, shortly; "an agreeable manner may set off handsome features, but can never alter plain ones. However, at any rate, as I have a great deal more at stake on this point than anybody else can have, I think it rather unnecessary in you to be advising me."

Anne had done; glad that it was over, and not absolutely hopeless of doing good. Elizabeth, though resenting the suspicion, might yet be made observant by it.

The last office of the four carriage-horses was to draw Sir Walter, Miss Elliot, and Mrs. Clay to Bath. The party drove off in very good spirits; Sir Walter prepared with condescending bows for all the afflicted tenantry and cottagers who might have had a hint to show themselves, and Anne walked up at the same time in a sort of desolate tranquillity to the Lodge, where she was to spend the first week.

Her friend was not in better spirits than herself. Lady Russell felt this break-up of the family exceedingly. Their respectability was as dear to her as her own, and a daily intercourse had become precious by habit. It was painful to look upon their deserted grounds, and still worse to anticipate the new hands they were to fall into; and to escape the solitariness and the melancholy of so altered a village, and be out of the way when Admiral and Mrs. Croft first arrived, she had determined to make her own absence from home begin when she must give up Anne. Accordingly their removal was made together, and Anne was set down at Uppercross Cottage, in the first stage of Lady Russell's journey.

Uppercross was a moderate-sized village, which a few years back had been completely in the old English style, containing only two houses superior in appearance to those of the yeomen and labourers; the mansion of the squire, with its high walls, great gates, and old trees, substantial and unmodernized, and the compact, tight parsonage, enclosed in its own neat garden, with a vine and a pear-tree trained round its casements; but upon the marriage of the young squire, it had received the improvement of a farmhouse, elevated into a cottage, for his residence, and Uppercross Cottage, with its verandah, French windows, and other prettinesses, was quite as likely to catch the traveller's eye as the more consistent and considerable aspect and premises of the Great House, about a quarter of a mile further on.

Here Anne had often been staying. She knew the ways of Uppercross as well as those of Kellynch. The two families were so continually meeting, so much in the habit of running in and out of each other's house at all hours, that it was rather a surprise to her to find Mary alone; but being alone, her being unwell and out of spirits was almost a matter of course. Though better endowed than the elder sister, Mary had not Anne's understanding nor temper. While well, and happy, and properly attended to, she had great good humour and excellent spirits; but any indisposition sunk her completely. She had no resources for solitude; and, inheriting a considerable share of the Elliot self-importance, was very prone to add to every other distress that of fancying herself neglected and ill-used. In person, she was inferior to both sisters, and had, even in her bloom, only reached the dignity of being "a fine girl." She was now lying on the faded sofa of the pretty little drawing-room, the once elegant furniture of which had been gradually growing shabby under the influence of four summers and two children; and, on Anne's appearing, greeted her with:

"So you are come at last! I began to think I should never see you. I am so ill I can hardly speak. I have not seen a creature the whole morning!"

"I am sorry to find you unwell," replied Anne. "You sent me such a good account of yourself on Thursday."

"Yes, I made the best of it; I always do: but I was very far from well at the time; and I do not think I ever was so ill in my life as I have been all this morning: very unfit to be left alone, I am sure. Suppose I were to be seized of a sudden in some dreadful way, and not able to ring the bell! So Lady Russell would not get out. I do not think she has been in this house three times this summer."

Anne said what was proper, and enquired after her husband. "Oh! Charles is out shooting. I have not seen him since seven o'clock. He would go, though I told him how ill I was. He said he should not stay out long; but he has never come back, and now it is almost one. I assure you I have not seen a soul this whole long morning."

"You have had your little boys with you?"

"Yes, as long as I could bear their noise; but they are so unmanageable that they do me more harm than good. Little Charles does not mind a word I say, and Walter is growing quite as bad."

"Well, you will soon be better now," replied Anne, cheerfully. "You know I always cure you when I come. How are your neighbours at the Great House?"

"I can give you no account of them. I have not seen one of them to-day, except Mr. Musgrove, who just stopped and spoke through the window, but without getting off his horse; and though I told him how ill I was, not one of them have been near me. It did not happen to suit the Miss Musgroves, I suppose, and they never put themselves out of their way."

"You will see them yet, perhaps, before the morning is gone. It is early."

"I never want them, I assure you. They talk and laugh a great deal too much for me. Oh! Anne, I am so very unwell! It was quite unkind of you not to come on Thursday."

"My dear Mary, recollect what a comfortable account you sent me of yourself! You wrote in the cheerfullest manner, and said you were perfectly well, and in no hurry for me; and that being the case, you must be aware that my wish would be to remain with Lady Russell to the last: and besides what I felt on her account, I have really been so busy, have had so much to do, that I could not very conveniently have left Kellynch sooner."

"Dear me! what can *you* possibly have to do?"

"A great many things, I assure you. More than I can recollect in a moment; but I can tell you some. I have been making a duplicate of the catalogue of my father's books and pictures. I have been several times in the garden with Mackenzie, trying to understand, and make him understand, which of Elizabeth's plants are for Lady Russell. I have had all my own little concerns to arrange, books and music to divide, and all my trunks to repack, from not having understood in time what was intended as to the waggons: and one thing I have had to do, Mary, of a more trying nature:

advantage, their faces were rather pretty, their spirits extremely good, their manners unembarrassed and pleasant; they were of consequence at home, and favourites abroad. Anne always contemplated them as some of the happiest creatures of her acquaintance: but still, saved as we all are, by some comfortable feeling of superiority from wishing for the possibility of exchange, she would not have given up her own more elegant and cultivated mind for all their enjoyments; and envied them nothing but that seemingly perfect good understanding and agreement together, that good-humoured mutual affection, of which she had known so little herself with either of her sisters.

They were received with great cordiality. Nothing seemed amiss on the side of the Great House family, which was generally, as Anne very well knew, the least to blame. The half hour was chatted away pleasantly enough; and she was not at all surprised, at the end of it, to have their walking party joined by both the Miss Musgroves, at Mary's particular invitation.

6

ANNE HAD NOT WANTED this visit to Uppercross to learn that a removal from one set of people to another, though at a distance of only three miles, will often include a total change of conversation, opinion, and idea. She had never been staying there before, without being struck by it, or without wishing that other Elliots could have her advantage in seeing how unknown, or unconsidered there, were the affairs which at Kellynch Hall were treated as of such general publicity and pervading interest; yet, with all this experience, she believed she must now submit to feel that another lesson, in the art of knowing our own nothingness beyond our own circle, was become necessary for her; for certainly, coming as she did, with a heart full of the subject which had been completely occupying both houses in Kellynch for many weeks, she had expected rather more curiosity and sympathy than she found in the separate, but very similar remark of Mr. and Mrs. Musgrove: "So, Miss Anne, Sir Walter and your sister are gone; and what part of Bath do you think they will settle in?" and this, without much waiting for an answer; or in the young ladies' addition of, "I hope *we* shall be in Bath in the winter; but remember, papa, if we do go, we must be in a good situation: none of your Queen Squares for us!" or in the anxious supplement from Mary, of—"Upon my word, I shall be pretty well off, when you are all gone away to be happy at Bath!"

She could only resolve to avoid such self-delusion in future, and think with heightened gratitude of the extraordinary blessing of having one such truly sympathising friend as Lady Russell.

The Mr. Musgroves had their own game to guard and to destroy, their own horses, dogs, and newspapers to engage them, and the females were fully occupied in all the other common subjects of housekeeping, neighbours, dress, dancing and music. She acknowledged it to be very fitting, that every little social commonwealth should dictate its own matters of discourse; and hoped, ere long, to become a not unworthy member of the one she was now transplanted into. With the prospect of spending at least two months at Uppercross, it was highly incumbent on her to clothe her imagination, her memory, and all her ideas in as much of Uppercross as possible.

She had no dread of these two months. Mary was not so repulsive and unsisterly as Elizabeth, nor so inaccessible to all influence of hers; neither was there anything among the other component parts of the Cottage inimical to comfort. She was always on friendly terms with her brother-in-law; and in the children, who loved her nearly as well, and respected her a great deal more than their mother, she had an object of interest, amusement, and wholesome exertion.

Charles Musgrove was civil and agreeable; in sense and temper he was undoubtedly superior to his wife, but not of

powers, or conversation, or grace to make the past, as they
were connected together, at all a dangerous contemplation;
though, at the same time, Anne could believe, with Lady
Russell, that a more equal match might have greatly improved him; and that a woman of real understanding might
have given more consequence to his character, and more
usefulness, rationality, and elegance to his habits and pursuits. As it was, he did nothing with much zeal, but sport;
and his time was otherwise trifled away, without benefit
from books or anything else. He had very good spirits,
which never seemed much affected by his wife's occasional
lowness, bore with her unreasonableness sometimes to
Anne's admiration, and upon the whole, though there was
very often a little disagreement (in which she had sometimes more share than she wished, being appealed to by
both parties), they might pass for a happy couple. They were
always perfectly agreed in the want of more money, and a
strong inclination for a handsome present from his father;
but here, as on most topics, he had the superiority, for while
Mary thought it a great shame that such a present was not
made, he always contended for his father's having many
other uses for his money, and a right to spend it as he liked.

As to the management of their children, his theory was
much better than his wife's, and his practice not so bad. "I
could manage them very well, if it were not for Mary's interference," was what Anne often heard him say, and had a
good deal of faith in; but when listening in turn to Mary's
reproach of, "Charles spoils the children so that I cannot get
them into any order," she never had the smallest temptation
to say, "Very true."

One of the least agreeable circumstances of her residence
there was her being treated with too much confidence by
all parties, and being too much in the secret of the com-

plaints of each house. Known to have some influence with her sister, she was continually requested, or at least receiving hints to exert it, beyond what was practicable. "I wish you could persuade Mary not to be always fancying herself ill," was Charles's language; and, in an unhappy mood, thus spoke Mary: "I do believe if Charles were to see me dying, he would not think there was anything the matter with me. I am sure, Anne, if you would, you might persuade him that I really am very ill—a great deal worse than I ever own."

Mary's declaration was, "I hate sending the children to the Great House, though their grandmamma is always wanting to see them, for she humours and indulges them to such a degree, and gives them so much trash and sweet things, that they are sure to come back sick and cross for the rest of the day." And Mrs. Musgrove took the first opportunity of being alone with Anne, to say, "Oh! Miss Anne, I cannot help wishing Mrs. Charles had a little of your method with those children. They are quite different creatures with you! But to be sure, in general, they are so spoilt! It is a pity you cannot put your sister in the way of managing them. They are as fine healthy children as ever were seen, poor little dears! without partiality; but Mrs. Charles knows no more how they should be treated—! Bless me! how troublesome they are sometimes. I assure you, Miss Anne, it prevents my wishing to see them at our house so often as I otherwise should. I believe Mrs. Charles is not quite pleased with my not inviting them oftener; but you know it is very bad to have children with one that one is obliged to be checking every moment; 'don't do this,' and 'don't do that'; or that one can only keep in tolerable order by more cake than is good for them."

She had this communication, moreover, from Mary: "Mrs. Musgrove thinks all her servants so steady, that it would be high treason to call it in question; but I am sure, without exaggeration, that her upper housemaid and laundrymaid, instead of being in their business, are gadding about the village all day long. I meet them wherever I go; and I declare I never go twice into my nursery without seeing something of them. If Jemima were not the trustiest, steadiest creature in the world, it would be enough to spoil her; for she tells me they are always tempting her to take a walk with them." And on Mrs. Musgrove's side it was, "I make a rule of never interfering in any of my daughter-in-law's concerns, for I know it would not do; but I shall tell *you,* Miss Anne, because you may be able to set things to rights, that I have no very good opinion of Mrs. Charles's nurserymaid: I hear strange stories of her; she is always upon the gad; and from my own knowledge, I can declare, she is such a fine-dressing lady, that she is enough to ruin any servants she comes near. Mrs. Charles quite swears by her, I know; but I just give you this hint, that you may be upon the watch; because, if you see anything amiss, you need not be afraid of mentioning it."

Again, it was Mary's complaint that Mrs. Musgrove was very apt not to give her the precedence that was her due, when they dined at the Great House with other families; and she did not see any reason why she was to be considered so much at home as to lose her place. And one day when Anne was walking with only the Miss Musgroves, one of them, after talking of rank, people of rank, and jealousy of rank, said, "I have no scruple of observing to *you,* how nonsensical some persons are about their place, because all the world knows how easy and indifferent you are about it; but I wish anybody would give Mary a hint that it would be a great deal better if she were not so very tenacious, especially if she would not be always putting herself forward to

take place of mamma. Nobody doubts her right to have precedence of mamma, but it would be more becoming in her
not to be always insisting on it. It is not that mamma cares
about it the least in the world, but I know it is taken notice
of by many persons."

How was Anne to set all these matters to rights? She
could do little more than listen patiently, soften every griev-
ance, and excuse each to the other; give them all hints of
the forbearance necessary between such near neighbours,
and make those hints broadest which were meant for her
sister's benefit.

In all other respects, her visit began and proceeded very
well. Her own spirits improved by change of place and subject, by being removed three miles from Kellynch; Mary's
ailments lessened by having a constant companion, and
their daily intercourse with the other family, since there was
neither superior affection, confidence nor employment in
the Cottage to be interrupted by it, was rather an advantage.
It was certainly carried nearly as far as possible, for they met
every morning, and hardly ever spent an evening asunder;
but she believed they should not have done so well without
the sight of Mr. and Mrs. Musgrove's respectable forms in
the usual places, or without the talking, laughing, and singing of their daughters.

She played a great deal better than either of the Miss
Musgroves, but having no voice, no knowledge of the harp,
and no fond parents, to sit by and fancy themselves delighted, her performance was little thought of, only out of
civility, or to refresh the others, as she was well aware. She
knew that when she played she was giving pleasure only to
herself; but this was no new sensation. Excepting one short
period of her life, she had never, since the age of fourteen,
never since the loss of her dear mother, known the happi-

ness of being listened to, or encouraged by any just appreciation or real taste. In music she had been always used to feel alone in the world; and Mr. and Mrs. Musgrove's fond partiality for their own daughters' performance, and total indifference to any other person's, gave her much more pleasure for their sakes, than mortification for her own.

The party at the Great House was sometimes increased by other company. The neighbourhood was not large, but the Musgroves were visited by everybody, and had more dinner-parties, and more callers, more visitors by invitation and by chance, than any other family. They were more completely popular.

The girls were wild for dancing; and the evenings ended, occasionally, in an unpremeditated little ball. There was a family of cousins within a walk of Uppercross, in less affluent circumstances, who depended on the Musgroves for all their pleasures; they would come at any time, or help to play at anything, or dance anywhere; and Anne, very much preferring the office of musician to a more active post, played country dances to them by the hour together; a kindness which always recommended her musical powers to the notice of Mr. and Mrs. Musgrove more than anything else, and often drew this compliment—"Well done, Miss Anne! very well done, indeed! Lord bless me! how those little fingers of yours fly about!"

So passed the first three weeks, Michaelmas came; and now Anne's heart must be in Kellynch again. A beloved home made over to others; all the precious rooms and furniture, groves and prospects, beginning to own other eyes and other limbs! She could not think of much else on the 29th of September; and she had this sympathetic touch in the evening from Mary, who, on having occasion to note down the day of the month, exclaimed, "Dear me, is not this the day the Crofts were to come to Kellynch? I am glad I did not think of it before. How low it makes me!"

The Crofts took possession with true naval alertness, and were to be visited. Mary deplored the necessity for herself. "Nobody knew how much she should suffer. She should put it off as long as she could"; but was not easy till she had talked Charles into driving her over on an early day, and was in a very animated, comfortable state of imaginary agitation when she came back. Anne had very sincerely rejoiced in there being no means of her going. She wished, however, to see the Crofts, and was glad to be within when the visit was returned. They came: the master of the house was not at home, but the two sisters were together; and as it chanced that Mrs. Croft fell to the share of Anne, while the Admiral sat by Mary, and made himself very agreeable by his good-humoured notice of her little boys, she was well able to watch for a likeness, and if it failed her in the features, to catch it in the voice, or in the turn of sentiment and expression.

Mrs. Croft, though neither tall nor fat, had a squareness, uprightness, and vigour of form, which gave importance to her person. She had bright dark eyes, good teeth, and altogether an agreeable face; though her reddened and weather-beaten complexion, the consequence of her having been almost as much at sea as her husband, made her seem to have lived some years longer in the world than her real eight-and-thirty. Her manners were open, easy, and decided, like one who had no distrust of herself, and no doubts of what to do; without any approach to coarseness, however, or any want of good humour. Anne gave her credit, indeed, for feelings of great consideration towards herself, in all that related to Kellynch, and it pleased her: especially, as she had satisfied herself in the very first half minute, in the instant even of introduction, that there was not the smallest symptom of any knowledge or suspicion on Mrs. Croft's side to give a bias of any sort. She was quite easy on that head, and consequently full of strength and courage, till for a moment electrified by Mrs. Croft's suddenly saying:

"It was you, and not your sister, I find, that my brother had the pleasure of being acquainted with, when he was in this country."

Anne hoped she had outlived the age of blushing; but the age of emotion she certainly had not.

"Perhaps you may not have heard that he is married?" added Mrs. Croft.

She could now answer as she ought; and was happy to feel, when Mrs. Croft's next words explained it to be Mr. Wentworth of whom she spoke, that she had said nothing which might not do for either brother. She immediately felt how reasonable it was, that Mrs. Croft should be thinking and speaking of Edward, and not of Frederick; and with shame at her own forgetfulness, applied herself to the knowledge of their former neighbour's present state with proper interest.

The rest was all tranquillity; till, just as they were moving, she heard the Admiral say to Mary:

"We are expecting a brother of Mrs. Croft's here soon; I dare say you know him by name?"

He was cut short by the eager attacks of the little boys, clinging to him like an old friend, and declaring he should not go; and being too much engrossed by proposals of carrying them away in his coat pocket, etc., to have another moment for finishing or recollecting what he had begun, Anne was left to persuade herself, as well as she could, that the same brother must still be in question. She could not, however, reach such a degree of certainty as not to be anxious to hear whether anything had been said on the subject at the other house, where the Crofts had previously been calling.

The folks of Great House were to spend the evening of this day at the Cottage; and it being now too late in the year for such visits to be made on foot, the coach was beginning to be listened for, when the youngest Miss Musgrove walked in. That she was coming to apologise, and that they should have to spend the evening by themselves, was the first black idea; and Mary was quite ready to be affronted, when Louisa made all right by saying, that she only came on foot, to leave more room for the harp, which was bringing in the carriage.

"And I will tell you our reason," she added, "and all about it. I am come on to give you notice, that papa and mamma are out of spirits this evening, especially mamma; she is thinking so much of poor Richard! And we agreed it would be best to have the harp, for it seems to amuse her more than the pianoforte. I will tell you why she is out of spirits. When the Crofts called this morning (they called here afterwards, did not they?), they happened to say that her brother, Captain Wentworth, is just returned to England, or paid off, or something, and is coming to see them almost directly; and most unluckily it came into mamma's head, when they were gone, that Wentworth, or something very like it, was the name of poor Richard's captain, at one time; I do not know when or where, but a great while before he died, poor fellow! And upon looking over his letters and things, she found it was so, and is perfectly sure that this must be the very man, and her head is quite full of it and of poor Richard! So we must all be as merry as we can, that she may not be dwelling upon such gloomy things."

The real circumstances of this pathetic piece of family history were, that the Musgroves had had the ill fortune of a very troublesome, hopeless son, and the good fortune to lose him before he reached his twentieth year; that he had been sent to sea because he was stupid and unmanageable on shore; that he had been very little cared for at any time by his family, though quite as much as he deserved; seldom heard of, and scarcely at all regretted, when the intelligence of his death abroad had worked its way to Uppercross, two years before.

He had, in fact, though his sisters were now doing all they could for him, by calling him "poor Richard," been nothing better than a thick-headed, unfeeling, unprofitable Dick Musgrove, who had never done anything to entitle himself to more than the abbreviation of his name, living or dead.

He had been several years at sea, and had, in the course of those removals to which all midshipmen are liable, and especially such midshipmen as every captain wishes to get rid of, been six months on board Captain Frederick Wentworth's frigate, the *Laconia;* and from the *Laconia* he had, under the influence of his captain, written the only two letters which his father and mother had ever received from him during the whole of his absence; that is to say, the only two disinterested letters: all the rest had been mere applications for money.

In each letter he had spoken well of his captain; but yet, so little were they in the habit of attending to such matters, so unobservant and incurious were they as to the names of men or ships, that it had made scarcely any impression at the time, and that Mrs. Musgrove should have been suddenly struck, this very day, with a recollection of the name of Wentworth, as connected with her son, seemed one of those extraordinary bursts of mind which do sometimes occur.

She had gone to her letters, and found it all as she supposed; and the re-perusal of these letters, after so long an
interval, her poor son gone for ever, and all the strength of
his faults forgotten, had affected her spirits exceedingly, and
thrown her into greater grief for him than she had known
on first hearing of his death. Mr. Musgrove was, in a lesser
degree, affected likewise; and when they reached the Cottage, they were evidently in want, first, of being listened to
anew on this subject, and afterwards, of all the relief which
cheerful companions could give.

To hear them talking so much of Captain Wentworth,
repeating his name so often, puzzling over past years, and
at last ascertaining that it *might,* that is probably *would,* turn
out to be the very same Captain Wentworth whom they recollected meeting, once or twice, after their coming back
from Clifton—a very fine young man—but they could not
say whether it was seven or eight years ago, was a new sort
of trial to Anne's nerves. She found, however, that it was one
to which she must inure herself. Since he actually was expected in the country, she must teach herself to be insensible on such points. And not only did it appear that he was
expected, and speedily, but the Musgroves, in their warm
gratitude for the kindness he had shown poor Dick, and very
high respect for his character, stamped as it was by poor
Dick's having been six months under his care, and mentioning him in strong, though not perfectly well-spelt praise, as
"a fine dashing fellow, only two perticular about the school-
master," were bent on introducing themselves, and seeking
his acquaintance as soon as they could hear of his arrival.

The resolution of doing so helped to form the comfort
of their evening.

7

A VERY FEW DAYS MORE, and Captain Wentworth was known to be at Kellynch, and Mr. Musgrove had called on him, and come back warm in his praise, and he was engaged with the Crofts to dine at Uppercross by the end of another week. It had been a great disappointment to Mr. Musgrove to find that no earlier day could be fixed, so impatient was he to show his gratitude, by seeing Captain Wentworth under his own roof, and welcoming him to all that was strongest and best in his cellars. But a week must pass; only a week, in Anne's reckoning, and then, she supposed, they must meet; and soon she began to wish that she could feel secure even for a week.

Captain Wentworth made a very early return to Mr. Musgrove's civility and she was all but calling there in the same half hour. She and Mary were actually setting forward for the Great House, where, as she afterwards learnt, they must inevitably have found him, when they were stopped by the eldest boy's being at that moment brought home in consequence of a bad fall. The child's situation put the visit entirely aside; but she could not hear of her escape with indifference, even in the midst of the serious anxiety which they afterwards felt on his account.

His collar-bone was found to be dislocated, and such injury received in the back, as roused the most alarming ideas. It was an afternoon of distress, and Anne had everything to do at once; the apothecary to send for, the father to have pursued and informed, the mother to support and keep from hysterics, the servants to control, the youngest child to banish, and the poor suffering one to attend and soothe; besides sending, as soon as she recollected it, proper notice to the other house, which brought her an accession rather of frightened inquiring companions, than of very useful assistants.

Her brother's return was the first comfort; he could take best care of his wife: and the second blessing was the arrival of the apothecary. Till he came and had examined the child, their apprehensions were the worse for being vague; they suspected great injury, but knew not where; but now the collar-bone was soon replaced, and though Mr. Robinson felt and felt, and rubbed, and looked grave, and spoke low words both to the father and the aunt, still they were all to hope the best, and to be able to part and eat their dinner in tolerable ease of mind; and then it was, just before they parted, that the two young aunts were able so far to digress from their nephew's state, as to give the information of Captain Wentworth's visit; staying five minutes behind their father and mother, to endeavour to express how perfectly delighted they were with him, how much handsomer, how infinitely more agreeable they thought him than any individual among their male acquaintance, who had been at all a favourite before. How glad they had been to hear papa invite him to stay to dinner, how sorry when he said it was quite out of his power, and how glad again when he had promised to reply to papa and mamma's further pressing invitations to come and dine with them on the morrow— actually on the morrow; and he had promised it in so pleasant a manner, as if he felt all the motive of their attention just as he ought. And in short, he had looked and said everything with such exquisite grace, that they could assure them all, their heads were both turned by him; and off they ran, quite as full of glee as of love, and apparently more full of Captain Wentworth than of little Charles.

The same story and the same raptures were repeated, when the two girls came with their father, through the gloom of the evening, to make enquiries; and Mr. Musgrove no longer under the first uneasiness about his heir, could add his confirmation and praise, and hope there would be now no occasion for putting Captain Wentworth off, and only be sorry to think that the Cottage party, probably, would not like to leave the little boy, to give him the meeting. "Oh! no; as to leaving the little boy," both father and mother were in much too strong and recent alarm to bear the thought; and Anne, in the joy of the escape, could not help adding her warm protestations to theirs.

Charles Musgrove, indeed, afterwards, showed more of inclination: "the child was going on so well, and he wished so much to be introduced to Captain Wentworth, that, perhaps, he might join them in the evening; he would not dine from home, but he might walk in for half an hour." But in this he was eagerly opposed by his wife, with "Oh! no, indeed, Charles, I cannot bear to have you go away. Only think, if anything should happen?"

The child had a good night, and was going on well the next day. It must be a work of time to ascertain that no injury had been done to the spine; but Mr. Robinson found nothing to increase alarm, and Charles Musgrove began, consequently, to feel no necessity for longer confinement. The child was to be kept in bed and amused as quietly as possible; but what was there for a father to do? This was quite a female case, and it would be highly absurd in him, who could be of no use at home, to shut himself up. His father very much wished him to meet Captain Wentworth, and there being no sufficient reason against it, he ought to go; and it ended in his making a bold, public declaration when he came in from shooting, of his meaning to dress directly, and dine at the other house.

"Nothing can be going on better than the child," said he; "so I told my father, just now, that I would come, and he thought me quite right. Your sister being with you, my love, I have no scruple at all. You would not like to leave him yourself, but you see I can be of no use. Anne will send for me if anything is the matter."

Husbands and wives generally understand when opposition will be vain. Mary knew, from Charles's manner of speaking, that he was quite determined on going, and that it would be of no use to tease him. She said nothing, therefore, till he was out of the room; but as soon as there was only Anne to hear—

"So you and I are to be left to shift by ourselves, with this poor sick child; and not a creature coming near us all the evening! I knew how it would be. This is always my luck. If there is anything disagreeable going on men are always sure to get out of it, and Charles is as bad as any of them. Very unfeeling! I must say it is very unfeeling of him to be running away from his poor little boy. Talks of his being going on so well! How does he know that he is going on well, or that there may not be a sudden change half an hour hence? I did not think Charles would have been so unfeeling. So here he is to go away and enjoy himself, and because I am the poor mother, I am not to be allowed to stir; and yet, I am sure, I am more unfit than anybody else to be about the child. My being the mother is the very reason why my feelings should not be tried. I am not at all equal to it. You saw how hysterical I was yesterday."

"But that was only the effect of the suddenness of your alarm — of the shock. You will not be hysterical again. I dare say we shall have nothing to distress us. I perfectly understand Mr. Robinson's directions, and have no fears; and, indeed, Mary, I cannot wonder at your husband. Nursing does not belong to a man; it is not his province. A sick child is always the mother's property: her own feelings generally make it so."

"I hope I am as fond of my child as any mother, but I do not know that I am of any more use in the sick-room than Charles, for I cannot be always scolding and teasing a poor child when it is ill; and you saw, this morning, that if I told him to keep quiet, he was sure to begin kicking about. I have not nerves for the sort of thing."

"But could you be comfortable yourself, to be spending the whole evening away from the poor boy?"

"Yes; you see his papa can, and why should not I? Jemima is so careful, and she could send us word every hour how he was. I really think Charles might as well have told his father we would all come. I am not more alarmed about little Charles now than he is. I was dreadfully alarmed yesterday, but the case is very different to-day."

"Well, if you do not think it too late to give notice for yourself, suppose you were to go, as well as your husband. Leave little Charles to my care. Mr. and Mrs. Musgrove cannot think it wrong while I remain with him."

"Are you serious?" cried Mary, her eyes brightening. "Dear me! that's a very good thought, very good, indeed. To be sure, I may just as well go as not, for I am of no use at home — am I? and it only harasses me. You, who have not a mother's feelings, are a great deal the properest person. You can make little Charles do anything; he always minds you at a word. It will be a great deal better than leaving him with only Jemima. Oh! I will certainly go; I am sure I ought if I can, quite as much as Charles, for they want me excessively to be acquainted with Captain Wentworth, and I know you do not mind being left alone. An excellent thought of yours, indeed, Anne. I will go and tell Charles, and get ready directly. You can send for us, you know, at a moment's notice, if anything is the matter; but I dare say there will be nothing to alarm you. I should not go, you may be sure, if I did not feel quite at ease about my dear child."

The next moment she was tapping at her husband's dressing-room door, and as Anne followed her upstairs, she was in time for the whole conversation, which began with Mary's saying, in a tone of great exultation:

"I mean to go with you, Charles, for I am of no more use at home than you are. If I were to shut myself up for ever with the child, I should not be able to persuade him to do anything he did not like. Anne will stay; Anne undertakes to stay at home and take care of him. It is Anne's own proposal, and so I shall go with you, which will be a great deal better, for I have not dined at the other house since Tuesday."

"This is very kind of Anne," was her husband's answer, "and I should be very glad to have you go; but it seems rather hard that she should be left at home by herself, to nurse our sick child."

Anne was now at hand to take up her own cause, and the

sincerity of her manner being soon sufficient to convince him, where conviction was at least very agreeable, he had no further scruples as to her being left to dine alone, though he still wanted her to join them in the evening, when the child might be at rest for the night, and kindly urged her to let him come and fetch her, but she was quite unpersuadable; and this being the case, she had ere long the pleasure of seeing them set off together in high spirits. They were gone, she hoped, to be happy, however oddly constructed such happiness might seem; as for herself, she was left with as many sensations of comfort, as were, perhaps, ever likely to be hers. She knew herself to be of the first utility to the child; and what was it to her if Frederick Wentworth were only half a mile distant, making himself agreeable to others?

She would have liked to know how he felt as to a meeting. Perhaps indifferent, if indifference could exist under such circumstances. He must be either indifferent or unwilling. Had he wished ever to see her again, he need not have waited till this time; he would have done what she could not but believe that in his place she should have done long ago, when events had been early giving him the independence which alone had been wanting.

Her brother and sister came back delighted with their new acquaintance, and their visit in general. There had been music, singing, talking, laughing, all that was most agreeable; charming manners in Captain Wentworth, no shyness or reserve; they seemed all to know each other perfectly, and he was coming the very next morning to shoot with Charles. He was to come to breakfast, but not at the Cottage, though that had been proposed at first; but then he had been pressed to come to the Great House instead, and he seemed afraid of being in Mrs. Charles Musgrove's way, on account of the child, and therefore somehow, they hardly knew how, it ended in Charles's being to meet him to breakfast at his father's.

Anne understood it. He wished to avoid seeing her. He had inquired after her, she found, slightly, as might suit a former slight acquaintance, seeming to acknowledge such as she had acknowledged, actuated, perhaps, by the same view of escaping introduction when they were to meet.

The morning hours of the Cottage were always later than those of the other house, and on the morrow the difference was so great that Mary and Anne were not more than beginning breakfast when Charles came in to say that they were just setting off, that he was come for his dogs, that his sisters were following with Captain Wentworth; his sisters meaning to visit Mary and the child, and Captain Wentworth proposing also to wait on her for a few minutes if not inconvenient; and though Charles had answered for the child's being in no such state as could make it inconvenient, Captain Wentworth would not be satisfied without his running on to give notice.

Mary, very much gratified by this attention, was delighted to receive him, while a thousand feelings rushed on Anne, of which this was the most consoling, that it would soon be over. And it was soon over. In two minutes after Charles's preparation, the others appeared; they were in the drawing-room. Her eye half met Captain Wentworth's, a bow, a curtsey passed; she heard his voice; he talked to Mary, said all that was right, said something to the Miss Musgroves, enough to mark an easy footing; the room seemed full, full of persons and voices, but a few minutes ended it. Charles showed himself at the window, all was ready, their visitor had bowed and was gone, the Miss Musgroves were gone too, suddenly resolving to walk to the end of the village with the sportsmen; the room was cleared, and Anne might finish her breakfast as she could.

"It is over! It is over!" she repeated to herself again and again, in nervous gratitude. "The worst is over!"

Mary talked, but she could not attend. She had seen him. They had met. They had been once more in the same room.

Soon, however, she began to reason with herself, and try to be feeling less. Eight years, almost eight years had passed, since all had been given up. How absurd to be resuming the agitation which such an interval had banished into distance and indistinctness! What might not eight years do? Events of every description, changes, alienations, removals — all, all must be comprised in it, and oblivion of the past — how natural, how certain too! It included nearly a third part of her own life.

Alas! with all her reasonings she found that to retentive feelings eight years may be little more than nothing.

Now, how were his sentiments to be read? Was this like wishing to avoid her? And the next moment she was hating herself for the folly which asked the question.

On one other question, which perhaps her utmost wisdom might not have prevented, she was soon spared all suspense; for, after the Miss Musgroves had returned and finished their visit at the Cottage, she had this spontaneous information from Mary:

"Captain Wentworth is not very gallant by you, Anne, though he was so attentive to me. Henrietta asked him what he thought of you, when they went away, and he said: 'You were so altered he should not have known you again.'"

Mary had no feelings to make her respect her sister's in a common way, but she was perfectly unsuspicious of being inflicting any peculiar wound.

"Altered beyond his knowledge." Anne fully submitted, in silent, deep mortification. Doubtless it was so, and she could take no revenge, for he was not altered, or not for the worse. She had already acknowledged it to herself, and she could not think differently, let him think of her as he would. No: the years which had destroyed her youth and bloom had only given him a more glowing, manly, open look, in no respect lessening his personal advantages. She had seen the same Frederick Wentworth.

"So altered that he should not have known her again!" These were words which could not but dwell with her. Yet she soon began to rejoice that she had heard them. They were of sobering tendency; they allayed agitation; they composed, and consequently must make her happier.

Frederick Wentworth had used such words, or something like them, but without an idea that they would be carried round to her. He had thought her wretchedly altered, and in the first moment of appeal, had spoken as he felt. He had not forgiven Anne Elliot. She had used him ill, deserted and disappointed him; and worse, she had shown a feebleness of character in doing so, which his own decided, confident temper could not endure. She had given him up to oblige others. It had been the effect of over-persuasion. It had been weakness and timidity.

He had been most warmly attached to her, and had never seen a woman since whom he thought her equal; but, except from some natural sensation of curiosity, he had no desire of meeting her again. Her power with him was gone for ever.

It was now his object to marry. He was rich, and being turned on shore, fully intended to settle as soon as he could be properly tempted; actually looking round, ready to fall in love with all the speed which a clear head and quick taste could allow. He had a heart for either of the Miss Musgroves, if they could catch it; a heart, in short, for any pleasing young woman who came in his way, excepting Anne Elliot. This was his only secret exception, when he said to his sister, in answer to her suppositions:

"Yes, here I am, Sophia, quite ready to make a foolish match. Anybody between fifteen and thirty may have me for asking. A little beauty, and a few smiles, and a few compliments to the navy, and I am a lost man. Should not this be enough for a sailor, who has had no society among women to make him nice?"

He said it, she knew, to be contradicted. His bright proud eye spoke the happy conviction that he was nice; and Anne Elliot was not out of his thoughts, when he more than seriously described the woman he should wish to meet with. "A strong mind, with sweetness of manner," made the first and the last of the description.

"That is the woman I want," said he. "Something a little inferior I shall of course put up with, but it must not be much. If I am a fool, I shall be a fool indeed, for I have thought on the subject more than most men."

8

FROM THIS TIME Captain Wentworth and Anne Elliot were repeatedly in the same circle. They were soon dining in company together at Mr. Musgrove's, for the little boy's state could no longer supply his aunt with a pretence for absenting herself; and this was but the beginning of other dinings and other meetings.

Whether former feelings were to be renewed must be brought to the proof; former times must undoubtedly be brought to the recollection of each; *they* could not but be reverted to; the year of their engagement could not but be named by him, in the little narratives or descriptions which conversation called forth. His profession qualified him, his disposition led him to talk; and " *That* was in the year six"; " *That* happened before I went to sea, in the year six," occurred in the course of the first evening they spent together; and though his voice did not falter, and though she had no reason to suppose his eye wandering towards her while he spoke, Anne felt the utter impossibility, from her knowledge of his mind, that he could be unvisited by remembrance any more than herself. There must be the same immediate association of thought, though she was very far from conceiving it to be of equal pain.

They had no conversation together, no intercourse but what the commonest civility required. Once so much to each other! Now nothing! There *had* been a time, when of all the large party now filling the drawing-room at Uppercross, they would have found it most difficult to cease to speak to one another. With the exception, perhaps, of Admiral and Mrs. Croft, who seemed particularly attached and happy (Anne could allow no other exception, even among the married couples), there could have been no two hearts so open, no tastes so similar, no feelings so in unison, no countenances so beloved. Now they were as strangers; nay, worse than strangers, for they could never become acquainted. It was a perpetual estrangement.

When he talked, she heard the same voice; and discerned the same mind. There was a very general ignorance of all naval matters throughout the party; and he was very much questioned, and especially by the two Miss Musgroves, who seemed hardly to have any eyes but for him, as to the manner of living on board, daily regulations, food, hours, etc.; and their surprise at his accounts, at learning the degree of accommodation and arrangement which was practicable, drew from him some pleasant ridicule, which reminded Anne of the early days when she too had been ignorant, and she too had been accused of supposing sailors to be living on board without anything to eat, or any cook to dress it if there were, or any servant to wait, or any knife and fork to use.

From thus listening and thinking, she was roused by a

whisper of Mrs. Musgrove's, who, overcome by fond regrets, could not help saying:

"Ah! Miss Anne, if it had pleased Heaven to spare my poor son, I dare say he would have been just such another by this time."

Anne suppressed a smile, and listened kindly, while Mrs. Musgrove relieved her heart a little more; and for a few minutes, therefore, could not keep pace with the conversation of the others.

When she could let her attention take its natural course again, she found the Miss Musgroves just fetching the Navy List (their own Navy List, the first that had ever been at Uppercross), and sitting down together to pore over it, with the professed view of finding out the ships which Captain Wentworth had commanded.

"Your first was the *Asp*, *I* remember; we will look for the *Asp*."

"You will not find her there. Quite worn out and broken up. I was the last man who commanded her. Hardly fit for service then. Reported fit for home service for a year or two, and so I was sent off to the West Indies."

The girls looked all amazement.

"The Admiralty," he continued, "entertain themselves now and then, with sending a few hundred men to sea in a ship not fit to be employed. But they have a great many to provide for; and among the thousands that may just as well go to the bottom as not, it is impossible for them to distinguish the very set who may be least missed."

"Phoo! phoo!" cried the Admiral, "what stuff these young fellows talk! Never was there a better sloop than the *Asp* in her day. For an old built sloop, you would not see her equal. Lucky fellow to get her! He knows there must have been twenty better men than himself applying for her at the same time. Lucky fellow to get anything so soon, with no more interest than his."

"I felt my luck, Admiral, I assure you," replied Captain Wentworth, seriously. "I was as well satisfied with my appointment as you can desire. It was a great object with me at that time to be at sea; a very great object, I wanted to be doing something."

"To be sure you did. What should a young fellow like you do ashore for half a year together? If a man has not a wife, he soon wants to be afloat again."

"But, Captain Wentworth," cried Louisa, "how vexed you must have been when you came to the *Asp*, to see what an old thing they had given you!"

"I knew pretty well what she was before that day," said he, smiling. "I had no more discoveries to make than you would have as to the fashion and strength of any old pelisse, which you had seen lent about among half your acquaintances ever since you could remember, and which at last, on some very wet day, is lent to yourself. Ah! she was a dear old *Asp* to me. She did all that I wanted. I knew she would. I knew that we should either go to the bottom together, or that she would be the making of me; and I never had two days of foul weather all the time I was at sea in her; and after taking privateers enough to be very entertaining, I had the good luck in my passage home, the next autumn, to fall in with the very French frigate I wanted. I brought her into Plymouth; and here was another instance of luck. We had not been six hours in the Sound, when a gale came on, which lasted four days and nights, and which would have done for poor old *Asp* in half the time; our touch with the Great Nation not having much improved our condition. Four-and-twenty hours later, and I should only have been a gallant Captain Wentworth, in a small paragraph at one corner of the newspapers; and being lost in only a sloop, nobody would have thought about me."

Anne's shudderings were to herself alone; but the Miss Musgroves could be as open as they were sincere, in their exclamations of pity and horror.

"And so then, I suppose," said Mrs. Musgrove, in a low voice, as if thinking aloud, "so then he went away to the *Laconia*, and there he met with our poor boy. Charles, my dear" (beckoning him to her), "do ask Captain Wentworth where it was he first met with your poor brother. I always forget."

"It was at Gibraltar, mother, I know. Dick had been left ill at Gibraltar, with a recommendation from his former captain to Captain Wentworth."

"Oh! but Charles, tell Captain Wentworth, he need not be afraid of mentioning poor Dick before me, for it would be rather a pleasure to hear him talked of by such a good friend."

Charles being somewhat more mindful of the probabilities of the case, only nodded in reply, and walked away.

The girls were now hunting for the *Laconia;* and Captain Wentworth could not deny himself the pleasure of taking the precious volume into his own hands to save them the trouble, and once more read aloud the little statement of her name and rate, and present non-commissioned class, observing over it that she too had been one of the best friends man ever had.

"Ah, those were pleasant days when I had the *Laconia*. How fast I made money in her! A friend of mine and I had such a lovely cruise together off the Western Islands. Poor Harville, sister! You know how much he wanted money; worse than myself. He had a wife. Excellent fellow! I shall never forget his happiness. He felt it all, so much for her sake. I wished for him again the next summer, when I had still the same luck in the Mediterranean."

"And I am sure, sir," said Mrs. Musgrove, "it was a lucky day for *us*, when you were put captain into that ship. *We* shall never forget what you did."

Her feelings made her speak low; and Captain Wentworth, hearing only in part, and probably not having Dick Musgrove at all near his thoughts, looked rather in suspense, and as if waiting for more.

"My brother," whispered one of the girls; "mamma is thinking of poor Richard."

"Poor dear fellow!" continued Mrs. Musgrove; "he was grown so steady, and such an excellent correspondent, while he was under your care! Ah! it would have been a happy thing, if he had never left you. I assure you, Captain Wentworth, we are very sorry he ever left you."

There was a momentary expression in Captain Wentworth's face at this speech, a certain glance of his bright eye, and curl of his handsome mouth, which convinced Anne, that instead of sharing in Mrs. Musgrove's kind wishes, as to her son, he had probably been at some pains to get rid of him; but it was too transient an indulgence of self-amusement to be detected by any who understood him less than herself; in another moment he was perfectly collected and serious, and almost instantly afterwards coming up to the sofa, on which she and Mrs. Musgrove were sitting, took a place by the latter, and entered into conversation with her, in a low voice, about her son, doing it with so much sympathy and natural grace, as showed the kindest consideration for all that was real and unabsurd in the parent's feelings.

They were actually on the same sofa, for Mrs. Musgrove

had most readily made room for him: they were divided only by Mrs. Musgrove. It was no insignificant barrier, indeed. Mrs. Musgrove was a comfortable substantial size, infinitely more fitted by nature to express good cheer and good humour than tenderness and sentiment; and while the agitations of Anne's slender form and pensive face may be considered as very completely screened, Captain Wentworth should be allowed some credit for the self-command with which he attended to her large fat sighings over the destiny of a son, whom alive nobody had cared for.

Personal size and mental sorrow have certainly no necessary proportions. A large bulky figure has as good a right to be in deep affliction as the most graceful set of limbs in the world. But, fair or not fair, there are unbecoming conjunctions, which reason will patronise in vain—which taste cannot tolerate—which ridicule will seize.

The Admiral, after taking two or three refreshing turns about the room with his hands behind him, being called to order by his wife, now came up to Captain Wentworth, and without any observation of what he might be interrupting, thinking only of his own thoughts, began with—

"If you had been a week later at Lisbon, last spring, Frederick, you would have been asked to give a passage to Lady Mary Grierson and her daughters."

"Should I? I am glad I was not a week later then!"

The Admiral abused him for his want of gallantry. He defended himself; though professing that he would never willingly admit any ladies on board a ship of his, excepting for a ball, or a visit, which a few hours might comprehend.

"But, if I know myself," said he, "this is from no want of gallantry towards them. It is rather from feeling how impossible it is, with all one's efforts, and all one's sacrifices, to make the accommodations on board such as women ought to have. There can be no want of gallantry, Admiral, in rating the claims of women to every personal comfort *high*, and this is what I do. I hate to hear of women on board; or to see them on board; and no ship under my command shall ever convey a family of ladies anywhere, if I can help it."

This brought his sister upon him.

"Oh! Frederick! But I cannot believe it of you. All idle refinement! Women may be as comfortable on board as in the best house in England. I believe I have lived as much on board as most women, and I know nothing superior to the accommodations of a man-of-war. I declare I have not a comfort or an indulgence about me, even at Kellynch Hall" (with a kind bow to Anne), "beyond what I always had in most of the ships I have lived in; and they have been five altogether."

"Nothing to the purpose," replied her brother. "You were living with your husband, and were the only woman on board."

"But you, yourself, brought Mrs. Harville, her sister, her cousin, and the three children, round from Portsmouth to Plymouth. Where was this superfine, extraordinary sort of gallantry of yours then?"

"All merged in my friendship, Sophia. I would assist any brother officer's wife that I could, and I would bring anything of Harville's from the world's end, if he wanted it. But do not imagine that I did not feel it an evil in itself."

"Depend upon it, they were all perfectly comfortable."

"I might not like them the better for that, perhaps. Such a number of women and children have no *right* to be comfortable on board."

"My dear Frederick, you are talking quite idly. Pray, what

would become of us poor sailor's wives, who often want to be conveyed to one port or another, after our husbands, if everybody had your feelings?"

"My feelings, you see, did not prevent my taking Mrs. Harville and all her family to Plymouth."

"But I hate to hear you talking so like a fine gentleman, and as if women were all fine ladies, instead of rational creatures. We none of us expect to be in smooth water all our days."

"Ah! my dear," said the Admiral, "when he has got a wife, he will sing a different tune. When he is married, if we have the good luck to live to another war, we shall see him do as you and I, and a great many others, have done. We shall have him very thankful to anybody that will bring him his wife."

"Ay, that we shall."

"Now I have done," cried Captain Wentworth. "When once married people begin to attack me with—'Oh! you will think very differently when you are married,' I can only say, 'No, I shall not'; and then they say again, 'Yes, you will,' and there is an end of it."

He got up and moved away.

"What a great traveller you must have been, ma'am!" said Mrs. Musgrove to Mrs. Croft.

"Pretty well, ma'am, in the fifteen years of my marriage; though many women have done more. I have crossed the Atlantic four times, and have been once to the East Indies and back again, and only once; besides being in different places about home: Cork, and Lisbon, and Gibraltar. But I never went beyond the Streights, and never was in the West Indies. We do not call Bermuda or Bahama, you know, the West Indies."

Mrs. Musgrove had not a word to say in dissent; she could not accuse herself of having ever called them anything in the whole course of her life.

"And I do assure you, ma'am," pursued Mrs. Croft, "that nothing can exceed the accommodations of a man-of-war; I speak, you know, of the higher rates. When you come to a frigate, of course, you are more confined; though any reasonable woman may be perfectly happy in one of them; and I can safely say that the happiest part of my life has been spent on board a ship. While we were together, you know, there was nothing to be feared. Thank God! I have always been blessed with excellent health, and no climate disagrees with me. A little disordered always the first twenty-four hours of going to sea, but never knew what sickness was afterwards. The only time that I ever really suffered in body or mind, the only time that I ever fancied myself unwell, or had any ideas of danger—was the winter that I passed by myself at Deal, when the Admiral (*Captain* Croft then) was in the North Seas. I lived in perpetual fright at that time, and had all manner of imaginary complaints from not knowing what to do with myself, or when I should hear from him next; but as long as we could be together, nothing ever ailed me, and I never met with the smallest inconvenience."

"Ay, to be sure. Yes, indeed, oh yes! I am quite of your opinion, Mrs. Croft," was Mrs. Musgrove's hearty answer. "There is nothing so bad as a separation. I am quite of your opinion. *I* know what it is, for Mr. Musgrove always attends the assizes, and I am so glad when they are over, and he is safe back again."

The evening ended with dancing. On its being proposed, Anne offered her services, as usual; and though her eyes would sometimes fill with tears as she sat at the instrument, she was extremely glad to be employed, and desired nothing in return but to be unobserved.

It was a merry, joyous party, and no one seemed in higher spirits than Captain Wentworth. She felt that he had everything to elevate him, which general attention and deference, and especially the attention of all the young women, could do. The Miss Hayters, the females of the family of cousins already mentioned, were apparently admitted to the honour of being in love with him; and as for Henrietta and Louisa, they both seemed so entirely occupied by him, that nothing but the continued appearance of the most perfect good-will between themselves could have made it credible that they were not decided rivals. If he were a little spoilt by such universal, such eager admiration, who could wonder?

These were some of the thoughts which occupied Anne, while her fingers were mechanically at work, proceeding for half an hour together, equally without error, and without consciousness. *Once* she felt that he was looking at herself, observing her altered features, perhaps, trying to trace in them the ruins of the face which had once charmed him; and *once* she knew that he must have spoken of her; she was hardly aware of it till she heard the answer; but then she was sure of his having asked his partner whether Miss Elliot never danced? The answer was, "Oh, no! never; she has quite given up dancing. She had rather play. She is never tired of playing." Once, too, he spoke to her. She had left the instrument on the dancing being over, and he had sat down to try to make out an air which he wished to give the Miss Musgroves an idea of. Unintentionally she returned to that part of the room; he saw her, and instantly rising, said, with studied politeness:

"I beg your pardon, madam, this is your seat;" and

though she immediately drew back with a decided negative, he was not to be induced to sit down again.

Anne did not wish for more of such looks and speeches. His cold politeness, his ceremonious grace, were worse than anything.

9

CAPTAIN WENTWORTH was come to Kellynch as to a home, to stay as long as he liked, being as thoroughly the object of the Admiral's fraternal kindness as of his wife's. He had intended, on first arriving, to proceed very soon into Shropshire, and visit the brother settled in that country, but the attractions of Uppercross induced him to put this off. There was so much of friendliness, and of flattery, and of everything most bewitching in his reception there; the old were so hospitable, the young so agreeable, that he could not but resolve to remain where he was, and take all the charms and perfections of Edward's wife upon credit a little longer.

It was soon Uppercross with him almost every day. The Musgroves could hardly be more ready to invite than he to come, particularly in the morning, when he had no companion at home; for the Admiral and Mrs. Croft were generally out of doors together, interesting themselves in their new possessions, their grass, and their sheep, and dawdling about in a way not endurable to a third person, or driving out in a gig, lately added to their establishment.

Hitherto there had been but one opinion of Captain Wentworth among the Musgroves and their dependencies. It was unvarying, warm admiration everywhere; but this intimate footing was not more than established, when a certain Charles Hayter returned among them, to be a good deal disturbed by it, and to think Captain Wentworth very much in the way.

Charles Hayter was the eldest of all the cousins, and a very amiable, pleasing young man, between whom and Henrietta there had been a considerable appearance of attachment previous to Captain Wentworth's introduction. He was in orders; and having a curacy in the neighbourhood, where residence was not required, lived at his father's house, only two miles from Uppercross. A short absence from home had left his fair one unguarded by his attentions at this critical period, and when he came back he had the pain of finding very altered manners, and of seeing Captain Wentworth.

Mrs. Musgrove and Mrs. Hayter were sisters. They had each had money, but their marriages had made a material difference in their degree of consequence. Mr. Hayter had some property of his own, but it was insignificant compared with Mr. Musgrove's; and while the Musgroves were in the first class of society in the country, the young Hayters would, from their parents' inferior, retired, and unpolished way of living, and their own defective education, have been hardly in any class at all, but for their connection with Uppercross, this eldest son of course excepted, who had chosen to be a scholar and a gentleman, and who was very superior in cultivation and manners to all the rest.

The two families had always been on excellent terms, there being no pride on one side, and no envy on the other, and only such a consciousness of superiority in the Miss Musgroves, as made them pleased to improve their cousins. Charles's attentions to Henrietta had been observed by her father and mother without any disapprobation. "It would not be a great match for her; but if Henrietta liked him,"— and Henrietta *did* seem to like him.

Henrietta fully thought so herself, before Captain Wentworth came; but from that time Cousin Charles had been very much forgotten.

Which of the two sisters was preferred by Captain Wentworth was as yet quite doubtful, as far as Anne's observation reached. Henrietta was perhaps the prettiest, Louisa had the higher spirits; and she knew not *now*, whether the more gentle or the more lively character were most likely to attract him.

Mr. and Mrs. Musgrove, either from seeing little, or from an entire confidence in the discretion of both their daughters, and of all the young men who came near them, seemed to leave everything to take its chance. There was not the smallest appearance of solicitude or remark about them in the Mansion House; but it was different at the Cottage; the young couple there were more disposed to speculate and wonder; and Captain Wentworth had not been above four or five times in the Miss Musgroves' company, and Charles Hayter had but just reappeared, when Anne had to listen to the opinions of her brother and sister, as to *which* was the one liked best. Charles gave it for Louisa, Mary for Henrietta, but quite agreeing that to have him marry either would be extremely delightful.

Charles "had never seen a pleasanter man in his life; and from what he had once heard Captain Wentworth himself say, was very sure that he had not made less than twenty thousand pounds by the war. Here was a fortune at once:

besides which, there would be the chance of what might be done in any future war; and he was sure Captain Wentworth was as likely a man to distinguish himself as any officer in the navy. Oh! it would be a capital match for either of his sisters."

"Upon my word it would," replied Mary. "Dear me! If he should rise to any very great honours! If he should ever be made a baronet! 'Lady Wentworth' sounds very well. That would be a noble thing, indeed, for Henrietta! She would take place of me then, and Henrietta would not dislike that. Sir Frederick and Lady Wentworth! It would be but a new creation, however, and I never think much of your new creations."

It suited Mary best to think Henrietta the one preferred on the very account of Charles Hayter, whose pretensions she wished to see put an end to. She looked down very decidedly upon the Hayters, and thought it would be quite a misfortune to have the existing connection between the families renewed—very sad for herself and her children.

"You know," said she, "I cannot think him at all a fit match for Henrietta; and considering the alliances which the Musgroves have made, she has no right to throw herself away. I do not think any young woman has a right to make a choice that may be disagreeable and inconvenient to the *principal* part of her family, and be giving bad connections to those who have not been used to them. And, pray, who is Charles Hayter? Nothing but a country curate. A most improper match for Miss Musgrove of Uppercross."

Her husband, however, would not agree with her here; for besides having a regard for his cousin, Charles Hayter was an eldest son, and he saw things as an eldest son himself.

"Now you are talking nonsense, Mary," was therefore his

answer. "It would not be a *great* match for Henrietta, but Charles has a very fair chance, through the Spicers, of getting something from the Bishop in the course of a year or two; and you will please to remember that he is the eldest son; whenever my uncle dies, he steps into very pretty property. The estate at Winthrop is not less than two hundred and fifty acres, besides the farm near Taunton, which is some of the best land in the country. I grant you, that any of them but Charles would be a very shocking match for Henrietta, and indeed it could not be; he is the only one that could be possible; but he is a very good-natured, good sort of a fellow; and whenever Winthrop comes into his hands, he will make a different sort of place of it, and live in a very different sort of way; and with that property he will never be a contemptible man—good freehold property. No, no; Henrietta might do worse than marry Charles Hayter; and if she has him and Louisa can get Captain Wentworth, I shall be very well satisfied."

"Charles may say what he pleases," cried Mary to Anne, as soon as he was out of the room, "but it would be shocking to have Henrietta marry Charles Hayter: a very bad thing for *her*, and still worse for *me*; and therefore it is very much to be wished that Captain Wentworth may soon put him quite out of her head, and I have very little doubt that he has. She took hardly any notice of Charles Hayter yesterday. I wish you had been there to see her behaviour. And as to Captain Wentworth's liking Louisa as well as Henrietta, it is nonsense to say so; for he certainly *does* like Henrietta a great deal the best. But Charles is so positive! I wish you had been with us yesterday, for then you might have decided between us; and I am sure you would have thought as I did, unless you had been determined to give it against me."

A dinner at Mr. Musgrove's had been the occasion when all these things should have been seen by Anne; but she had stayed at home, under the mixed plea of a headache of her own, and some return of indisposition in little Charles. She had thought only of avoiding Captain Wentworth; but an escape from being appealed to as umpire was now added to the advantages of a quiet evening.

As to Captain Wentworth's views, she deemed it of more consequence that he should know his own mind early enough not to be endangering the happiness of either sister, or impeaching his own honour, than that he should prefer Henrietta to Louisa, or Louisa to Henrietta. Either of them would, in all probability, make him an affectionate, good-humoured wife. With regard to Charles Hayter, she had delicacy which must be pained by any lightness of conduct in a well-meaning young woman, and a heart to sympathise in any of the sufferings it occasioned; but if Henrietta found herself mistaken in the nature of her feelings, the alteration could not be understood too soon.

Charles Hayter had met with much to disquiet and mortify him in his cousin's behaviour. She had too old a regard for him to be so wholly estranged as might in two meetings extinguish every past hope, and leave him nothing to do but to keep away from Uppercross: but there was such a change as became very alarming, when such a man as Captain Wentworth was to be regarded as the probable cause. He had been absent only two Sundays, and when they parted, had left her interested, even to the height of his wishes, in his prospect of soon quitting his present curacy, and obtaining that of Uppercross instead. It had then seemed the object nearest her heart, that Dr. Shirley, the rector, who for more than forty years had been zealously discharging all the duties of his office, but was now growing too infirm for many of them, should be quite fixed on engaging a curate; should make his curacy quite as good as he could afford, and should give Charles Hayter the promise of it. The advantage of his having to come only to Uppercross, instead of going six miles another way; of his having, in every respect, a better curacy; of his belonging to their dear Dr. Shirley; and of dear, good Dr. Shirley's being relieved from the duty which he could no longer get through without most injurious fatigue, had been a great deal, even to Louisa, but had been almost everything to Henrietta. When he came back, alas! the zeal of the business was gone by. Louisa could not listen at all to his account of a conversation which he had just held with Dr. Shirley: she was at the window, looking out for Captain Wentworth; and even Henrietta had at best only a divided attention to give, and seemed to have forgotten all the former doubt and solicitude of the negotiation.

"Well, I am very glad, indeed; but I always thought you would have it; I always thought you sure. It did not appear to me that—in short, you know, Dr. Shirley *must* have a curate, and you had secured his promise. Is he coming, Louisa?"

One morning, very soon after the dinner at the Musgroves', at which Anne had not been present, Captain Wentworth walked into the drawing-room at the Cottage, where were only herself and the little invalid Charles, who was lying on the sofa.

The surprise of finding himself almost alone with Anne Elliot deprived his manners of their usual composure: he started, and could only say, "I thought the Miss Musgroves had been here: Mrs. Musgrove told me I should find them here," before he walked to the window to recollect himself, and feel how he ought to behave.

"They are upstairs with my sister: they will be down in a

few moments, I dare say," had been Anne's reply, in all the confusion that was natural; and if the child had not called her to come and do something for him, she would have been out of the room the next moment, and released Captain Wentworth as well as herself.

He continued at the window; and after calmly and politely saying, "I hope the little boy is better," was silent.

She was obliged to kneel down by the sofa, and remain there to satisfy her patient; and thus they continued a few minutes, when, to her very great satisfaction, she heard some other person crossing the little vestibule. She hoped, on turning her head, to see the master of the house; but it proved to be one much less calculated for making matters easy—Charles Hayter, probably not at all better pleased by the sight of Captain Wentworth, than Captain Wentworth had been by the sight of Anne.

She only attempted to say, "How do you do? Will not you sit down? The others will be here presently."

Captain Wentworth, however, came from his window, apparently not ill-disposed for conversation; but Charles Hayter soon put an end to his attempts, by seating himself near the table, and taking up the newspaper; and Captain Wentworth returned to his window.

Another minute brought another addition. The younger boy, a remarkably stout, forward child, of two years old, having got the door opened for him by some one without, made his determined appearance among them, and went straight to the sofa to see what was going on, and put in his claim to anything good that might be giving away.

There being nothing to be eat, he could only have some play; and as his aunt would not let him tease his sick brother, he began to fasten himself upon her, as she knelt, in such a way that, busy as she was about Charles, she could not shake him off. She spoke to him, ordered, entreated, and insisted in vain. Once did she contrive to push him away, but the boy had the greater pleasure in getting upon her back again directly.

"Walter," said she, "get down this moment. You are extremely troublesome. I am very angry with you."

"Walter," cried Charles Hayter, "why do you not do as you are bid? Do not you hear your aunt speak? Come to me, Walter; come to cousin Charles."

But not a bit did Walter stir.

In another moment, however, she found herself in the state of being released from him; some one was taking him from her, though he had bent down her head so much, that his little sturdy hands were unfastened from around her neck, and he was resolutely borne away, before she knew that Captain Wentworth had done it.

Her sensations on the discovery made her perfectly speechless. She could not even thank him. She could only hang over little Charles, with most disordered feelings. His kindness in stepping forward to her relief, the manner, the silence in which it had passed, the little particulars of the circumstance, with the conviction soon forced on her by the noise he was studiously making with the child, that he meant to avoid hearing her thanks, and rather sought to testify that her conversation was the last of his wants, produced such a confusion of varying, but very painful agitation as she could not recover from, till enabled, by the entrance of Mary and the Miss Musgroves, to make over her little patient to their cares, and leave the room. She could not stay. It might have been an opportunity of watching the loves and jealousies of the four—they were now all together; but she could stay for none of it. It was evident that Charles Hayter was not well inclined towards Captain Wentworth.

She had a strong impression of his having said, in a vexed tone of voice, after Captain Wentworth's interference, "You ought to have minded *me,* Walter; I told you not to tease your aunt;" and could comprehend his regretting that Captain Wentworth should do what he ought to have done himself. But neither Charles Hayter's feelings, nor anybody's feelings, could interest her, till she had a little better arranged her own. She was ashamed of herself, quite ashamed of being so nervous, so overcome by such a trifle; but so it was, and it required a long application of solitude and reflection to recover her.

10

OTHER OPPORTUNITIES of making her observations could not fail to occur. Anne had soon been in company with all the four together often enough to have an opinion, though too wise to acknowledge as much at home, where she knew it would have satisfied neither husband nor wife; for while she considered Louisa to be rather the favourite, she could not but think, as far as she might dare to judge from memory and experience, that Captain Wentworth was not in love with either. They were more in love with him; yet there it was not love. It was a little fever of admiration; but it might, probably must, end in love with some. Charles Hayter seemed aware of being slighted, and yet Henrietta had sometimes the air of being divided between them. Anne longed for the power of representing to them all what they were about, and of pointing out some of the evils they were exposing themselves to. She did not attribute guile to any. It was the highest satisfaction to her to believe Captain Wentworth not in the least aware of the pain he was occasioning. There was no triumph, no pitiful triumph in his manner. He had, probably, never heard, and never thought of any claims of Charles Hayter. He was only wrong in accepting the attentions (for accepting must be the word) of two young women at once.

After a short struggle, however, Charles Hayter seemed to quit the field. Three days had passed without his coming once to Uppercross; a most decided change. He had even refused one regular invitation to dinner; and having been found on the occasion by Mr. Musgrove with some large books before him, Mr. and Mrs. Musgrove were sure all could not be right, and talked, with grave faces, of his studying himself to death. It was Mary's hope and belief that he had received a positive dismissal from Henrietta, and her husband lived under the constant dependence of seeing him to-morrow. Anne could only feel that Charles Hayter was wise.

One morning, about this time, Charles Musgrove and Captain Wentworth being gone a-shooting together, as the sisters in the Cottage were sitting quietly at work, they were visited at the window by the sisters from the Mansion House.

It was a very fine November day, and the Miss Musgroves came through the little grounds, and stopped for no other purpose than to say, that they were going to take a *long* walk, and therefore concluded Mary could not like to go with them; and when Mary immediately replied, with some jealousy at not being supposed a good walker, "Oh, yes! I should like to join you very much, I am very fond of a long walk," Anne felt persuaded, by the looks of the two girls, that it was precisely what they did not wish, and admired again the sort of necessity which the family habits seemed to produce, of everything being to be communicated, and everything being to be done together, however undesired and inconvenient. She tried to dissuade Mary from going, but in vain; and that being the case, thought it best to accept the Miss Musgroves' much more cordial invitation to herself to go likewise, as she might be useful in turning back with her sister, and lessening the interference in any plan of their own.

"I cannot imagine why they should suppose I should not like a long walk," said Mary, as she went upstairs. "Everybody is always supposing that I am not a good walker; and yet they would not have been pleased if we had refused to join them. When people come in this manner on purpose to ask us, how can one say no?"

Just as they were setting off, the gentlemen returned. They had taken out a young dog, which had spoilt their sport, and sent them back early. Their time, and strength, and spirits, were, therefore, exactly ready for this walk, and they entered into it with pleasure. Could Anne have foreseen such a junction, she would have stayed at home; but, from some feelings of interest and curiosity, she fancied now that it was too late to retract, and the whole six set forward together in the direction chosen by the Miss Musgroves, who evidently considered the walk as under their guidance.

Anne's object was, not to be in the way of anybody; and where the narrow paths across the fields made many separations necessary, to keep with her brother and sister. Her *pleasure* in the walk must arise from the exercise and the day, from the view of the last smiles of the year upon the tawny leaves and withered hedges, and from repeating to herself some few of the thousand poetical descriptions extant of autumn, that season of peculiar and inexhaustible influence on the mind of taste and tenderness, that season which has drawn from every poet, worthy of being read, some attempt at description, or some lines of feeling. She occupied her mind as much as possible in such like musings and quotations; but it was not possible, that when within reach of Captain Wentworth's conversation with either of the Miss Musgroves, she should not try to hear it; yet she caught little very remarkable. It was mere lively chat, such as any young persons, on an intimate footing, might fall into. He was more engaged with Louisa, than with Henrietta. Louisa certainly put more forward for his notice than her sister. This distinction appeared to increase, and there was one speech of Louisa's which struck her. After one of the many praises of the day, which were continually bursting forth, Captain Wentworth added:

"What glorious weather for the Admiral and my sister! They meant to take a long drive this morning; perhaps we may hail them from some of these hills. They talked of coming into this side of the country. I wonder whereabouts they will upset to-day. Oh! it does happen very often, I assure you; but my sister makes nothing of it; she would as lieve be tossed out as not."

"Ah! you make the most of it, I know," cried Louisa; "but if it were really so, I should do just the same in her place. If I loved a man as she loves the Admiral, I would always be with him, nothing should ever separate us, and I would rather be overturned by him, than driven safely by anybody else."

It was spoken with enthusiasm.

"Had you?" cried he, catching the same tone; "I honour you!" And there was silence between them for a little while.

Anne could not immediately fall into a quotation again. The sweet scenes of autumn were for a while put by, unless some tender sonnet, fraught with the apt analogy of the declining year with declining happiness, and the images of youth, and hope, and spring, all gone together, blessed her memory. She roused herself to say, as they struck by order into another path, "Is not this one of the ways to Winthrop?" But nobody heard, or, at least, nobody answered her.

Winthrop, however, or its environs — for young men are sometimes to be met with, strolling about near home — was their destination; and after another half mile of gradual ascent through large enclosures, where the ploughs at work, and the fresh made path spoke the farmer counteracting the sweets of poetical despondence, and meaning to have spring again, they gained the summit of the most considerable hill, which parted Uppercross and Winthrop, and soon commanded a full view of the latter, at the foot of the hill on the other side.

Winthrop, without beauty and without dignity, was stretched before them — an indifferent house, standing low, and hemmed in by the barns and buildings of a farmyard.

Mary exclaimed, "Bless me! here is Winthrop. I declare I had no idea! Well now, I think we had better turn back; I am excessively tired."

Henrietta, conscious and ashamed, and seeing no cousin Charles walking along any path, or leaning against any gate, was ready to do as Mary wished; but "No!" said Charles Musgrove, and "No, no!" cried Louisa, more eagerly, and taking her sister aside, seemed to be arguing the matter warmly.

Charles, in the meanwhile, was very decidedly declaring his resolution of calling on his aunt, now that he was so near; and very evidently, though more fearfully, trying to induce his wife to go too. But this was one of the points on which the lady showed her strength; and when he recommended the advantage of resting herself a quarter of an hour at Winthrop, as she felt so tired, she resolutely answered, "Oh, no, indeed! walking up that hill again would do her more harm than any sitting down could do her good"; and in short, her look and manner declared, that go she would not.

After a little succession of these sort of debates and consultations, it was settled between Charles and his two sisters, that he and Henrietta should just run down for a few minutes, to see their aunt and cousins, while the rest of the party waited for them at the top of the hill. Louisa seemed the principal arranger of the plan; and, as she went a little way with them down the hill, still talking to Henrietta, Mary took the opportunity of looking scornfully around her, and saying to Captain Wentworth:

"It is very unpleasant having such connections! But, I assure you, I have never been in the house above twice in my life."

She received no other answer than an artificial, assenting smile, followed by a contemptuous glance, as he turned away, which Anne perfectly knew the meaning of.

The brow of the hill, where they remained, was a cheerful spot; Louisa returned; and Mary, finding a comfortable seat for herself on the step of a stile, was very well satisfied so long as the others all stood about her; but when Louisa drew Captain Wentworth away, to try for a gleaning of nuts in an adjoining hedge-row, and they were gone by degrees quite out of sight and sound, Mary was happy no longer: she quarrelled with her own seat, was sure Louisa had got a much better somewhere, and nothing could prevent her from going to look for a better also. She turned through the same gate, but could not see them. Anne found a nice seat for her, on a dry sunny bank, under the hedge-row, in which she had no doubt of their still being, in some spot or other. Mary sat down for a moment, but it would not do; she was sure Louisa had found a better seat somewhere else, and she would go on till she overtook her.

Anne, really tired herself, was glad to sit down; and she very soon heard Captain Wentworth and Louisa in the hedge-row behind her, as if making their way back along the rough, wild sort of channel, down the centre. They were speaking as they drew near. Louisa's voice was the first distinguished. She seemed to be in the middle of some eager speech. What Anne first heard was:

"And so, I made her go. I could not bear that she should be frightened from the visit by such nonsense. What! would I be turned back from doing a thing that I had determined to do, and that I knew to be right, by the airs and interference of such a person, or of any persons, I may say? No, I have no idea of being so easily persuaded. When I have made up my mind, I have made it; and Henrietta seemed entirely to have made up hers to call at Winthrop to-day; and yet, she was as near giving it up out of nonsensical complaisance!"

"She would have turned back, then, but for you?"

"She would indeed. I am almost ashamed to say it."

"Happy for her, to have such a mind as yours at hand! After the hints you gave just now, which did but confirm my own observations, the last time I was in company with him, I need not affect to have no comprehension of what is going on. I see that more than a mere dutiful morning visit to your aunt was in question; and woe betide him, and her too, when it comes to things of consequence, when they are placed in circumstances requiring fortitude and strength of mind, if she have not resolution enough to resist idle interference in such a trifle as this. Your sister is an amiable creature; but *yours* is the character of decision and firmness, I see. If you value her conduct or happiness, infuse as much of your own spirit into her as you can. But this, no doubt, you have been always doing. It is the worst evil of too yielding and indecisive a character, that no influence over it can be depended on. You are never sure of a good impression being durable; everybody may sway it. Let those who would be happy be firm. Here is a nut," said he, catching one down from an upper bough, "to exemplify: a beautiful glossy nut, which, blessed with original strength, has outlived all the storms of autumn. Not a puncture, not a weak spot anywhere. This nut," he continued, with playful solemnity, "while so many of its brethren have fallen and been trodden under foot, is still in possession of all the happiness that a hazel nut can be supposed capable of." Then returning to his former earnest tone—"My first wish for all whom I am interested in, is that they should be firm. If Louisa Musgrove would be beautiful and happy in her November of life, she will cherish all her present powers of mind."

He had done, and was unanswered. It would have surprised Anne if Louisa could have readily answered such a speech: words of such interest, spoken with such serious warmth! She could imagine what Louisa was feeling. For herself, she feared to move, lest she should be seen. While she remained, a bush of low rambling holly protected her, and they were moving on. Before they were beyond her hearing, however, Louisa spoke again.

"Mary is good-natured enough in many respects," said she; "but she does sometimes provoke me excessively by her nonsense and pride—the Elliot pride. She has a great deal too much of the Elliot pride. We do so wish that Charles had married Anne instead. I suppose you know he wanted to marry Anne?"

After a moment's pause, Captain Wentworth said:

"Do you mean that she refused him?"

"Oh! yes; certainly."

"When did that happen?"

"I do not exactly know, for Henrietta and I were at school at the time; but I believe about a year before he married Mary. I wish she had accepted him. We should all have liked her a great deal better; and papa and mamma always think it was her great friend Lady Russell's doing that she did not. They think Charles might not be learned and bookish enough to please Lady Russell, and that, therefore, she persuaded Anne to refuse him."

The sounds were retreating, and Anne distinguished no more. Her own emotions still kept her fixed. She had much to recover from before she could move. The listener's proverbial fate was not absolutely hers: she had heard no evil of herself, but she had heard a great deal of very painful import. She saw how her own character was considered by Captain Wentworth, and there had been just that degree of feeling and curiosity about her in his manner which must give her extreme agitation.

As soon as she could, she went after Mary, and having found and walked back with her to their former station by the stile, felt some comfort in their whole party being immediately afterwards collected, and once more in motion together. Her spirits wanted the solitude and silence which only numbers could give.

Charles and Henrietta returned, bringing, as may be conjectured, Charles Hayter with them. The minutiæ of the business Anne could not attempt to understand; even Captain Wentworth did not seem admitted to perfect confidence here; but that there had been a withdrawing on the gentleman's side, and a relenting on the lady's, and that they were now very glad to be together again, did not admit a doubt. Henrietta looked a little ashamed, but very well pleased;

Charles Hayter exceedingly happy: and they were devoted to each other almost from the first instant of their all setting forward for Uppercross.

Everything now marked out Louisa for Captain Wentworth: nothing could be plainer; and where many divisions were necessary, or even where they were not, they walked side by side nearly as much as the other two. In a long strip of meadow land, where there was ample space for all, they were thus divided, forming three distinct parties; and to that party of the three which boasted least animation, and least complaisance, Anne necessarily belonged. She joined Charles and Mary, and was tired enough to be very glad of Charles's other arm; but Charles, though in very good humour with her, was out of temper with his wife. Mary had shown herself disobliging to him, and was now to reap the consequence, which consequence was his dropping her arm almost every moment to cut off the heads of some nettles in the hedge with his switch; and when Mary began to complain of it, and lament her being ill-used, according to custom, it being on the hedge side, while Anne was never incommoded on the other, he dropped the arms of both, to hunt after a weasel, which he had a momentary glance of, and they could hardly get him along at all.

This long meadow bordered a lane which their footpath, at the end of it, was to cross, and when the party had all reached the gate of exit, the carriage advancing in the same direction, which had been some time heard, was just coming up, and proved to be Admiral Croft's gig. He and his wife had taken their intended drive, and were returning home. Upon hearing how long a walk the young people had engaged in, they kindly offered a seat to any lady who might be particularly tired; it would save her full a mile, and they were going through Uppercross. The invitation was general and generally declined. The Miss Musgroves were not at all tired, and Mary was either offended by not being asked before any of the others, or what Louisa called the Elliot pride could not endure to make a third in a one-horse chaise.

The walking party had crossed the lane, and were surmounting an opposite stile, and the Admiral was putting his horse into motion again, when Captain Wentworth cleared the hedge in a moment, to say something to his sister. The something might be guessed by its effects.

"Miss Elliot, I am sure *you* are tired," cried Mrs. Croft. "Do let us have the pleasure of taking you home. Here is excellent room for three, I assure you. If we were all like you, I believe we might sit four. You must, indeed, you must."

Anne was still in the lane, and though instinctively beginning to decline, she was not allowed to proceed. The Admiral's kind urgency came in support of his wife's: they would not be refused: they compressed themselves into the smallest possible space to leave her a corner, and Captain Wentworth, without saying a word, turned to her, and quietly obliged her to be assisted into the carriage.

Yes; he had done it. She was in the carriage, and felt that he had placed her there, that his will and his hands had done it, that she owed it to his perception of her fatigue, and his resolution to give her rest. She was very much affected by the view of his disposition towards her, which all these things made apparent. This little circumstance seemed the completion of all that had gone before. She understood him. He could not forgive her, but he could not be unfeeling. Though condemning her for the past, and considering it with high and unjust resentment, though perfectly careless of her, and though becoming attached to another, still he could not see her suffer without the desire of giving her relief. It was a remainder of former sentiment; it was an impulse of pure, though unacknowledged friendship; it was a proof of his own warm and amiable heart, which she could not contemplate without emotions so compounded of pleasure and pain, that she knew not which prevailed.

Her answers to the kindness and the remarks of her companions were at first unconsciously given. They had travelled half their way along the rough lane before she was quite awake to what they said. She then found them talking of "Frederick."

"He certainly means to have one or other of those two girls, Sophy," said the Admiral; "but there is no saying which. He has been running after them, too, long enough, one would think, to make up his mind. Ay, this comes of the peace. If it were war now, he would have settled it long ago. We sailors, Miss Elliot, cannot afford to make long courtships in time of war. How many days was it, my dear, between the first time of my seeing you and our sitting down together in our lodgings at North Yarmouth?"

"We had better not talk about it, my dear," replied Mrs. Croft, pleasantly; "for if Miss Elliot were to hear how soon we came to an understanding, she would never be persuaded that we could be happy together. I had known you by character, however, long before."

"Well, and I had heard of you as a very pretty girl, and what were we to wait for besides? I do not like having such things so long in hand. I wish Frederick would spread a little more canvas, and bring us home one of these young ladies to Kellynch. Then there would always be company for them. And very nice young ladies they both are; I hardly know one from the other."

"Very good humoured, unaffected girls, indeed," said

Mrs. Croft, in a tone of calmer praise, such as made Anne suspect that her keener powers might not consider either of them as quite worthy of her brother; "and a very respectable family. One could not be connected with better people. My dear Admiral, that post; we shall certainly take that post."

But by coolly giving the reins a better direction herself they happily passed the danger; and by once afterwards judiciously putting out her hand they neither fell into a rut, nor ran foul of a dung-cart; and Anne, with some amusement at their style of driving, which she imagined no bad representation of the general guidance of their affairs, found herself safely deposited by them at the Cottage.

11

THE TIME NOW APPROACHED for Lady Russell's return: the day was even fixed; and Anne, being engaged to join her as soon as she was resettled, was looking forward to an early removal to Kellynch, and beginning to think how her own comfort was likely to be affected by it.

It would place her in the same village with Captain Wentworth, within half a mile of him; they would have to frequent the same church, and there must be intercourse between the two families. This was against her; but on the other hand, he spent so much of his time at Uppercross that in removing thence she might be considered rather as leaving him behind, than as going towards him; and upon the whole, she believed she must, on this interesting question, be the gainer, almost as certainly as in her change of domestic society, in leaving poor Mary for Lady Russell.

She wished it might be possible for her to avoid ever seeing Captain Wentworth at the Hall: those rooms had witnessed former meetings which would be brought too painfully before her; but she was yet more anxious for the possibility of Lady Russell and Captain Wentworth never meeting anywhere. They did not like each other, and no renewal of acquaintance now could do any good; and were Lady Russell to see them together, she might think that he had too much self-possession, and she too little.

These points formed her chief solicitude in anticipating her removal from Uppercross, where she felt she had been stationed quite long enough. Her usefulness to little Charles would always give some sweetness to the memory of her two months' visit there, but he was gaining strength apace, and she had nothing else to stay for.

The conclusion of her visit, however, was diversified in a way which she had not at all imagined. Captain Wentworth, after being unseen and unheard of at Uppercross for two whole days, appeared again among them to justify himself by a relation of what had kept him away.

A letter from his friend, Captain Harville, having found him out at last, had brought intelligence of Captain Harville's being settled with his family at Lyme for the winter; of their being, therefore, quite unknowingly, within twenty miles of each other. Captain Harville had never been in good health since a severe wound which he received two years before, and Captain Wentworth's anxiety to see him had determined him to go immediately to Lyme. He had been there for four-and-twenty hours. His acquittal was complete, his friendship warmly honoured, a lively interest excited for his friend, and his description of the fine country about Lyme so feelingly attended to by the party, that an earnest desire to see Lyme themselves, and a project for going thither was the consequence.

The young people were all wild to see Lyme. Captain Wentworth talked of going there again himself, it was only seventeen miles from Uppercross; though November, the weather was by no means bad; and, in short, Louisa, who was the most eager of the eager, having formed the resolution to go, and besides the pleasure of doing as she liked, being now armed with the idea of merit in maintaining her own way, bore down all the wishes of her father and mother for putting it off till summer; and to Lyme they were to go— Charles, Mary, Anne, Henrietta, Louisa, and Captain Wentworth.

The first heedless scheme had been to go in the morning and return at night; but to this Mr. Musgrove, for the sake of his horses, would not consent; and when it came to be rationally considered, a day in the middle of November would not leave much time for seeing a new place, after deducting seven hours, as the nature of the country required, for going and returning. They were consequently, to stay the night there, and not to be expected back till the next day's dinner. This was felt to be a considerable amendment; and though they all met at the Great House at rather an early breakfast hour, and set off very punctually, it was so much past noon before the two carriages, Mr. Musgrove's coach containing the four ladies, and Charles's curricle, in which he drove Captain Wentworth, were descending the long hill into Lyme, and entering upon the still steeper street of the town itself, that it was very evident they would not have more than time for looking about them, before the light and warmth of the day were gone.

After securing accommodations, and ordering a dinner at one of the inns, the next thing to be done was unquestionably to walk directly down to the sea. They were come too late in the year for any amusement or variety which Lyme, as a public place, might offer. The rooms were shut up, the lodgers almost all gone, scarcely any family but of the residents left; and, as there is nothing to admire in the buildings themselves, the remarkable situation of the town, the principal street almost hurrying into the water, the walk to the Cobb, skirting round the pleasant little bay, which, in the season, is animated with bathing machines and company; the Cobb itself, its old wonders and new improvements, with the very beautiful line of cliffs stretching out to the east of the town, are what the stranger's eye will seek; and a very strange stranger it must be, who does not see charms in the immediate environs of Lyme, to make him wish to know it better. The scenes in its neighbourhood, Charmouth, with its high grounds and extensive sweeps of country, and still more, its sweet, retired bay, backed by dark cliffs, where fragments of low rock among the sands make it the happiest spot for watching the flow of the tide, for sitting in unwearied contemplation; the wooded varieties of the cheerful village of Up Lyme; and, above all, Pinny, with its green chasms between romantic rocks, where the scattered forest trees and orchards of luxuriant growth declare that many a generation must have passed away since the first partial falling of the cliff prepared the ground for such a state, where a scene so wonderful and so lovely is exhibited as may more than equal any of the resembling scenes of the far-famed Isle of Wight: these places must be visited, and visited again to make the worth of Lyme understood.

The party from Uppercross passing down by the now deserted and melancholy looking rooms, and still descending, soon found themselves on the sea-shore; and lingering only as all must linger, and gaze on a first return to the sea, who ever deserve to look on it at all, proceeded towards the Cobb, equally their object in itself and on Captain Wentworth's account: for in a small house, near the foot of an old pier of unknown date, were the Harvilles settled. Captain

Wentworth turned in to call on his friend: the others walked on, and he was to join them on the Cobb.

They were by no means tired of wondering and admiring; and not even Louisa seemed to feel that they had parted with Captain Wentworth long, when they saw him coming after them with three companions, all well known already, by description, to be Captain and Mrs. Harville, and a Captain Benwick, who was staying with them.

Captain Benwick had some time ago been first lieutenant of the *Laconia;* and the account which Captain Wentworth had given of him, on his return from Lyme before, his warm praise of him as an excellent young man and an officer whom he had always valued highly, which must have stamped him well in the esteem of every listener, had been followed by a little history of his private life, which rendered him perfectly interesting in the eyes of all the ladies. He had been engaged to Captain Harville's sister, and was now mourning her loss. They had been a year or two waiting for fortune and promotion. Fortune came, his prize-money as lieutenant being great; promotion, too, came at *last;* but Fanny Harville did not live to know it. She had died the preceding summer while he was at sea. Captain Wentworth believed it impossible for man to be more attached to woman than poor Benwick had been to Fanny Harville, or to be more deeply afflicted under the dreadful change. He considered his disposition as of the sort which must suffer heavily, uniting very strong feelings with quiet, serious, and retiring manners, and a decided taste for reading, and sedentary pursuits. To finish the interest of the story, the friendship between him and the Harvilles seemed, if possible, augmented by the event which closed all their views of alliance, and Captain Benwick was now living with them entirely. Captain Harville had taken his present house for half a year;

his taste, and his health, and his fortune, all directing him to a residence unexpensive, and by the sea; and the grandeur of the country, and the retirement of Lyme in the winter, appeared exactly adapted to Captain Benwick's state of mind. The sympathy and good-will excited towards Captain Benwick was very great.

"And yet," said Anne to herself, as they now moved forward to meet the party, "he has not, perhaps, a more sorrowing heart than I have. I cannot believe his prospects so blighted for ever. He is younger than I am; younger in feeling, if not in fact; younger as a man. He will rally again, and be happy with another."

They all met, and were introduced. Captain Harville was a tall, dark man, with a sensible, benevolent countenance: a little lame; and from strong features and want of health, looking much older than Captain Wentworth. Captain Benwick looked, and was, the youngest of the three, and, compared with either of them, a little man. He had a pleasing face and a melancholy air, just as he ought to have, and drew back from conversation.

Captain Harville, though not equalling Captain Wentworth in manners, was a perfect gentleman, unaffected, warm, and obliging. Mrs. Harville, a degree less polished than her husband, seemed, however, to have the same good feelings; and nothing could be more pleasant than their desire of considering the whole party as friends of their own, because the friends of Captain Wentworth, or more kindly hospitable than their entreaties for their all promising to dine with them. The dinner, already ordered at the inn, was at last, though unwillingly, accepted as an excuse; but they seemed almost hurt that Captain Wentworth should have brought any such party to Lyme without considering it as a thing of course that they should dine with them.

There was so much attachment to Captain Wentworth in all this, and such a bewitching charm in a degree of hospitality so uncommon, so unlike the usual style of give-and-take invitations, and dinners of formality and display, that Anne felt her spirits not likely to be benefitted by an increasing acquaintance among his brother-officers. "These would have been all my friends," was her thought; and she had to struggle against a great tendency to lowness.

On quitting the Cobb, they all went indoors with their new friends, and found rooms so small as none but those who invite from the heart could think capable of accommodating so many. Anne had a moment's astonishment on the subject herself; but it was soon lost in the pleasanter feelings which sprang from the sight of all the ingenious contrivances and nice arrangements of Captain Harville, to turn the actual space to the best possible account, to supply the deficiencies of lodging-house furniture, and defend the windows and doors against the winter storms to be expected. The varieties in the fitting up of the rooms, where the common necessaries provided by the owner, in the common indifferent plight, were contrasted with some few articles of a rare species of wood, excellently worked up, and with something curious and valuable from all the distant countries Captain Harville had visited, were more than amusing to Anne: connected as it all was with his profession, the fruit of its labours, the effect of its influence on his habits, the picture of repose and domestic happiness it presented, made it to her a something more, or less, than gratification.

Captain Harville was no reader; but he had contrived excellent accommodations, and fashioned very pretty shelves, for a tolerable collection of well-bound volumes, the property of Captain Benwick. His lameness prevented him from

taking much exercise; but a mind of usefulness and inge-
nuity seemed to furnish him with constant employment
within. He drew, he varnished, he carpentered, he glued;
he made toys for the children; he fashioned new netting-
needles and pins with improvements; and if everything else
was done, sat down to his large fishing-net at one corner of
the room.

Anne thought she left great happiness behind her when
they quitted the house; and Louisa, by whom she found
herself walking, burst forth into raptures of admiration and
delight on the character of the navy; their friendliness, their
brotherliness, their openness, their uprightness; protesting
that she was convinced of sailors having more worth and
warmth than any other set of men in England; that they only
knew how to live, and they only deserved to be respected
and loved.

They went back to dress and dine; and so well had the
scheme answered already that nothing was found amiss;
though its being "so entirely out of the season," and the "no
thoroughfare of Lyme," and the "no expectation of company," had brought many apologies from the heads of the
inn.

Anne found herself by this time growing so much more
hardened to being in Captain Wentworth's company than
she had at first imagined could ever be, that the sitting down
to the same table with him now, and the interchange of the
common civilities attending on it (they never got beyond),
was become a mere nothing.

The nights were too dark for the ladies to meet again till
the morrow, but Captain Harville had promised them a visit
in the evening; and he came, bringing his friend also, which
was more than had been expected, it having been agreed
that Captain Benwick had all the appearance of being op-

pressed by the presence of so many strangers. He ventured among them again, however, though his spirits certainly did not seem fit for the mirth of the party in general.

While Captains Wentworth and Harville led the talk on one side of the room, and by recurring to former days, supplied anecdotes in abundance to occupy and entertain the others, it fell to Anne's lot to be placed rather apart with Captain Benwick; and a very good impulse of her nature obliged her to begin an acquaintance with him. He was shy, and disposed to abstraction; but the engaging mildness of her countenance, and gentleness of her manner, soon had their effect; and Anne was well repaid the first trouble of exertion. He was evidently a young man of considerable taste in reading, though principally in poetry; and besides the persuasion of having given him at least an evening's indulgence in the discussion of subjects, which his usual companions had probably no concern in, she had the hope of being of real use to him in some suggestions as to the duty and benefit of struggling against affliction, which had naturally grown out of their conversation. For, though shy, he did not seem reserved: it had rather the appearance of feelings glad to burst their usual restraints; and having talked of poetry, the richness of the present age, and gone through a brief comparison of opinion as to the first-rate poets, trying to ascertain whether *Marmion* or *The Lady of the Lake* were to be preferred, and how ranked the *Giaour* and *The Bride of Abydos,* and moreover, how the *Giaour* was to be pronounced, he showed himself so intimately acquainted with all the tenderest songs of the one poet, and all the impassioned descriptions of hopeless agony of the other; he repeated, with such tremulous feeling, the various lines which imaged a broken heart, or a mind destroyed by wretchedness, and looked so entirely as if he meant to be understood, that she ventured to hope he did not always read only poetry, and to say that she thought it was the misfortune of poetry to be seldom safely enjoyed by those who enjoyed it completely; and that the strong feelings which alone could estimate it truly were the very feelings which ought to taste it but sparingly.

His looks showing him not pained, but pleased with this allusion to his situation, she was emboldened to go on; and feeling in herself the right of seniority of mind, she ventured to recommend a larger allowance of prose in his daily study; and on being requested to particularise, mentioned such works of our best moralists, such collections of the finest letters, such memoirs of characters of worth and suffering, as occurred to her at the moment as calculated to rouse and fortify the mind by the highest precepts and the strongest examples of moral and religious endurances.

Captain Benwick listened attentively, and seemed grateful for the interest implied; and though with a shake of the head, and sighs which declared his little faith in the efficacy of any books on grief like his, noted down the names of those she recommended, and promised to procure and read them.

When the evening was over, Anne could not but be amused at the idea of her coming to Lyme to preach patience and resignation to a young man whom she had never seen before; nor could she help fearing, on more serious reflection, that, like many other great moralists and preachers, she had been eloquent on a point in which her own conduct would ill bear examination.

12

ANNE AND HENRIETTA, finding themselves the earliest of the party the next morning, agreed to stroll down to the sea before breakfast. They went to the sands, to watch the flowing of the tide, which a fine south-easterly breeze was bringing in with all the grandeur which so flat a shore admitted. They praised the morning; gloried in the sea; sympathised in the delight of the fresh-feeling breeze—and were silent; till Henrietta suddenly began again, with:

"Oh, yes! I am quite convinced that, with very few exceptions, the sea-air always does good. There can be no doubt of its having been of the greatest service to Dr. Shirley, after his illness, last spring twelvemonth. He declares himself, that coming to Lyme for a month did him more good than all the medicine he took; and that being by the sea always makes him feel young again. Now, I cannot help thinking it a pity that he does not live entirely by the sea. I do think he had better leave Uppercross entirely, and fix at Lyme. Do not you, Anne? Do not you agree with me, that it is the best thing he could do, both for himself and Mrs. Shirley? She has cousins here, you know, and many acquaintances, which would make it cheerful for her, and I am sure she would be glad to get a place where she could have medical attendance at hand, in case of his having another seizure. Indeed, I think it quite melancholy to have such excellent people as Dr. and Mrs. Shirley, who have been doing good all their lives, wearing out their last days in a place like Uppercross, where, excepting our family, they seem shut out from all the world. I wish his friends would propose it to him. I really think they ought. And, as to procuring a dispensation, there could be no difficulty at his time of life and with his character. My only doubt is, whether anything could persuade him to leave his parish. He is so very strict and scrupulous in his notions; over-scrupulous I must say. Do not you think, Anne, it is being over-scrupulous? Do not you think it is quite a mistaken point of conscience, when a clergyman sacrifices his health for the sake of duties which may be just as well performed by another person? And at Lyme, too, only seventeen miles off, he would be near enough to hear if people thought there was anything to complain of."

Anne smiled more than once to herself during this speech, and entered into the subject, as ready to do good by entering into the feelings of a young lady as of a young man, though here it was good of a lower standard, for what could be offered but general acquiescence? She said all that was reasonable and proper on the business; felt the claims of Dr. Shirley to repose as she ought; saw how very desirable it was that he should have some active, respectable young man as a resident curate, and was even courteous enough to hint at the advantage of such resident curate's being married.

"I wish," said Henrietta, very well pleased with her companion, "I wish Lady Russell lived at Uppercross, and were intimate with Dr. Shirley. I have always heard of Lady Russell as a woman of the greatest influence with everybody! I always look upon her as able to persuade a person to anything! I am afraid of her, as I told you before, quite afraid of her, because she is so very clever; but I respect her amazingly, and wish we had such a neighbour at Uppercross."

Anne was amused by Henrietta's manner of being grateful, and amused also that the course of events and the new interest of Henrietta's views should have placed her friend at all in favour with any of the Musgrove family; she had only time, however, for a general answer, and a wish that such another woman were at Uppercross, before all subjects suddenly ceased, on seeing Louisa and Captain Wentworth coming towards them. They came also for a stroll till breakfast was likely to be ready; but Louisa recollecting immediately afterwards that she had something to procure at a shop, invited them all to go back with her into the town. They were all at her disposal.

When they came to the steps, leading upwards from the beach, a gentleman, at the same moment preparing to come down, politely drew back, and stopped to give them way. They ascended and passed him; and as they passed, Anne's face caught his eye, and he looked at her with a degree of earnest admiration which she could not be insensible of. She was looking remarkably well; her very regular, very pretty features, having the bloom and freshness of youth restored by the fine wind which had been blowing on her complexion, and by the animation of eye which it had also produced. It was evident that the gentleman (completely a gentleman in manner) admired her exceedingly. Captain Wentworth looked round at her instantly in a way which showed his noticing of it. He gave her a momentary glance, a glance of brightness, which seemed to say, "That man is struck with you, and even I, at this moment, see something like Anne Elliot again."

After attending Louisa through her business, and loitering about a little longer, they returned to the inn; and Anne, in passing afterwards quickly from her own chamber to their dining-room, had nearly run against the very same gentleman, as he came out of an adjoining apartment. She had before conjectured him to be a stranger like themselves, and determined that a well-looking groom, who was strolling about near the two inns as they came back, should be his servant. Both master and man being in mourning assisted the idea. It was now proved that he belonged to the same inn as themselves; and this second meeting, short as it was, also proved again, by the gentleman's looks, that he thought hers very lovely, and by the readiness and propriety of his apologies, that he was a man of exceedingly good manners. He seemed about thirty, and though not handsome, had an agreeable person. Anne felt that she should like to know who he was.

They had nearly done breakfast, when the sound of a carriage (almost the first they had heard since entering Lyme), drew half the party to the window. It was a gentleman's carriage, a curricle, but only coming round from the stable-yard to the front door; somebody must be going away. It was driven by a servant in mourning.

The word curricle made Charles Musgrove jump up that he might compare it with his own; the servant in mourning roused Anne's curiosity, and the whole six were collected to look, by the time the owner of the curricle was to be seen issuing from the door, amidst the bows and civilities of the household, and taking his seat, to drive off.

"Ah!" cried Captain Wentworth, instantly, and with half a glance at Anne, "it is the very man we passed."

The Miss Musgroves agreed to it; and having all kindly

watched him as far up the hill as they could, they returned to the breakfast table. The waiter came into the room soon afterwards.

"Pray," said Captain Wentworth, immediately, "can you tell us the name of the gentleman who is just gone away?"

"Yes, sir, a Mr. Elliot, a gentleman of large fortune, came in last night from Sidmouth. Dare say you heard the carriage, sir, while you were at dinner; and going on now for Crewkherne, on his way to Bath and London."

"Elliot!" Many had looked on each other, and many had repeated the name, before all this had been got through, even by the smart rapidity of a waiter.

"Bless me!" cried Mary, "it must be our cousin; it must be our Mr. Elliot, it must, indeed! Charles, Anne, must not it? In mourning, you see, just as our Mr. Elliot must be. How very extraordinary! In the very same inn with us! Anne, must not it be our Mr. Elliot? My father's next heir? Pray, sir," turning to the waiter, "did not you hear, did not his servant say whether he belonged to the Kellynch family?"

"No, ma'am, he did not mention no particular family; but he said his master was a very rich gentleman, and would be a baronet some day."

"There! you see!" cried Mary in an ecstasy; "just as I said! Heir to Sir Walter Elliot! I was sure that would come out, if it was so. Depend upon it, that is a circumstance which his servants take care to publish, wherever he goes. But, Anne, only conceive how extraordinary! I wish I had looked at him more. I wish we had been aware in time who it was, that he might have been introduced to us. What a pity that we should not have been introduced to each other! Do you think he had the Elliot countenance? I hardly looked at him, I was looking at the horses; but I think he had something of the Elliot countenance. I wonder the arms did not strike me! Oh! the great-coat was hanging over the panel, and hid the arms, so it did; otherwise, I am sure, I should have observed them, and the livery too; if the servant had not been in mourning, one should have known him by the livery."

"Putting all these very extraordinary circumstances together," said Captain Wentworth, "we must consider it to be the arrangement of Providence that you should not be introduced to your cousin."

When she could command Mary's attention, Anne quietly tried to convince her that their father and Mr. Elliot had not, for many years, been on such terms as to make the power of attempting an introduction at all desirable.

At the same time, however, it was a secret gratification to herself to have seen her cousin, and to know that the future owner of Kellynch was undoubtedly a gentleman, and had an air of good sense. She would not, upon any account, mention her having met with him the second time; luckily Mary did not much attend to their having passed close by him in their early walk, but she would have felt quite ill-used by Anne's having actually run against him in the passage, and received his very polite excuses, while she had never been near him at all; no, that cousinly little interview must remain a perfect secret.

"Of course," said Mary, "you will mention our seeing Mr. Elliot the next time you write to Bath. I think my father certainly ought to hear of it; do mention all about him."

Anne avoided a direct reply, but it was just the circumstance which she considered as not merely unnecessary to be communicated, but as what ought to be suppressed. The offence which had been given her father, many years back, she knew; Elizabeth's particular share in it she suspected; and that Mr. Elliot's idea always produced irritation in both was beyond a doubt. Mary never wrote to Bath herself; all

the toil of keeping up a slow and unsatisfactory correspondence with Elizabeth fell on Anne.

Breakfast had not been long over when they were joined
by Captain and Mrs. Harville and Captain Benwick; with
whom they had appointed to take their last walk about
Lyme. They ought to be setting off for Uppercross by one,
and in the meanwhile were to be all together, and out of
doors as long as they could.

Anne found Captain Benwick getting near her, as soon
as they were all fairly in the street. Their conversation the
preceding evening did not disincline him to seek her again;
and they walked together some time, talking as before of
Mr. Scott and Lord Byron, and still as unable as before, and
as unable as any other two readers, to think exactly alike of
the merits of either, till something occasioned an almost
general change amongst their party, and instead of Captain
Benwick, she had Captain Harville by her side.

"Miss Elliot," said he, speaking rather low, "you have
done a good deed in making that poor fellow talk so much.
I wish he could have such company oftener. It is bad for
him, I know, to be shut up as he is; but what can we do? We
cannot part."

"No," said Anne, "that I can easily believe to be impossible; but in time, perhaps—we know what time does in
every case of affliction, and you must remember, Captain
Harville, that your friend may yet be called a young
mourner—only last summer, understand."

"Ay, true enough" (with a deep sigh), "only June."

"And not known to him, perhaps, so soon."

"Not till the first week in August, when he came home
from the Cape, just made into the *Grappler*. I was at Plymouth dreading to hear of him; he sent in letters, but the
Grappler was under orders for Portsmouth. There the news

must follow him, but who was to tell it? Not I. I would as soon have been run up to the yard-arm. Nobody could do it, but that good fellow" (pointing to Captain Wentworth). "The *Laconia* had come into Plymouth the week before; no danger of her being sent to sea again. He stood his chance for the rest; wrote up for leave of absence, but without waiting the return, travelled night and day till he got to Portsmouth, rowed off to the *Grappler* that instant, and never left the poor fellow for a week. That's what he did, and nobody else could have saved poor James. You may think, Miss Elliot, whether he is dear to us!"

Anne did think on the question with perfect decision, and said as much in reply as her own feelings could accomplish, or as his seemed able to bear, for he was too much affected to renew the subject, and when he spoke again, it was of something totally different.

Mrs. Harville's giving it as her opinion that her husband would have quite walking enough by the time he reached home, determined the direction of all the party in what was to be their last walk; they would accompany them to their door, and then return and set off themselves. By all their calculations there was just time for this; but as they drew near the Cobb, there was such a general wish to walk along it once more, all were so inclined, and Louisa soon grew so determined, that the difference of a quarter of an hour, it was found, would be no difference at all; so with all the kind leave-taking, and all the kind interchange of invitations and promises which may be imagined, they parted from Captain and Mrs. Harville at their own door, and still accompanied by Captain Benwick, who seemed to cling to them to the last, proceeded to make the proper adieux to the Cobb.

Anne found Captain Benwick again drawing near her.

Lord Byron's "dark blue seas" could not fail of being brought forward by their present view, and she gladly gave him all her attention as long as attention was possible. It was soon drawn, perforce, another way.

There was too much wind to make the high part of the new Cobb pleasant for the ladies, and they agreed to get down the steps to the lower, and all were contented to pass quietly and carefully down the steep flight, excepting Louisa; she must be jumped down them by Captain Wentworth. In all their walks he had had to jump her from the stiles; the sensation was delightful to her. The hardness of the pavement for her feet made him less willing upon the present occasion; he did it, however. She was safely down, and instantly, to show her enjoyment, ran up the steps to be jumped down again. He advised her against it, thought the jar too great; but no, he reasoned and talked in vain, she smiled and said, "I am determined I will:" he put out his hands; she was too precipitate by half a second, she fell on the pavement on the Lower Cobb, and was taken up lifeless! There was no wound, no blood, no visible bruise; but her eyes were closed, she breathed not, her face was like death. The horror of that moment to all who stood around!

Captain Wentworth, who had caught her up, knelt with her in his arms, looking on her with a face as pallid as her own in an agony of silence. "She is dead! She is dead!" screamed Mary, catching hold of her husband, and contributing with his own horror to make him immovable; and in another moment, Henrietta, sinking under the conviction, lost her senses too, and would have fallen on the steps but for Captain Benwick and Anne, who caught and supported her between them.

"Is there no one to help me?" were the first words which burst from Captain Wentworth, in a tone of despair, and as if all his own strength were gone.

"Go to him, go to him," cried Anne, "for heaven's sake, go to him. I can support her myself. Leave me, and go to him. Rub her hands, rub her temples; here are salts: take them, take them."

Captain Benwick obeyed, and Charles at the same moment disengaging himself from his wife, they were both with him; and Louisa was raised up and supported more firmly between them, and everything was done that Anne had prompted, but in vain; while Captain Wentworth, staggering against the wall for his support, exclaimed in the bitterest agony:

"Oh God! her father and mother!"

"A surgeon!" said Anne.

He caught the word: it seemed to rouse him at once; and saying only: "True, true, a surgeon this instant," was darting away, when Anne eagerly suggested:

"Captain Benwick, would not it better for Captain Benwick? He knows where a surgeon is to be found."

Every one capable of thinking felt the advantage of the idea, and in a moment (it was all done in rapid moments) Captain Benwick had resigned the poor corpse-like figure entirely to the brother's care, and was off for the town with the utmost rapidity.

As to the wretched party left behind, it could scarcely be said which of the three, who were completely rational, was suffering most: Captain Wentworth, Anne, or Charles, who, really a very affectionate brother, hung over Louisa with sobs of grief, and could only turn his eyes from one sister to see the other in a state as insensible, or to witness the hysterical agitations of his wife, calling on him for help which he could not give.

Anne, attending with all the strength, and zeal, and thought, which instinct supplied, to Henrietta, still tried, at intervals, to suggest comfort to the others, tried to quiet

Mary, to animate Charles, to assuage the feelings of Captain Wentworth. Both seemed to look to her for directions.

"Anne, Anne," cried Charles, "what is to be done next? What, in heaven's name, is to be done next?"

Captain Wentworth's eyes were also turned towards her.

"Had not she better be carried to the inn? Yes, I am sure: carry her gently to the inn."

"Yes, yes, to the inn," repeated Captain Wentworth, comparatively collected, and eager to be doing something. "I will carry her myself. Musgrove, take care of the others."

By this time the report of the accident had spread among the workmen and boatmen about the Cobb, and many were collected near them, to be useful if wanted; at any rate, to enjoy the sight of a dead young lady, nay, two dead young ladies, for it proved twice as fine as the first report. To some of the best-looking of these good people Henrietta was consigned, for, though partially revived, she was quite helpless; and in this manner, Anne walking by her side, and Charles attending to his wife, they set forward, treading back, with feelings unutterable, the ground which so lately, so very lately, and so light of heart, they had passed along.

They were not off the Cobb before the Harvilles met them. Captain Benwick had been seen flying by their house, with a countenance which showed something to be wrong; and they had set off immediately, informed and directed as they passed, towards the spot. Shocked as Captain Harville was, he brought senses and nerves that could be instantly useful; and a look between him and his wife decided what was to be done. She must be taken to their house; all must go to their house; and wait the surgeon's arrival there. They would not listen to scruples: he was obeyed: they were all beneath his roof; and while Louisa, under Mrs. Harville's direction, was conveyed upstairs, and given possession of her own bed, assistance, cordials, restoratives were supplied by her husband to all who needed them.

Louisa had once opened her eyes, but soon closed them again, without apparent consciousness. This had been a proof of life, however, of service to her sister; and Henrietta, though perfectly incapable of being in the same room with Louisa, was kept, by the agitation of hope and fear, from a return of her own insensibility. Mary, too, was growing calmer.

The surgeon was with them almost before it had seemed possible. They were sick with horror, while he examined; but he was not hopeless. The head had received a severe contusion, but he had seen greater injuries recovered from; he was by no means hopeless; he spoke cheerfully.

That he did not regard it as a desperate case, that he did not say a few hours must end it, was at first felt beyond the hope of most; and the ecstasy of such a reprieve, the rejoicing, deep and silent, after a few fervent ejaculations of gratitude to Heaven had been offered, may be conceived.

The tone, the look, with which "Thank God!" was uttered by Captain Wentworth, Anne was sure could never be forgotten by her; nor the sight of him afterwards, as he sat near a table, leaning over it with folded arms, and face concealed, as if overpowered by the various feelings of his soul, and trying by prayer and reflection to calm them.

Louisa's limbs had escaped. There was no injury but to the head.

It now became necessary for the party to consider what was best to be done, as to their general situation. They were now able to speak to each other and consult. That Louisa must remain where she was, however distressing to her friends to be involving the Harvilles in such trouble, did not admit a doubt. Her removal was impossible. The Harvilles

silenced all scruples, and, as much as they could, all gratitude. They had looked forward and arranged everything
before the others began to reflect. Captain Benwick must
give up his room to them and get a bed elsewhere; and the
whole was settled. They were only concerned that the house
could accommodate no more; and yet, perhaps, by "putting
the children away in the maid's room, or swinging a cot
somewhere," they could hardly bear to think of not finding
room for two or three besides, supposing they might wish
to stay; though, with regard to any attendance on Miss Musgrove, there need not be the least uneasiness in leaving her
to Mrs. Harville's care entirely. Mrs. Harville was a very ex-
perienced nurse, and her nursery-maid, who had lived with
her long, and gone about with her everywhere, was just such
another. Between those two she could want no possible attendance by day or night. And all this was said with a truth
and sincerity of feeling irresistible.

Charles, Henrietta, and Captain Wentworth were the
three in consultation, and for a little while it was only an
interchange of perplexity and terror. "Uppercross, the necessity of someone's going to Uppercross, the news to be
conveyed; how it could be broken to Mr. and Mrs. Musgrove; the lateness of the morning; an hour already gone
since they ought to have been off; the impossibility of being
in tolerable time." At first they were capable of nothing more
to the purpose than such exclamations; but after a while
Captain Wentworth, exerting himself, said:

"We must be decided, and without the loss of another
minute. Every minute is valuable. Someone must resolve on
being off for Uppercross instantly. Musgrove, either you or
I must go."

Charles agreed, but declared his resolution of not going
away. He would be as little encumbrance as possible to Cap-

tain and Mrs. Harville; but as to leaving his sister in such a state, he neither ought nor would. So far it was decided; and Henrietta at first declared the same. She, however, was soon persuaded to think differently. The usefulness of her staying! She, who had not been able to remain in Louisa's room, or to look at her, without sufferings which made her worse than helpless! She was forced to acknowledge that she could do no good, yet was still unwilling to be away, till, touched by the thought of her father and mother, she gave it up; she consented, she was anxious to be at home.

The plan had reached this point, when Anne, coming quietly down from Louisa's room, could not but hear what followed, for the parlour door was open.

"Then it is settled, Musgrove," cried Captain Wentworth, "that you stay, and that I take care of your sister home. But as to the rest, as to the others, if one stays to assist Mrs. Harville, I think it need be only one. Mrs. Charles Musgrove will, of course, wish to get back to her children; but if Anne will stay, no one so proper, so capable as Anne."

She paused a moment to recover from the emotion of hearing herself so spoken of. The other two warmly agreed to what he said, and she then appeared.

"You will stay, I am sure; you will stay and nurse her," cried he, turning to her and speaking with a glow, and yet a gentleness, which seemed almost restoring the past. She coloured deeply, and he recollected himself and moved away. She expressed herself most willing, ready, happy to remain. "It was what she had been thinking of, and wishing to be allowed to do. A bed on the floor in Louisa's room would be sufficient for her, if Mrs. Harville would but think so."

One thing more, and all seemed arranged. Though it was rather desirable that Mr. and Mrs. Musgrove should be pre-

viously alarmed by some share of delay; yet the time required by the Uppercross horses to take them back, would
be a dreadful extension of suspense; and Captain Wentworth proposed, and Charles Musgrove agreed, that it
would be much better for him to take a chaise from the inn,
and leave Mr. Musgrove's carriage and horses to be sent
home the next morning early, when there could be the further advantage of sending an account of Louisa's night.

Captain Wentworth now hurried off to get everything
ready on his part, and to be soon followed by the two ladies.
When the plan was made known to Mary, however, there
was an end of all peace in it. She was so wretched, and so
vehement, complained so much of injustice in being expected to go away instead of Anne; Anne, who was nothing
to Louisa, while she was her sister, and had the best right
to stay in Henrietta's stead! Why was not she to be as useful
as Anne? And to go home without Charles, too, without her
husband! No, it was too unkind. And in short, she said more
than her husband could long withstand, and as none of the
others could oppose when he gave way, there was no help
for it: the change of Mary for Anne was inevitable.

Anne had never submitted more reluctantly to the jealous and ill-judging claims of Mary; but so it must be, and
they set off for the town, Charles taking care of his sister,
and Captain Benwick attending to her. She gave a moment's
recollection, as they hurried along, to the little circumstances which the same spots had witnessed earlier in the
morning. There she had listened to Henrietta's schemes for
Dr. Shirley's leaving Uppercross; farther on, she had first
seen Mr. Elliot; a moment seemed all that could now be
given to anyone but Louisa, or those who were wrapped up
in her welfare.

Captain Benwick was most considerately attentive to her; and, united as they all seemed by the distress of the day, she felt an increasing degree of goodwill towards him, and a pleasure even in thinking that it might, perhaps, be the occasion of continuing their acquaintance.

Captain Wentworth was on the watch for them, and a chaise and four in waiting, stationed for their convenience in the lowest part of the street; but his evident surprise and vexation at the substitution of one sister for the other, the change of his countenance, the astonishment, the expressions begun and suppressed, with which Charles was listened to, made but a mortifying reception of Anne; or must at least convince her that she was valued only as she could be useful to Louisa.

She endeavoured to be composed, and to be just. Without emulating the feelings of an Emma towards her Henry, she would have attended on Louisa with a zeal above the common claims of regard, for his sake; and she hoped he would not long be so unjust as to suppose she would shrink unnecessarily from the office of a friend.

In the meanwhile she was in the carriage. He had handed them both in, and placed himself between them; and in this manner, under these circumstances, full of astonishment and emotion to Anne, she quitted Lyme. How the long stage would pass; how it was to affect their manners; what was to be their sort of intercourse, she could not foresee. It was all quite natural, however. He was devoted to Henrietta; always turning towards her; and when he spoke at all, always with the view of supporting her hopes and raising her spirits. In general, his voice and manner were studiously calm. To spare Henrietta from agitation seemed the governing principle. Once only, when she had been grieving over the last ill-judged, ill-fated walk to the Cobb, bitterly lamenting that it ever had been thought of, he burst forth, as if wholly overcome:

"Don't talk of it, don't talk of it," he cried. "Oh, God! that I had not given way to her at the fatal moment! Had I done as I ought! But so eager and so resolute! Dear, sweet Louisa!"

Anne wondered whether it ever occurred to him now, to question the justness of his own previous opinion as to the universal felicity and advantage of firmness of character; and whether it might not strike him that, like all other qualities of the mind, it should have its proportions and limits. She thought it could scarcely escape him to feel that a persuadable temper might sometimes be as much in favour of happiness as a very resolute character.

They got on fast. Anne was astonished to recognise the same hills and the same objects so soon. Their actual speed, heightened by some dread of the conclusion, made the road appear but half as long as on the day before. It was growing quite dusk, however, before they were in the neighbourhood of Uppercross, and there had been total silence among them for some time, Henrietta leaning back in the corner, with a shawl over her face, giving the hope of her having cried herself to sleep; when, as they were going up their last hill, Anne found herself all at once addressed by Captain Wentworth. In a low cautious voice, he said:

"I have been considering what we had best do. She must not appear at first. She could not stand it. I have been thinking whether you had not better remain in the carriage with her, while I go in and break it to Mr. and Mrs. Musgrove. Do you think this a good plan?"

She did: he was satisfied, and said no more. But the remembrance of the appeal remained a pleasure to her, as a proof of friendship, and of deference for her judgment, a great pleasure; and when it became a sort of parting proof, its value did not lessen.

When the distressing communication at Uppercross was over, and he had seen the father and mother quite as composed as could be hoped, and the daughter all the better for being with them, he announced his intention of returning in the same carriage to Lyme; and when the horses were baited, he was off.

13

THE REMAINDER OF Anne's time at Uppercross, comprehending only two days, was spent entirely at the Mansion House; and she had the satisfaction of knowing herself extremely useful there, both as an immediate companion, and as assisting in all those arrangements for the future, which, in Mr. and Mrs. Musgrove's distressed state of spirits, would have been difficulties.

They had an early account from Lyme the next morning. Louisa was much the same. No symptoms worse than before had appeared. Charles came a few hours afterwards to bring a later and more particular account. He was tolerably cheerful. A speedy cure must not be hoped, but everything was going on as well as the nature of the case admitted. In speaking of the Harvilles, he seemed unable to satisfy his own sense of their kindness, especially of Mrs. Harville's exertions as a nurse. "She really left nothing for Mary to do. He and Mary had been persuaded to go early to their inn last night. Mary had been hysterical again this morning. When he came away, she was going to walk out with Captain Benwick, which he hoped would do her good. He almost wished she had been prevailed on to come home the day before; but the truth was, that Mrs. Harville left nothing for anybody to do."

Charles was to return to Lyme the same afternoon, and his father had at first half a mind to go with him, but the ladies could not consent. It would be going only to multiply trouble to the others, and increase his own distress; and a much better scheme followed, and was acted upon. A chaise was sent for from Crewkherne, and Charles conveyed back a far more useful person in the old nursery-maid of the family, one who, having brought up all the children, and seen the very last, the lingering and long-petted Master Harry, sent to school after his brothers, was now living in her deserted nursery to mend stockings, and dress all the blains and bruises she could get near her, and who, consequently, was only too happy in being allowed to go and help nurse dear Miss Louisa. Vague wishes of getting Sarah thither had occurred before to Mrs. Musgrove and Henrietta; but without Anne, it would hardly have been resolved on, and found practicable so soon.

They were indebted, the next day, to Charles Hayter, for all the minute knowledge of Louisa, which it was so essential to obtain every twenty-four hours. He made it his business to go to Lyme, and his account was still encouraging. The intervals of sense and consciousness were believed to be stronger. Every report agreed in Captain Wentworth's appearing fixed in Lyme.

Anne was to leave them on the morrow, an event which they all dreaded. "What should they do without her? They were wretched comforters for one another." And so much was said in this way, that Anne thought she could not do better than impart among them the general inclination to which she was privy, and persuade them all to go to Lyme at once. She had little difficulty; it was soon determined that they would go: go to-morrow, fix themselves at the inn, or get into lodgings, as it suited, and there remain till dear Louisa could be moved. They must be taking off some trouble from the good people she was with: they might at least relieve Mrs. Harville from the care of her own children: and in short, they were so happy in the decision, that Anne was delighted with what she had done, and felt that she could not spend her last morning at Uppercross better than in assisting their preparations, and sending them off at an early hour, though her being left to the solitary range of the house was the consequence.

She was the last, excepting the little boys at the Cottage, she was the very last, the only remaining one of all that had filled and animated both houses, of all that had given Uppercross its cheerful character. A few days had made a change indeed!

If Louisa recovered, it would all be well again. More than former happiness would be restored. There could not be a doubt, to her mind there was none, of what would follow her recovery. A few months hence and the room now so deserted, occupied but by her silent, pensive self, might be filled again with all that was happy and gay, all that was glowing and bright in prosperous love, all that was most unlike Anne Elliot!

An hour's complete leisure for such reflections as these, on a dark November day, a small thick rain almost blotting out the very objects ever to be discerned from the windows, was enough to make the sound of Lady Russell's carriage exceedingly welcome; and yet, though desirous to be gone, she could not quit the Mansion House, or look an adieu to the Cottage, with its black, dripping and comfortless verandah, or even notice through the misty glasses the last humble tenements of the village, without a saddened heart. Scenes had passed in Uppercross which made it precious. It stood the record of many sensations of pain, once severe, but now softened; and of some instances of relenting feeling, some breathings of friendship and reconciliation, which could never be looked for again, and which could never cease to be dear. She left it all behind her, all but the recollection that such things had been.

Anne had never entered Kellynch since her quitting Lady Russell's house in September. It had not been necessary, and the few occasions of its being possible for her to go to the Hall she had contrived to evade and escape from. Her first return was to resume her place in the modern and elegant apartments of the Lodge, and to gladden the eyes of its mistress.

There was some anxiety mixed with Lady Russell's joy in meeting her. She knew who had been frequenting Uppercross. But happily, either Anne was improved in plumpness and looks, or Lady Russell fancied her so; and Anne, in receiving her compliments on the occasion, had the amusement of connecting them with the silent admiration of her cousin, and of hoping that she was to be blessed with a second spring of youth and beauty.

When they came to converse, she was soon sensible of some mental change. The subjects of which her heart had been full on leaving Kellynch, and which she had felt slighted, and been compelled to smother among the Musgroves, were now become but of secondary interest. She had lately lost sight even of her father, and sister, and Bath. Their concerns had been sunk under those of Uppercross; and when Lady Russell reverted to their former hopes and fears, and spoke her satisfaction in the house in Camden Place which had been taken, and her regret that Mrs. Clay should still be with them, Anne would have been ashamed to have it known how much more she was thinking of Lyme and Louisa Musgrove, and all her acquaintances there; how much more interesting to her was the home and the friendship of the Harvilles and Captain Benwick, than her own father's house in Camden Place, or her own sister's intimacy with Mrs. Clay. She was actually forced to exert herself to meet Lady Russell with anything like the appearance of equal solicitude, on topics which had by nature the first claim on her.

There was a little awkwardness at first in their discourse on another subject. They must speak of the accident at Lyme. Lady Russell had not been arrived five minutes the day before, when a full account of the whole had burst on her; but still it must be talked of, she must make enquiries, she must regret the imprudence, lament the result, and Captain Wentworth's name must be mentioned by both. Anne was conscious of not doing it so well as Lady Russell. She could not speak the name, and look straight forward to Lady Russell's eye, till she had adopted the expedient of telling her briefly what she thought of the attachment between him and Louisa. When this was told, his name distressed her no longer.

Lady Russell had only to listen composedly, and wish them happy, but internally her heart revelled in angry pleasure, in pleased contempt, that the man who at twenty-three had seemed to understand somewhat of the value of an Anne Elliot, should, eight years afterwards, be charmed by a Louisa Musgrove.

The first three or four days passed most quietly, with no circumstance to mark them excepting the receipt of a note or two from Lyme, which found their way to Anne, she could not tell how, and brought a rather improving account of Louisa. At the end of that period, Lady Russell's politeness could repose no longer, and the fainter self-threatenings of the past became in a decided tone, "I must call on Mrs. Croft; I really must call upon her soon. Anne, have you courage to go with me and pay a visit in that house? It will be some trial to us both."

Anne did not shrink from it: on the contrary, she truly felt as she said, in observing:

"I think you are very likely to suffer the most of the two; your feelings are less reconciled to the change than mine. By remaining in the neighbourhood, I am become enured to it."

She could have said more on the subject, for she had in fact so high an opinion of the Crofts, and considered her father so very fortunate in his tenants, felt the parish to be so sure of a good example, and the poor of the best attention and relief, that however sorry and ashamed for the necessity of the removal, she could not but in conscience feel that they were gone who deserved not to stay, and that Kellynch Hall had passed into better hands than its owners. These convictions must unquestionably have their own pain, and severe was its kind; but they precluded that pain which Lady Russell would suffer in entering the house again, and returning through the well-known apartments.

In such moments Anne had no power of saying to herself, "These rooms ought to belong only to us. Oh, how fallen in their destination! How unworthily occupied! An ancient family to be so driven away! Strangers filling their place!" No, except when she thought of her mother, and remembered where she had been used to sit and preside, she had no sigh of that description to heave.

Mrs. Croft always met her with a kindness which gave her the pleasure of fancying herself a favourite, and on the present occasion, receiving her in that house, there was particular attention.

The sad accident at Lyme was soon the prevailing topic, and on comparing their latest accounts of the invalid, it appeared that each lady dated her intelligence from the same hour of yestermorn; that Captain Wentworth had been in Kellynch yesterday (the first time since the accident), had brought Anne the last note, which she had not been able to trace the exact steps of; and stayed a few hours, and then returned again to Lyme, and without any present intention of quitting it any more. He had enquired after her, she found particularly; had expressed his hope of Miss Elliot's not being the worse for her exertions, and had spoken of those exertions as great. This was handsome, and gave her more pleasure than almost anything else could have done.

As to the sad catastrophe itself, it could be canvassed only in one style by a couple of steady, sensible women, whose judgments had to work on ascertained events; and it was perfectly decided that it had been the consequence of much thoughtlessness and much imprudence; that its effects were most alarming, and that it was frightful to think how long Miss Musgrove's recovery might yet be doubtful, and how liable she would still remain to suffer from the concussion hereafter! The Admiral wound it all up summarily by exclaiming:

"Ay, a very bad business, indeed. A new sort of way this, for a young fellow to be making love, by breaking his mistress's head, is not it, Miss Elliot? This is breaking a head and giving a plaster, truly!"

Admiral Croft's manners were not quite of the tone to

suit Lady Russell, but they delighted Anne. His goodness of heart and simplicity of character were irresistible.

"Now, this must be very bad for you," said he, suddenly rousing from a little reverie, "to be coming and finding us here. I had not recollected it before, I declare, but it must be very bad. But now, do not stand upon ceremony. Get up and go over all the rooms in the house, if you like it."

"Another time, sir, I thank you; not now."

"Well, whenever it suits you. You can slip in from the shrubbery at any time; and there you will find we keep our umbrellas hanging up by that door. A good place, is not it? But" (checking himself), "you will not think it a good place, for yours were always kept in the butler's room. Ay, so it always is, I believe. One man's ways may be as good as another's, but we all like our own best; and so you must judge for yourself, whether it would be better for you to go about the house or not."

Anne, finding she might decline it, did so very gratefully.

"We have made very few changes either," continued the Admiral, after thinking a moment. "Very few. We told you about the laundry-door at Uppercross. That has been a very great improvement. The wonder was, how any family upon earth could bear with the inconvenience of its opening as it did so long! You will tell Sir Walter what we have done, and that Mr. Shepherd thinks it the greatest improvement the house ever had. Indeed, I must do ourselves the justice to say, that the few alterations we have made have been all very much for the better. My wife should have the credit of them, however. I have done very little besides sending away some of the large looking-glasses from my dressing-room, which was your father's. A very good man, and very much the gentleman, I am sure; but I should think, Miss Elliot" (looking with serious reflection), "I should think he must be rather a dressy man for his time of life. Such a number of looking-glasses! oh, Lord! there was no getting away from one's self. So I got Sophy to lend me a hand, and we soon shifted their quarters; and now I am quite snug, with my little shaving-glass in one corner, and another great thing that I never go near."

Anne, amused in spite of herself, was rather distressed for an answer; and the Admiral, fearing he might not have been civil enough, took up the subject again, to say:

"The next time you write to your good father, Miss Elliot, pray give my compliments and Mrs. Croft's, and say that we are settled here quite to our liking, and have no fault at all to find with the place. The breakfast-room chimney smokes a little, I grant you, but it is only when the wind is due north and blows hard, which may not happen three times a winter. And take it altogether, now that we have been into most of the houses hereabouts and can judge, there is not one that we like better than this. Pray say so, with my compliments. He will be glad to hear it."

Lady Russell and Mrs. Croft were very well pleased with each other: but the acquaintance which this visit began was fated not to proceed far at present; for when it was returned, the Crofts announced themselves to be going away for a few weeks, to visit their connections in the north of the county, and probably might not be at home again before Lady Russell would be removing to Bath.

So ended all danger to Anne of meeting Captain Wentworth at Kellynch Hall, or of seeing him in company with her friend. Everything was safe enough, and she smiled over the many anxious feelings she had wasted on the subject.

14

Though Charles and Mary had remained at Lyme much longer after Mr. and Mrs. Musgrove's going than Anne conceived they could have been at all wanted, they were yet the first of the family to be at home again; and as soon as possible after their return to Uppercross they drove over to the Lodge. They had left Louisa beginning to sit up; but her head, though clear, was exceedingly weak, and her nerves susceptible to the highest extreme of tenderness; and though she might be pronounced to be altogether doing very well, it was still impossible to say when she might be able to bear the removal home; and her father and mother, who must return in time to receive their younger children for the Christmas holidays, had hardly a hope of being allowed to bring her with them.

They had been all in lodgings together. Mrs. Musgrove had got Mrs. Harville's children away as much as she could, every possible supply from Uppercross had been furnished, to lighten the inconvenience to the Harvilles, while the Harvilles had been wanting them to come to dinner every day; and, in short, it seemed to have been only a struggle on each side, as to which should be most disinterested and hospitable.

Mary had had her evils; but upon the whole, as was evident by her staying so long, she had found more to enjoy than to suffer. Charles Hayter had been at Lyme oftener than suited her; and when they dined with the Harvilles there had been only a maid-servant to wait, and at first Mrs. Harville had always given Mrs. Musgrove precedence; but then she had received so very handsome an apology from her on finding out whose daughter she was, and there had been so much going on every day, there had been so many walks between their lodgings and the Harvilles, and she had got books from the library, and changed them so often, that the balance had certainly been much in favour of Lyme. She had been taken to Charmouth too, and she had bathed, and she had gone to church, and there were a great many more people to look at in the church at Lyme than at Uppercross; and all this, joined to the sense of being so very useful, had made really an agreeable fortnight.

Anne inquired after Captain Benwick. Mary's face was clouded directly. Charles laughed.

"Oh! Captain Benwick is very well, I believe, but he is a very odd young man. I do not know what he would be at. We asked him to come home with us for a day or two: Charles undertook to give him some shooting, and he seemed quite delighted, and, for my part, I thought it was all settled, when, behold! on Tuesday night, he made a very awkward sort of an excuse; 'he never shot,' and he had 'been quite misunderstood,' and he had promised this and he had promised that, and the end of it was, I found, that he did not mean to come. I suppose he was afraid of finding it dull;

but upon my word I should have thought we were lively enough at the Cottage for such a heartbroken man as Captain Benwick."

Charles laughed again, and said, "Now, Mary, you know very well how it really was. It was all your doing" (turning to Anne). "He fancied that if he went with us he should find you close by: he fancied everybody to be living in Uppercross; and when he discovered that Lady Russell lived three miles off, his heart failed him, and he had not courage to come. That is the fact, upon my honour. Mary knows it is."

But Mary did not give into it very graciously, whether from not considering Captain Benwick entitled by birth and situation to be in love with an Elliot, or from not wanting to believe Anne a greater attraction to Uppercross than herself, must be left to be guessed. Anne's goodwill, however, was not to be lessened by what she heard. She boldly acknowledged herself flattered, and continued her enquiries.

"Oh! he talks of you," cried Charles, "in such terms—" Mary interrupted him. "I declare, Charles, I never heard him mention Anne twice all the time I was there. I declare, Anne, he never talks of you at all."

"No," admitted Charles, "I do not know that he ever does, in a general way; but, however, it is a very clear thing that he admires you exceedingly. His head is full of some books that he is reading upon your recommendation, and he wants to talk to you about them; he has found out something or other in one of them which he thinks—oh! I cannot pretend to remember it, but it was something very fine—I overheard him telling Henrietta all about it; and then 'Miss Elliot' was spoken of in the highest terms! Now, Mary, I declare it was so, I heard it myself, and you were in the other room. 'Elegance, sweetness, beauty.' Oh! there was no end of Miss Elliot's charms."

"And I am sure," cried Mary, warmly, "it was very little to his credit if he did. Miss Harville only died last June. Such a heart is very little worth having, is it, Lady Russell? I am sure you will agree with me."

"I must see Captain Benwick before I decide," said Lady Russell, smiling.

"And that you are very likely to do very soon, I can tell you, ma'am," said Charles. "Though he had not nerves for coming away with us, and setting off again afterwards to pay a formal visit here, he will make his way over to Kellynch one day by himself, you may depend on it. I told him the distance and the road, and I told him of the church's being so very well worth seeing; for as he has a taste for those sort of things, I thought that would be a good excuse, and he listened with all his understanding and soul; and I am sure, from his manner, that you will have him calling here soon. So, I give you notice, Lady Russell."

"Any acquaintance of Anne's will be always welcome to me," was Lady Russell's kind answer.

"Oh! as to being Anne's acquaintance," said Mary, "I think he is rather my acquaintance, for I have been seeing him every day this last fortnight."

"Well, as your joint acquaintance, then, I shall be very happy to see Captain Benwick."

"You will not find anything very agreeable in him, I assure you, ma'am. He is one of the dullest young men that ever lived. He has walked with me, sometimes, from one end of the sands to the other, without saying a word. He is not at all a well-bred young man. I am sure you will not like him."

"There we differ, Mary," said Anne. "I think Lady Russell would like him. I think she would be so much pleased with his mind, that she would very soon see no deficiency in his manner."

"So do I, Anne," said Charles. "I am sure Lady Russell would like him. He is just Lady Russell's sort. Give him a book, and he will read all day long."

"Yes, that he will!" exclaimed Mary, tauntingly. "He will sit poring over his book, and not know when a person speaks to him, or when one drops one's scissors, or anything that happens. Do you think Lady Russell would like that?"

Lady Russell could not help laughing. "Upon my word," said she, "I should not have supposed that my opinion of any one could have admitted of such difference of conjecture, steady and matter of fact as I may call myself. I have really a curiosity to see the person who can give occasion to such directly opposite notions. I wish he may be induced to call here. And when he does, Mary, you may depend upon hearing my opinion; but I am determined not to judge him beforehand."

"You will not like him; I will answer for it."

Lady Russell began talking of something else. Mary spoke with animation of their meeting with, or rather missing Mr. Elliot so extraordinarily.

"He is a man," said Lady Russell, "whom I have no wish to see. His declining to be on cordial terms with the head of his family has left a very strong impression in his disfavour with me."

This decision checked Mary's eagerness, and stopped her short in the midst of the Elliot countenance.

With regard to Captain Wentworth, though Anne hazarded no enquiries, there was voluntary communication sufficient. His spirits had been greatly recovering lately, as might be expected. As Louisa improved, he had improved, and he was now quite a different creature from what he had been the first week. He had not seen Louisa; and was so extremely fearful of any ill consequence to her from an interview, that he did not press for it at all; and, on the contrary, seemed to have a plan of going away for a week or ten days, till her head was stronger. He had talked of going down to Plymouth for a week, and wanted to persuade Captain Benwick to go with him; but, as Charles maintained to the last, Captain Benwick seemed much more disposed to ride over to Kellynch.

There can be no doubt that Lady Russell and Anne were both occasionally thinking of Captain Benwick, from this time. Lady Russell could not hear the door-bell without feeling that it might be his herald; nor could Anne return from any stroll of solitary indulgence in her father's grounds, or any visit of charity in the village, without wondering whether she might see him or hear of him. Captain Benwick came not, however. He was either less disposed for it than Charles had imagined, or he was too shy; and after giving him a week's indulgence, Lady Russell determined him to be unworthy of the interest which he had been beginning to excite.

The Musgroves came back to receive their happy boys and girls from school, bringing with them Mrs. Harville's little children, to improve the noise of Uppercross, and lessen that of Lyme. Henrietta remained with Louisa, but all the rest of the family were again in their usual quarters.

Lady Russell and Anne paid their compliments to them once, when Anne could not but feel that Uppercross was already quite alive again. Though neither Henrietta, nor Louisa, nor Charles Hayter, nor Captain Wentworth were there, the room presented as strong a contrast as could be wished to the last state she had seen it in.

Immediately surrounding Mrs. Musgrove were the little Harvilles, whom she was sedulously guarding from the tyranny of the two children from the Cottage, expressly arrived to amuse them. On one side was a table occupied by some chattering girls, cutting up silk and gold paper; and on the other were tressels and trays, bending under the weight of brawn and cold pies, where riotous boys were holding high revel; the whole completed by a roaring Christmas fire, which seemed determined to be heard in spite of all the noise of the others. Charles and Mary also came in, of course, during their visit, and Mr. Musgrove made a point of paying his respects to Lady Russell, and sat down close to her for ten minutes, talking with a very raised voice, but, from the clamour of the children on his knees, generally in vain. It was a fine family-piece.

Anne, judging from her own temperament, would have deemed such a domestic hurricane a bad restorative of the nerves, which Louisa's illness must have so greatly shaken. But Mrs. Musgrove, who got Anne near her on purpose to thank her most cordially, again and again, for all her attentions to them, concluded a short recapitulation of what she had suffered herself by observing, with a happy glance round the room, that after all she had gone through, nothing was so likely to do her good as a little quiet cheerfulness at home.

Louisa was now recovering apace. Her mother could even think of her being able to join their party at home before her brothers and sisters went to school again. The Harvilles had promised to come with her and stay at Uppercross whenever she returned. Captain Wentworth was gone for the present, to see his brother in Shropshire.

"I hope I shall remember, in future," said Lady Russell,

as soon as they were reseated in the carriage, "not to call at Uppercross in the Christmas holidays."

Everybody has their taste in noises as well as in other matters; and sounds are quite innoxious or most distressing, by their sort rather than their quantity. When Lady Russell, not long afterwards, was entering Bath on a wet afternoon, and driving through the long course of streets from the Old Bridge to Camden Place, midst the dash of other carriages, the heavy rumble of carts and drays, the bawling of newsmen, muffin-men, and milkmen, and the ceaseless clink of pattens, she made no complaint. No, these were noises which belonged to the winter pleasures; her spirits rose under their influence; and like Mrs. Musgrove, she was feeling, though not saying, that after being long in the country, nothing could be so good for her as a little quiet cheerfulness.

Anne did not share these feelings. She persisted in a very determined, though very silent disinclination for Bath; caught the first dim view of the extensive buildings, smoking in rain, without any wish of seeing them better; felt their progress through the streets to be, however disagreeable, yet too rapid; for who would be glad to see her when she arrived? And looked back with fond regret to the bustles of Uppercross and the seclusion of Kellynch.

Elizabeth's last letter had communicated a piece of news of some interest. Mr. Elliot was in Bath. He had called in Camden Place; had called a second time, a third; had been pointedly attentive. If Elizabeth and her father did not deceive themselves, had been taking as much pains to seek the acquaintance, and proclaim the value of the connection, as he had formerly taken pains to show neglect. This was very wonderful if it were true; and Lady Russell was in a state of very agreeable curiosity and perplexity about Mr. Elliot, already recanting the sentiment she had so lately expressed to Mary, of his being "a man whom she had no wish to see." She had a great wish to see him. If he really sought to reconcile himself like a dutiful branch, he must be forgiven for having dismembered himself from the paternal tree.

Anne was not animated to an equal pitch by the circumstance, but she felt that she would rather see Mr. Elliot again than not, which was more than she could say for many other persons in Bath.

She was put down in Camden Place, and Lady Russell then drove to her own lodgings in Rivers Street.

15

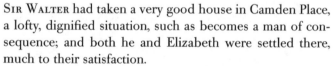

Sᴉʀ Wᴀʟᴛᴇʀ had taken a very good house in Camden Place, a lofty, dignified situation, such as becomes a man of consequence; and both he and Elizabeth were settled there, much to their satisfaction.

Anne entered it with a sinking heart, anticipating an imprisonment of many months, and anxiously saying to herself, "Oh! when shall I leave you again?" A degree of unexpected cordiality, however, in the welcome she received, did her good. Her father and sister were glad to see her, for the sake of showing her the house and furniture, and met her with kindness. Her making a fourth, when they sat down to dinner, was noticed as an advantage.

Mrs. Clay was very pleasant and very smiling, but her courtesies and smiles were more a matter of course. Anne had always felt that she would pretend what was proper on her arrival, but the complaisance of the others was unlooked for. They were evidently in excellent spirits, and she was soon to listen to the causes. They had no inclination to listen to her. After laying out for some compliments of being deeply regretted in their old neighbourhood, which Anne could not pay, they had only a few faint enquiries to make, before the talk must be all their own. Uppercross excited no interest, Kellynch very little: it was all Bath.

They had the pleasure of assuring her that Bath more than answered their expectations in every respect. Their house was undoubtedly the best in Camden Place, their drawing-rooms had many decided advantages over all the others which they had either seen or heard of, and the superiority was not less in the style of the fitting-up or the taste of the furniture. Their acquaintance was exceedingly sought after. Everybody was wanting to visit them. They had drawn back from many introductions, and still were perpetually having cards left by people of whom they knew nothing.

Here were funds of enjoyment! Could Anne wonder that her father and sister were happy? She might not wonder, but she must sigh that her father should feel no degradation in his change, should see nothing to regret in the duties and dignity of the resident landholder, should find so much to be vain of in the littlenesses of a town; and she must sigh, and smile, and wonder too, as Elizabeth threw open the folding-doors, and walked with exultation from one drawing-room to the other, boasting of their space: at the possibility of that woman, who had been mistress of Kellynch Hall, finding extent to be proud of between two walls, perhaps thirty feet asunder.

But this was not all which they had to make them happy. They had Mr. Elliot too. Anne had a great deal to hear of Mr. Elliot. He was not only pardoned, they were delighted with him. He had been in Bath about a fortnight (he had passed through Bath in November, in his way to London, when the intelligence of Sir Walter's being settled there had of course reached him, though only twenty-four hours in the place, but he had not been able to avail himself of it); but he had now been a fortnight in Bath, and his first object on arriving had been to leave his card in Camden Place, following it up by such assiduous endeavours to meet, and when they did meet, by such great openness of conduct, such readiness to apologize for the past, such solicitude to be received as a relation again, that their former good understanding was completely re-established.

They had not a fault to find in him. He had explained away all the appearance of neglect on his own side. It had originated in misapprehension entirely. He had never had an idea of throwing himself off; he had feared that he was thrown off, but knew not why, and delicacy had kept him silent. Upon the hint of having spoken disrespectfully or carelessly of the family and the family honours, he was quite indignant. He, who had ever boasted of being an Elliot, and whose feelings, as to connection, were only too strict to suit the unfeudal tone of the present day. He was astonished, indeed, but his character and general conduct must refute it. He could refer Sir Walter to all who knew him; and certainly, the pains he had been taking on this, the first opportunity of reconciliation, to be restored to the footing of a relation and heir-presumptive, was a strong proof of his opinions on the subject.

The circumstances of his marriage, too, were found to admit of much extenuation. This was an article not to be entered on by himself; but a very intimate friend of his, a Colonel Wallis, a highly respectable man, perfectly the gentleman (and not an ill-looking man, Sir Walter added), who was living in very good style in Marlborough Buildings, and had, at his own particular request, been admitted to their acquaintance through Mr. Elliot, had mentioned one or two things relative to the marriage, which made a material difference in the discredit of it.

Colonel Wallis had known Mr. Elliot long, had been well acquainted also with his wife, had perfectly understood the whole story. She was certainly not a woman of family, but well educated, accomplished, rich and excessively in love with his friend. There had been the charm. She had sought him. Without that attraction, not all her money would have tempted Elliot, and Sir Walter was, moreover, assured of her having been a very fine woman. Here was a great deal to soften the business. A very fine woman with a large fortune, in love with him! Sir Walter seemed to admit it as complete apology; and though Elizabeth could not see the circumstance in quite so favourable a light, she allowed it to be a great extenuation.

Mr. Elliot had called repeatedly, had dined with them once, evidently delighted by the distinction of being asked for they gave no dinners in general; delighted, in short, by every proof of cousinly notice, and placing his whole happiness in being on intimate terms in Camden Place.

Anne listened, but without quite understanding it. Allowances, large allowances, she knew, must be made for the ideas of those who spoke. She heard it all under embellishment. All that sounded extravagant or irrational in the progress of the reconciliation might have no origin but in the language of the relators. Still, however, she had the sensation of there being something more than immediately appeared, in Mr. Elliot's wishing, after an interval of so many years, to be well received by them. In a worldly view, he had nothing to gain by being on terms with Sir Walter; nothing to risk by a state of variance. In all probability he was already the richer of the two, and the Kellynch estate would as

surely be his hereafter as the title. A sensible man, and he
looked like a *very* sensible man, why should it be an object
to him? She could only offer one solution: it was, perhaps,
for Elizabeth's sake. There might really have been a liking
formerly, though convenience and accident had drawn him
a different way; and now that he could afford to please himself, he might mean to pay his addresses to her. Elizabeth
was certainly very handsome, with well-bred, elegant manners, and her character might never have been penetrated
by Mr. Elliot, knowing her but in public, and when very
young himself. How her temper and understanding might
bear the investigation of his present keener time of life was
another concern and rather a fearful one. Most earnestly
did she wish that he might not be too nice, or too observant
if Elizabeth were his object; and that Elizabeth was disposed to believe herself so, and that her friend, Mrs. Clay,
was encouraging the idea, seemed apparent by a glance or
two between them, while Mr. Elliot's frequent visits were
talked of.

Anne mentioned the glimpses she had had of him at
Lyme, but without being much attended to. "Oh! yes, perhaps, it had been Mr. Elliot. They did not know. It might be
him, perhaps." They could not listen to her description of
him. They were describing him themselves; Sir Walter especially. He did justice to his very gentleman-like appearance, his air of elegance and fashion, his good-shaped face,
his sensible eye; but, at the same time, "must lament his
being very much under-hung, a defect which time seemed
to have increased; nor could he pretend to say that the years
had not altered almost every feature for the worse. Mr. Elliot
appeared to think that he (Sir Walter) was looking exactly
as he had done when they last parted;" but Sir Walter had
"not been able to return the compliment entirely, which had

embarrassed him. He did not mean to complain, however. Mr. Elliot was better to look at than most men, and he had no objection to being seen with him anywhere."

Mr. Elliot, and his friends in Marlborough Buildings, were talked of the whole evening. "Colonel Wallis had been so impatient to be introduced to them! and Mr. Elliot so anxious that he should!" and there was a Mrs. Wallis, at present known only to them by description, as she was in daily expectation of her confinement; but Mr. Elliot spoke of her as "a most charming woman, quite worthy of being known in Camden Place," and as soon as she recovered they were to be acquainted. Sir Walter thought much of Mrs. Wallis; she was said to be an excessively pretty woman, beautiful. "He longed to see her. He hoped she might make some amends for the many very plain faces he was continually passing in the streets. The worst of Bath was the number of its plain women. He did not mean to say that there were no pretty women, but the number of the plain was out of all proportion. He had frequently observed, as he walked, that one handsome face would be followed by thirty, or five-and-thirty frights; and once, as he had stood in a shop in Bond Street, he had counted eighty-seven women go by, one after another, without there being a tolerable face among them. It had been a frosty morning, to be sure, a sharp frost, which hardly one woman in a thousand could stand the test of. But still, there certainly were a dreadful multitude of ugly women in Bath; and as for the men! they were infinitely worse. Such scarecrows as the streets were full of! It was evident how little the women were used to the sight of anything tolerable, by the effect which a man of decent appearance produced. He had never walked anywhere arm-in-arm with Colonel Wallis (who was a fine military figure, though sandy-haired) without observing that every woman's eye was upon him; every woman's eye was sure to be upon Colonel Wallis." Modest Sir Walter! He was not allowed to escape, however. His daughter and Mrs. Clay united in hinting that Colonel Wallis's companion might have as good a figure as Colonel Wallis, and certainly was not sandy-haired.

"How is Mary looking?" said Sir Walter, in the height of his good humour. "The last time I saw her she had a red nose, but I hope that may not happen every day."

"Oh! no, that must have been quite accidental. In general she has been in very good health and very good looks since Michaelmas."

"If I thought it would not tempt her to go out in sharp winds, and grow coarse, I would send her a new hat and pelisse."

Anne was considering whether she should venture to suggest that a gown, or a cap, would not be liable to any such misuse, when a knock at the door suspended everything. "A knock at the door! and so late! It was ten o'clock. Could it be Mr. Elliot? They knew he was to dine in Lansdown Crescent. It was possible that he might stop in his way home to ask them how they did. They could think of no one else. Mrs. Clay decidedly thought it Mr. Elliot's knock." Mrs. Clay was right. With all the state which a butler and foot-boy could give, Mr. Elliot was ushered into the room.

It was the same, the very same man, with no difference but of dress. Anne drew a little back, while the others received his compliments, and her sister his apologies for calling at so unusual an hour, but "he could not be so near without wishing to know that neither she nor her friend had taken cold the day before," etc., etc.; which was all as politely done, and as politely taken, as possible, but her part must follow then. Sir Walter talked of his youngest daughter; "Mr.

16

THERE WAS ONE POINT which Anne, on returning to her family, would have been more thankful to ascertain even than Mr. Elliot's being in love with Elizabeth, which was, her father's not being in love with Mrs. Clay; and she was very far from easy about it, when she had been at home a few hours. On going down to breakfast the next morning she found there had just been a decent pretense on the lady's side of meaning to leave them. She could imagine Mrs. Clay to have said, that "now Miss Anne was come, she could not suppose herself at all wanted;" for Elizabeth was replying in a sort of whisper, "That must not be any reason, indeed. I assure you I feel it none. She is nothing to me, compared with you;" and she was in full time to hear her father say, "My dear madam, this must not be. As yet, you have seen nothing of Bath. You have been here only to be useful. You must not run away from us now. You must stay to be acquainted with Mrs. Wallis, the beautiful Mrs. Wallis. To your fine mind, I well know the sight of beauty is a real gratification."

He spoke and looked so much in earnest, that Anne was not surprised to see Mrs. Clay stealing a glance at Elizabeth and herself. Her countenance, perhaps, might express some watchfulness; but the praise of the fine mind did not appear to excite a thought in her sister. The lady could not but yield to such joint entreaties, and promise to stay.

In the course of the same morning, Anne and her father chancing to be alone together, he began to compliment her on her improved looks; he thought her "less thin in her person, in her cheeks; her skin, her complexion greatly improved; clearer, fresher. Had she been using anything in particular?" "No, nothing." "Merely Gowland," he supposed. "No, nothing at all." "Ha! he was surprised at that"; and added, "certainly you cannot do better than continue as you are; you cannot be better than well; or I should recommend Gowland, the constant use of Gowland, during the spring months. Mrs. Clay has been using it at my recommendation, and you see what it has done for her. You see how it has carried away her freckles."

If Elizabeth could but have heard this! Such personal praise might have struck her, especially as it did not appear to Anne that the freckles were at all lessened. But everything must take its chance. The evil of the marriage would be much diminished, if Elizabeth were also to marry. As for herself, she might always command a home with Lady Russell.

Lady Russell's composed mind and polite manners were put to some trial on this point, in her intercourse in Camden Place. The sight of Mrs. Clay in such favour, and of Anne so overlooked, was a perpetual provocation to her there; and vexed her as much when she was away, as a person in Bath who drinks the water, gets all the new publications, and has a very large acquaintance, has time to be vexed.

As Mr. Elliot became known to her, she grew more charitable, or more indifferent, towards the others. His manners were an immediate recommendation; and on conversing with him she found the solid so fully supporting the superficial, that she was at first, as she told Anne, almost ready to exclaim: "Can this be Mr. Elliot?" and could not seriously picture to herself a more agreeable or estimable man. Everything united in him; good understanding, correct opinions, knowledge of the world, and a warm heart. He had strong feelings of family attachment and family honour, without pride or weakness; he lived with the liberality of a man of fortune, without display; he judged for himself in everything essential, without defying public opinion in any point of world decorum. He was steady, observant, moderate, candid; never run away with by spirits or by selfishness, which fancied itself strong feeling; and yet, with a sensibility to what was amiable and lovely, and a value for all the felicities of domestic life, which characters of fancied enthusiasm and violent agitation seldom really possess. She was sure that he had not been happy in marriage. Colonel Wallis said it, and Lady Russell saw it; but it had been no unhappiness to sour his mind, nor (she began pretty soon to suspect) to prevent his thinking of a second choice. Her satisfaction in Mr. Elliot outweighed all the plague of Mrs. Clay.

It was now some years since Anne had begun to learn that she and her excellent friend could sometimes think differently; and it did not surprise her, therefore, that Lady Russell should see nothing suspicious or inconsistent, nothing to require more motives than appeared in Mr. Elliot's great desire of a reconciliation. In Lady Russell's view, it was perfectly natural that Mr. Elliot, at a mature time of life, should feel it a most desirable object, and what would very generally recommend him among all sensible people, to be on good terms with the head of his family; the simplest process in the world of time upon a head naturally clear, and only erring in the heyday of youth. Anne presumed, however, still to smile about it, and at last to mention "Elizabeth." Lady Russell listened, and looked, and made only this cautious reply:—"Elizabeth! very well; time will explain."

It was a reference to the future, which Anne, after a little observation, felt she must submit to. She could determine nothing at present. In that house Elizabeth must be first; and she was in the habit of such general observance as "Miss Elliot," that any particularity of attention seemed almost impossible. Mr. Elliot, too, it must be remembered, had not been a widower seven months. A little delay on his side might be very excusable. In fact, Anne could never see the crape round his hat, without fearing that she was the inexcusable one, in attributing to him such imaginations; for though his marriage had not been very happy, still it had existed so many years that she could not comprehend a very rapid recovery from the awful impression of its being dissolved.

However it might end, he was without any question their pleasantest acquaintance in Bath: she saw nobody equal to him; and it was a great indulgence now and then to talk to him about Lyme, which he seemed to have as lively a wish to see again, and to see more of, as herself. They went through the particulars of their first meeting a great many times. He gave her to understand that he had looked at her with some earnestness. She knew it well; and she remembered another person's look also.

They did not always think alike. His value for rank and

connection she perceived to be greater than hers. It was not merely complaisance, it must be a liking to the cause, which made him enter warmly into her father and sister's solicitudes on a subject which she thought unworthy to excite them. The Bath paper one morning announced the arrival of the Dowager Viscountess Dalrymple, and her daughter, the Honourable Miss Carteret; and all the comfort of No. — Camden Place, was swept away for many days; for the Dalrymples (in Anne's opinion, most unfortunate) were cousins of the Elliots; and the agony was how to introduce themselves properly.

Anne had never seen her father and sister before in contact with nobility, and she must acknowledge herself disappointed. She had hoped better things from their high ideas of their own situation in life, and was reduced to form a wish which she had never foreseen; a wish that they had more pride; for "our cousins, Lady Dalrymple and Miss Carteret"; "our cousins the Dalrymples," sounded in her ears all day long.

Sir Walter had once been in company with the late viscount, but had never seen any of the rest of the family; and the difficulties of the case arose from there having been a suspension of all intercourse by letters of ceremony, ever since the death of that said late viscount, when, in consequence of a dangerous illness of Sir Walter's at the same time, there had been an unlucky omission at Kellynch. No letter of condolence had been sent to Ireland. The neglect had been visited on the head of the sinner; for when poor Lady Elliot died herself, no letter of condolence was received at Kellynch, and, consequently, there was but too much reason to apprehend that the Dalrymples considered the relationship as closed. How to have this anxious business set to rights, and be admitted as cousins again, was the question: and it was a question which, in a more rational manner, neither Lady Russell nor Mr. Elliot thought unimportant. "Family connections were always worth preserving, good company always worth seeking; Lady Dalrymple had taken a house, for three months, in Laura Place, and would be living in style. She had been at Bath the year before, and Lady Russell had heard her spoken of as a charming woman. It was very desirable that the connection should be renewed, if it could be done, without any compromise of propriety on the side of the Elliots."

Sir Walter, however, would choose his own means and at last wrote a very fine letter of ample explanation, regret, and entreaty, to his right honourable cousin. Neither Lady Russell nor Mr. Elliot could admire the letter; but it did all that was wanted, in bringing three lines of scrawl from the Dowager Viscountess. "She was very much honoured, and should be happy in their acquaintance." The toils of the business were over, the sweets began. They visited in Laura Place, they had the cards of Dowager Viscountess Dalrymple, and the Honourable Miss Carteret, to be arranged wherever they might be most visible: and "Our cousins in Laura Place,"—"Our cousins, Lady Dalrymple and Miss Carteret," were talked of to everybody.

Anne was ashamed. Had Lady Dalrymple and her daughter even been very agreeable, she would still have been ashamed of the agitation they created, but they were nothing. There was no superiority of manner, accomplishment, or understanding. Lady Dalrymple had acquired the name of "a charming woman," because she had a smile and a civil answer for everybody. Miss Carteret, with still less to say, was so plain and so awkward, that she would never have been tolerated in Camden Place but for her birth.

Lady Russell confessed that she had expected something better; but yet "it was an acquaintance worth having;" and when Anne ventured to speak her opinion of them to Mr. Elliot, he agreed to their being nothing in themselves, but still maintained that, as a family connection, as good company, as those who would collect good company around them, they had their value. Anne smiled and said:

"My idea of good company, Mr. Elliot, is the company of clever, well-informed people, who have a great deal of conversation; that is what I call good company."

"You are mistaken," said he, gently, "that is not good company; that is the best. Good company requires only birth, education, and manners, and with regard to education is not very nice. Birth and good manners are essential; but a little learning is by no means a dangerous thing in good company; on the contrary, it will do very well. My cousin Anne shakes her head. She is not satisfied. She is fastidious. My dear cousin" (sitting down by her), "you have a better right to be fastidious than almost any other woman I know; but will it answer? Will it make you happy? Will it not be wiser to accept the society of these good ladies in Laura Place, and enjoy all the advantages of the connection as far as possible? You may depend upon it, that they will move in the first set in Bath this winter, and as rank is rank, your being known to be related to them will have its use in fixing your family (our family let me say) in that degree of consideration which we must all wish for."

"Yes," sighed Anne, "we shall, indeed, be known to be related to them!" then recollecting herself, and not wishing to be answered she added, "I certainly do think there has been by far too much trouble taken to procure the acquaintance. I suppose" (smiling) "I have more pride than any of you; but I confess it does vex me, that we should be so solicitous to have the relationship acknowledged, which we may be very sure is a matter of perfect indifference to them."

"Pardon me, my dear cousin, you are unjust to your own claims. In London, perhaps, in your present quiet style of living, it might be as you say; but in Bath, Sir Walter Elliot and his family will always be worth knowing: always acceptable as acquaintance."

"Well," said Anne, "I certainly am proud, too proud to enjoy a welcome which depends so entirely upon place."

"I love your indignation," said he; "it is very natural. But here you are in Bath, and the object is to be established here with all the credit and dignity which ought to belong to Sir Walter Elliot. You talk of being proud; I am called proud, I know, and I shall not wish to believe myself otherwise; for our pride, if investigated, would have the same object, I have no doubt, though the kind may seem a little different. In one point I am sure, my dear cousin" (he continued, speaking lower, though there was no one else in the room), "in one point I am sure we must feel alike. We must feel that every addition to your father's society, among his equals or superiors, may be of use in diverting his thoughts from those who are beneath him."

He looked as he spoke, to the seat which Mrs. Clay had been lately occupying: a sufficient explanation of what he particularly meant; and though Anne could not believe in their having the same sort of pride, she was pleased with him for not liking Mrs. Clay; and her conscience admitted that his wishing to promote her father's getting great acquaintance was more than excusable in the view of defeating her.

17

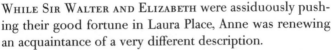

WHILE SIR WALTER AND ELIZABETH were assiduously pushing their good fortune in Laura Place, Anne was renewing an acquaintance of a very different description.

She had called on her former governess, and had heard from her of there being an old schoolfellow in Bath, who had the two strong claims on her attention of past kindness and present suffering. Miss Hamilton, now Mrs. Smith, had shown her kindness in one of those periods of her life when it had been most valuable. Anne had gone unhappy to school, grieving for the loss of a mother whom she had dearly loved, feeling her separation from home, and suffering as a girl of fourteen, of strong sensibility and not high spirits, must suffer at such a time; and Miss Hamilton, three years older than herself, but still from the want of near relations and a settled home, remaining another year at school, had been useful and good to her in a way which had considerably lessened her misery, and could never be remembered with indifference.

Miss Hamilton had left school, had married not long afterwards, was said to have married a man of fortune, and
this was all that Anne had known of her, till now that their
governess's account brought her situation forward in a more
decided but very different form.

She was a widow and poor. Her husband had been extravagant; and at his death, about two years before, had left
his affairs dreadfully involved. She had had difficulties of
every sort to contend with, and in addition to these distresses had been afflicted with a severe rheumatic fever,
which, finally settling in her legs, had made her for the present a cripple. She had come to Bath on that account, and
was now in lodgings near the hot baths, living in a very
humble way, unable even to afford herself the comfort of a
servant, and of course almost excluded from society.

Their mutual friend answered for the satisfaction which
a visit from Miss Elliot would give Mrs. Smith, and Anne
therefore lost no time in going. She mentioned nothing of
what she had heard, or what she intended at home. It would
excite no proper interest there. She only consulted Lady
Russell, who entered thoroughly into her sentiments, and
was most happy to convey her as near to Mrs. Smith's lodgings, in Westgate Buildings, as Anne chose to be taken.

The visit was paid, their acquaintance re-established,
their interest in each other more than rekindled. The first
ten minutes had its awkwardness and its emotion. Twelve
years were gone since they had parted, and each presented
a somewhat different person from what the other had imagined. Twelve years had changed Anne from the blooming,
silent, unformed girl of fifteen, to the elegant little woman
of seven-and-twenty, with every beauty excepting bloom,
and with manners as consciously right as they were invariably gentle; and twelve years had transformed the fine-

looking, well-grown Miss Hamilton, in all the glow of health
and confidence of superiority, into a poor, infirm, helpless
widow, receiving the visit of her former protégée as a favour;
but all that was uncomfortable in the meeting had soon
passed away, and left only the interesting charm of remembering former partialities and talking over old times.

Anne found in Mrs. Smith the good sense and agreeable
manners which she had almost ventured to depend on, and
a disposition to converse and be cheerful beyond her expectation. Neither the dissipations of the past—and she had
lived very much in the world—nor the restrictions of the
present, neither sickness nor sorrow seemed to have closed
her heart or ruined her spirits.

In the course of a second visit she talked with great openness, and Anne's astonishment increased. She could scarcely
imagine a more cheerless situation in itself than Mrs. Smith's.
She had been very fond of her husband: she had buried
him. She had been used to affluence: it was gone. She had
no child to connect her with life and happiness again, no
relations to assist in the arrangement of perplexed affairs,
no health to make all the rest supportable. Her accommodations were limited to a noisy parlour, and a dark bedroom
behind, with no possibility of moving from one to the other
without assistance, which there was only one servant in the
house to afford, and she never quitted the house but to be
conveyed into the warm bath. Yet, in spite of all this, Anne
had reason to believe that she had moments only of languor
and depression to hours of occupation and enjoyment. How
could it be? She watched, observed, reflected, and finally
determined that this was not a case of fortitude or of resignation only. A submissive spirit might be patient, a strong
understanding would supply resolution, but here was something more; here was that elasticity of mind, that disposition

to be comforted, that power of turning readily from evil to good, and of finding employment which carried her out of herself, which was from nature alone. It was the choicest gift of Heaven; and Anne viewed her friend as one of those instances in which, by a merciful appointment, it seems designed to counterbalance almost every other want.

There had been a time, Mrs. Smith told her, when her spirits had nearly failed. She could not call herself an invalid now, compared with her state on first reaching Bath. Then she had, indeed, been a pitiable object; for she had caught cold on the journey, and had hardly taken possession of her lodgings before she was again confined to her bed, and suffering under severe and constant pain; and all this among strangers, with the absolute necessity of having a regular nurse, and finances at that moment particularly unfit to meet any extraordinary expense. She had weathered it, however, and could truly say that it had done her good. It had increased her comforts by making her feel herself to be in good hands. She had seen too much of the world to expect sudden or disinterested attachment anywhere, but her illness had proved to her that her landlady had a character to preserve, and would not use her ill; and she had been particularly fortunate in her nurse, as a sister of her landlady, a nurse by profession, and who had always a home in that house when unemployed, chanced to be at liberty just in time to attend her. "And she," said Mrs. Smith, "besides nursing me most admirably, has really proved an invaluable acquaintance. As soon as I could use my hands she taught me to knit, which has been a great amusement; and she put me in the way of making these little thread-cases, pin-cushions, and card-racks, which you always find me so busy about, and which supply me with the means of doing a little good to one or two very poor families in this neighbourhood. She has a large acquaintance, of course professionally, among those who can afford to buy, and she disposes of my merchandise. She always takes the right time for applying. Everybody's heart is open, you know, when they have recently escaped from severe pain, or are recovering the blessing of health, and Nurse Rooke thoroughly understands when to speak. She is a shrewd, intelligent, sensible woman. Hers is a line for seeing human nature; and she has a fund of good sense and observation, which, as a companion, make her infinitely superior to thousands of those who, having only received 'the best education in the world,' know nothing worth attending to. Call it gossip, if you will, but when Nurse Rooke has half an hour's leisure to bestow on me, she is sure to have something to relate that is entertaining and profitable: something that makes one know one's species better. One likes to hear what is going on, to be *au fait* as to the newest modes of being trifling and silly. To me, who live so much alone, her conversation, I assure you, is a treat."

Anne, far from wishing to cavil at the pleasure, replied, "I can easily believe it. Women of that class have great opportunities, and if they are intelligent may be well worth listening to. Such varieties of human nature as they are in the habit of witnessing! And it is not merely in its follies that they are well read; for they see it occasionally under every circumstance that can be most interesting or affecting. What instances must pass before them of ardent, disinterested, self-denying attachment, of heroism, fortitude, patience, resignation; of all the conflicts and all the sacrifices that ennoble us most. A sick chamber may often furnish the worth of volumes."

"Yes," said Mrs. Smith, more doubtingly, "sometimes it may, though I fear its lessons are not often in the elevated style you describe. Here and there, human nature may be great in times of trial; but generally speaking it is its weakness and not its strength that appears in a sick chamber: it is selfishness and impatience, rather than generosity and fortitude, that one hears of. There is so little real friendship in the world! and unfortunately" (speaking low and tremulously), "there are so many who forget to think seriously till it is almost too late."

Anne saw the misery of such feelings. The husband had not been what he ought, and the wife had been led among that part of mankind which made her think worse of the world than she hoped it deserved. It was but a passing emotion, however, with Mrs. Smith; she shook it off, and soon added in a different tone:

"I do not suppose the situation my friend Mrs. Rooke is in at present will furnish much either to interest or edify me. She is only nursing Mrs. Wallis, of Marlborough Buildings; a mere pretty, silly, expensive, fashionable woman, I believe; and of course will have nothing to report but of lace and finery. I mean to make my profit of Mrs. Wallis, however. She has plenty of money, and I intend she shall buy all the high-priced things I have in hand now."

Anne had called several times on her friend, before the existence of such a person was known in Camden Place. At last, it became necessary to speak of her. Sir Walter, Elizabeth and Mrs. Clay, returned one morning from Laura Place, with a sudden invitation from Lady Dalrymple for the same evening, and Anne was already engaged to spend that evening in Westgate Buildings. She was not sorry for the excuse. They were only asked, she was sure, because Lady Dalrymple, being kept at home by a bad cold, was glad to make use of the relationship which had been so pressed on her; and she declined on her own account with great alacrity: "She was engaged to spend the evening with an old schoolfellow." They were not much interested in anything relative to Anne; but still there were questions enough asked to make it understood what this old schoolfellow was; and Elizabeth was disdainful! and Sir Walter severe.

"Westgate Buildings!" said he; "and who is Miss Anne Elliott to be visiting in Westgate Buildings? A Mrs. Smith. A widow Mrs. Smith; and who was her husband? One of the five thousand Mr. Smiths whose names are to be met with everywhere. And what is her attraction? That she is old and sickly. Upon my word, Miss Anne Elliot, you have the most extraordinary taste! Everything that revolts other people, low company, paltry rooms, foul air, disgusting associations, are inviting to you. But surely you may put off this old lady till to-morrow; she is not so near her end, I presume, but that she may hope to see another day. What is her age? Forty?"

"No, sir, she is not one-and-thirty; but I do not think I can put off my engagement, because it is the only evening for some time which will at once suit her and myself. She goes into the warm bath to-morrow; and for the rest of the week, you know, we are engaged."

"But what does Lady Russell think of this acquaintance?" asked Elizabeth.

"She sees nothing to blame in it," replied Anne; "on the contrary, she approves it, and has generally taken me when I have called on Mrs. Smith."

"Westgate Buildings must have been rather surprised by the appearance of a carriage drawn up near its pavement," observed Sir Walter. "Sir Henry Russell's widow, indeed, has no honours to distinguish her arms, but still it is a handsome equipage, and no doubt is well known to convey a Miss Elliot. A widow Mrs. Smith, lodging in Westgate Buildings!

A poor widow, barely able to live, between thirty and forty; a mere Mrs. Smith, an every-day Mrs. Smith, of all people and all names in the world, to be the chosen friend of Miss Anne Elliot, and to be preferred by her to her own family connections among the nobility of England and Ireland! Mrs. Smith! Such a name!"

Mrs. Clay, who had been present while all this passed, now thought it advisable to leave the room, and Anne could have said much, and did long to say a little in defence of *her* friend's not very dissimilar claims to theirs, but her sense of personal respect to her father prevented her. She made no reply. She left it to himself to recollect, that Mrs. Smith was not the only widow in Bath between thirty and forty, with little to live on, and no surname of dignity.

Anne kept her appointment, the others kept theirs, and of course she heard the next morning that they had had a delightful evening. She had been the only one of the set absent, for Sir Walter and Elizabeth had not only been quite at her ladyship's service themselves, but had actually been happy to be employed by her in collecting others, and had been at the trouble of inviting both Lady Russell and Mr. Elliot; and Mr. Elliot had made a point of leaving Colonel Wallis early, and Lady Russell had fresh arranged all her evening engagements, in order to wait on her. Anne had the whole history of all that such an evening could supply from Lady Russell. To her, its greatest interest must be, in having been very much talked of between her friend and Mr. Elliot; in having been wished for, regretted, and at the same time honoured for staying away in such a cause. Her kind, compassionate visits to this old schoolfellow, sick and reduced, seemed to have quite delighted Mr. Elliot. He thought her a most extraordinary young woman: in her temper, manners, mind, a model of female excellence. He could meet even

Lady Russell in a discussion of her merits; and Anne could not be given to understand so much by her friend, could not know herself to be so highly rated by a sensible man, without many of those agreeable sensations which her friend meant to create.

Lady Russell was now perfectly decided in her opinion of Mr. Elliot. She was as much convinced of his meaning to gain Anne in time as of his deserving her, and was beginning to calculate the number of weeks which would free him from all the remaining restraints of widowerhood, and leave him at liberty to exert his most open powers of pleasing. She would not speak to Anne with half the certainty she felt on the subject, she would venture on little more than hints of what might be hereafter, of a possible attachment on his side, of the desirableness of the alliance, supposing such an attachment to be real and returned. Anne heard her, and made no violent exclamations; she only smiled, blushed, and gently shook her head.

"I am no match-maker, as you well know," said Lady Russell, "being much too well aware of the uncertainty of all human events and calculations. I only mean that if Mr. Elliot should some time hence pay his addresses to you, and if you should be disposed to accept him, I think there would be every possibility of your being happy together. A most suitable connection everybody must consider it, but I think it might be a very happy one."

"Mr. Elliot is an exceedingly agreeable man, and in many respects I think highly of him," said Anne; "but we should not suit."

Lady Russell let this pass, and only said in rejoinder, "I own that to be able to regard you as the future mistress of Kellynch, the future Lady Elliot, to look forward and see you occupying your dear mother's place, succeeding to all her rights, and all her popularity, as well as to all her virtues, would be the highest possible gratification to me. You are your mother's self in countenance and disposition; and if I might be allowed to fancy you such as she was, in situation, and name, and home, presiding and blessing in the same spot, and only superior to her in being more highly valued, my dearest Anne, it would give me more delight than is often felt at my time of life."

Anne was obliged to turn away, to rise, to walk to a distant table, and, leaning there in pretended employment, try to subdue the feelings this picture excited. For a few moments her imagination and her heart were bewitched. The idea of becoming what her mother had been; of having the precious name of "Lady Elliot" first revived in herself; of being restored to Kellynch, calling it her home again, her home for ever, was a charm which she could not immediately resist. Lady Russell said not another word, willing to leave the matter to its own operation; and believing that, could Mr. Elliot at that moment with propriety have spoken for himself!— she believed, in short, what Anne did not believe. The same image of Mr. Elliot speaking for himself brought Anne to composure again. The charm of Kellynch and of "Lady Elliot" all faded away. She never could accept him. And it was not only that her feelings were still adverse to any man save one; her judgment, on a serious consideration of the possibilities of such a case, was against Mr. Elliot.

Though they had now been acquainted a month, she could not be satisfied that she really knew his character. That he was a sensible man, an agreeable man, that he talked well, professed good opinions, seemed to judge properly and as a man of principle, this was all clear enough. He certainly knew what was right, nor could she fix on any one article of moral duty evidently transgressed; but yet she would have been afraid to answer for his conduct. She distrusted the past, if not the present. The names which occasionally dropped of former associates, the allusions to former practices and pursuits, suggested suspicions not favourable of what he had been. She saw that there had been bad habits; that Sunday travelling had been a common thing; that there had been a period of his life (and probably not a short one) when he had been, at least, careless on all serious matters; and, though he might now think very differently, who could answer for the true sentiments of a clever, cautious man grown old enough to appreciate a fair character? How could it ever be ascertained that his mind was truly cleansed?

Mr. Elliot was rational, discreet, polished, but he was not open. There was never any burst of feeling, any warmth of indignation or delight, at the evil or good of others. This, to Anne, was a decided imperfection. Her early impressions were incurable. She prized the frank, the open-hearted, the eager character beyond all others. Warmth and enthusiasm did captivate her still. She felt that she could so much more depend upon the sincerity of those who sometimes looked or said a careless or a hasty thing, than of those whose presence of mind never varied, whose tongue never slipped.

Mr. Elliot was too generally agreeable. Various as were the tempers in her father's house, he pleased them all. He endured too well, stood too well with everybody. He had spoken to her with some degree of openness of Mrs. Clay; had appeared completely to see what Mrs. Clay was about, and to hold her in contempt; and yet Mrs. Clay found him as agreeable as anybody.

Lady Russell saw either less or more than her young friend, for she saw nothing to excite distrust. She could not imagine a man more exactly what he ought to be than Mr. Elliot; nor did she ever enjoy a sweeter feeling than the hope of seeing him receive the hand of her beloved Anne in Kellynch church, in the course of the following autumn.

18

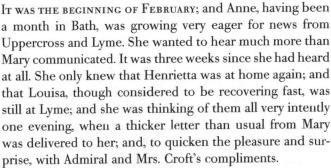

It was the beginning of February; and Anne, having been a month in Bath, was growing very eager for news from Uppercross and Lyme. She wanted to hear much more than Mary communicated. It was three weeks since she had heard at all. She only knew that Henrietta was at home again; and that Louisa, though considered to be recovering fast, was still at Lyme; and she was thinking of them all very intently one evening, when a thicker letter than usual from Mary was delivered to her; and, to quicken the pleasure and surprise, with Admiral and Mrs. Croft's compliments.

The Crofts must be in Bath! A circumstance to interest her. They were people whom her heart turned to very naturally.

"What is this?" cried Sir Walter. "The Crofts arrived in Bath? The Crofts who rent Kellynch? What have they brought you?"

"A letter from Uppercross Cottage, sir."

"Oh! those letters are convenient passports. They secure

an introduction. I should have visited Admiral Croft, however, at any rate. I know what is due to my tenant."

Anne could listen no longer; she could not even have
told how the poor Admiral's complexion escaped; her letter
engrossed her. It had been begun several days back.

February 1st —.

My Dear Anne,—

I make no apology for my silence, because I know
how little people think of letters in such a place as
Bath. You must be a great deal too happy to care for
Uppercross, which, as you well know, affords little to
write about. We have had a very dull Christmas; Mr.
and Mrs. Musgrove have not had one dinner-party
all the holidays. I do not reckon the Hayters as anybody. The holidays, however, are over at last: I believe no children ever had such long ones. I am sure
I had not. The house was cleared yesterday, except
of the little Harvilles; but you will be surprised to
hear that they have never gone home. Mrs. Harville
must be an odd mother to part with them so long. I
do not understand it. They are not at all nice children, in my opinion; but Mrs. Musgrove seems to
like them quite as well, if not better, than her grand-
children. What dreadful weather we have had! It
may not be felt in Bath, with your nice pavements;
but in the country it is of some consequence. I have
not had a creature call on me since the second week
in January, except Charles Hayter, who has been
calling much oftener than was welcome. Between
ourselves, I think it a great pity Henrietta did not remain at Lyme as long as Louisa; it would have kept
her a little out of his way. The carriage is gone to-

day, to bring Louisa and the Harvilles to-morrow.
We are not asked to dine with them, however, till the
day after, Mrs. Musgrove is so afraid of her being fa-
tigued by the journey, which is not very likely, considering the care that will be taken of her; and it
would be much more convenient to me to dine
there to-morrow. I am glad you find Mr. Elliot so
agreeable, and wish I could be acquainted with him
too; but I have my usual luck: I am always out of the
way when anything desirable is going on; always the
last of my family to be noticed. What an immense
time Mrs. Clay has been staying with Elizabeth! Does
she never mean to go away? But, perhaps, if she
were to leave the room vacant, we might not be invited. Let me know what you think of this. I do not
expect my children to be asked, you know. I can
leave them at the Great House very well, for a
month or six weeks. I have this moment heard that
the Crofts are going to Bath almost immediately:
they think the Admiral gouty. Charles heard it quite
by chance: they have not had the civility to give me
any notice, or offer to take anything. I do not think
they improve at all as neighbours. We see nothing of
them, and this is really an instance of gross inatten-
tion. Charles joins me in love, and everything
proper. Yours affectionately,

MARY M——.

I am sorry to say that I am very far from well; and
Jemima has just told me that the butcher says there
is a bad sore-throat very much about. I dare say I
shall catch it; and my sore-throats, you know, are always worse than anybody's.

So ended the first part, which had been afterwards put into an envelope, containing nearly as much more.

I kept my letter open, that I might send you word how Louisa bore her journey, and now I am extremely glad I did, having a great deal to add. In the first place, I had a note from Mrs. Croft yesterday, offering to convey anything to you; a very kind, friendly note indeed, addressed to me, just as it ought; I shall therefore be able to make my letter as long as I like. The Admiral does not seem very ill, and I sincerely hope Bath will do him all the good he wants. I shall be truly glad to have them back again. Our neighbourhood cannot spare such a pleasant family. But now for Louisa. I have something to communicate that will astonish you not a little. She and the Harvilles came on Tuesday very safely, and in the evening we went to ask her how she did, when we were rather surprised not to find Captain Benwick of the party, for he had been invited as well as the Harvilles; and what do you think was the reason? Neither more nor less than his being in love with Louisa, and not choosing to venture to Uppercross till he had had an answer from Mr. Musgrove; for it was all settled between him and her before she came away, and he had written to her father by Captain Harville. True, upon my honour! Are not you astonished? I shall be surprised at least if you ever received a hint of it, for I never did. Mrs. Musgrove protests solemnly that she knew nothing of the matter. We are all very well pleased, however; for though it is not equal to her marrying Captain Wentworth, it is infinitely better than Charles Hayter; and Mr. Musgrove has written his consent, and Captain Benwick is expected to-day. Mrs. Harville says her husband feels a good deal on his poor sister's account; but, however, Louisa is a great favourite with both. Indeed, Mrs. Harville and I quite agree that we love her the better for having nursed her. Charles wonders what Captain Wentworth will say; but if you remember, I never thought him attached to Louisa; I never could see anything of it. And this is the end, you see, of Captain Benwick's being supposed to be an admirer of yours. How Charles could take such a thing into his head was always incomprehensible to me. I hope he will be more agreeable now. Certainly not a great match for Louisa Musgrove, but a million times better than marrying among the Hayters.

Mary need not have feared her sister's being in any degree prepared for the news. She had never in her life been more astonished. Captain Benwick and Louisa Musgrove! It was almost too wonderful for belief, and it was with the greatest effort that she could remain in the room, preserve an air of calmness, and answer the common questions of the moment. Happily for her, they were not many. Sir Walter wanted to know whether the Crofts travelled with four horses, and whether they were likely to be situated in such a part of Bath as it might suit Miss Elliot and himself to visit in; but had little curiosity beyond.

"How is Mary?" said Elizabeth; and without waiting for an answer, "And pray what brings the Crofts to Bath?"

"They come on the Admiral's account. He is thought to be gouty."

"Gout and decrepitude!" said Sir Walter. "Poor old gentleman!"

"Have they any acquaintances here?" asked Elizabeth.

"I do not know; but I can hardly suppose that, at Admiral Croft's time of life, and in his profession, he should not have many acquaintances in such a place as this."

"I suspect," said Sir Walter, coolly, "that Admiral Croft will be best known in Bath as the renter of Kellynch Hall. Elizabeth, may we venture to present him and his wife in Laura Place?"

"Oh no! I think not. Situated as we are with Lady Dalrymple, cousins, we ought to be very careful not to embarrass her with acquaintances she might not approve. If we were not related it would not signify; but as cousins, she would feel scrupulous as to any proposal of ours. We had better leave the Crofts to find their own level. There are several odd-looking men walking about here, who, I am told, are sailors. The Crofts will associate with them."

This was Sir Walter and Elizabeth's share of interest in the letter; when Mrs. Clay had paid her tribute of more decent attention, in an enquiry after Mrs. Charles Musgrove and her fine little boys, Anne was at liberty.

In her own room she tried to comprehend it. Well might Charles wonder how Captain Wentworth would feel! Perhaps he had quitted the field, had given Louisa up, had ceased to love, had found he did not love her. She could not endure the idea of treachery or levity, or anything akin to ill usage between him and his friend. She could not endure that such a friendship as theirs should be severed unfairly.

Captain Benwick and Louisa Musgrove! The high-spirited, joyous-talking Louisa Musgrove, and the dejected, thinking, feeling, reading Captain Benwick, seemed each of them everything that would not suit the other. Their minds most dissimilar! Where could have been the attraction? The answer soon presented itself. It had been in situation. They had been thrown together several weeks; they had been living in the same small family party: since Henrietta's coming away, they must have been depending almost entirely on each other, and Louisa, just recovering from illness, had been in an interesting state, and Captain Benwick was not inconsolable. That was a point which Anne had not been able to avoid suspecting before; and instead of drawing the same conclusion as Mary, from the present course of events, they served only to confirm the idea of his having felt some dawning of tenderness toward herself. She did not mean, however, to derive much more from it to gratify her vanity than Mary might have allowed. She was persuaded that any tolerably pleasing young woman who had listened and seemed to feel for him would have received the same compliment. He had an affectionate heart. He must love somebody.

She saw no reason against their being happy. Louisa had fine naval fervour to begin with, and they would soon grow more alike. He would gain cheerfulness, and she would learn to be an enthusiast for Scott and Lord Byron; nay, that was probably learnt already; of course they had fallen in love over poetry. The idea of Louisa Musgrove turned into a person of literary taste and sentimental reflection was amusing, but she had no doubt of its being so. The day at Lyme, the fall from the Cobb, might influence her health, her nerves, her courage, her character to the end of her life, as thoroughly as it appeared to have influenced her fate.

The conclusion of the whole was, that if the woman who had been sensible of Captain Wentworth's merits could be allowed to prefer another man, there was nothing in the engagement to excite lasting wonder; and if Captain Wentworth lost no friend by it, certainly nothing to be regretted. No, it was not regret which made Anne's heart beat in spite of herself, and brought the colour into her cheeks when she thought of Captain Wentworth unshackled and free. She had some feelings which she was ashamed to investigate. They were too much like joy, senseless joy!

She longed to see the Crofts; but when the meeting took place, it was evident that no rumour of the news had yet reached them. The visit of ceremony was paid and returned; and Louisa Musgrove was mentioned, and Captain Benwick, too, without even half a smile.

The Crofts had placed themselves in lodgings in Gay Street, perfectly to Sir Walter's satisfaction. He was not at all ashamed of the acquaintance, and did, in fact, think and talk a great deal more about the Admiral than the Admiral ever thought or talked about him.

The Crofts knew quite as many people in Bath as they wished for, and considered their intercourse with the Elliots as a mere matter of form, and not in the least likely to afford them any pleasure. They brought with them their country habit of being always together. He was ordered to walk to keep off the gout, and Mrs. Croft seemed to go shares with him in everything, and to walk for her life to do him good. Anne saw them wherever she went. Lady Russell took her out in her carriage almost every morning, and she never failed to think of them, and never failed to see them. Knowing their feelings as she did, it was a most attractive picture of happiness to her. She always watched them as long as she could, delighted to fancy she understood what they might be talking of, as they walked along in happy independence, or equally delighted to see the Admiral's hearty shake of the hand when he encountered an old friend, and observe their eagerness of conversation when occasionally forming into a little knot of the navy, Mrs. Croft looking as intelligent and keen as any of the officers around her.

Anne was too much engaged with Lady Russell to be often walking herself; but it so happened that one morning, about a week or ten days after the Crofts' arrival, it suited her best to leave her friend, or her friend's carriage, in the lower part of the town, and return alone to Camden Place, and in walking up Milsom Street she had the good fortune to meet with the Admiral. He was standing by himself, at a printshop window, with his hands behind him, in earnest contemplation of some print, and she not only might have passed him unseen, but was obliged to touch as well as address him before she could catch his notice. When he did perceive and acknowledge her, however, it was done with all his usual frankness and good-humour. "Ha! is it you? Thank you, thank you. This is treating me like a friend. Here I am, you see, staring at a picture. I can never get by this shop without stopping. But what a thing here is, by way of a boat! Do look at it. Did you ever see the like? What queer fellows your fine painters must be, to think that anybody would venture their lives in such a shapeless old cockle-shell as that? And yet here are two gentlemen stuck up in it mightily at their ease, and looking about them at the rocks and mountains, as if they were not to be upset the next moment, which they certainly must be. I wonder where that boat was built!" (laughing heartily); "I would not venture over a horsepond in it. Well" (turning away), "now, where are you bound? Can I go anywhere for you, or with you? Can I be of any use?"

"None, I thank you, unless you will give me the pleasure of your company the little way our road lies together. I am going home."

"That I will, with all my heart, and further too. Yes, yes, we will have a snug walk together, and I have something to tell you as we go along. There, take my arm; that's right; I do not feel comfortable if I have not a woman there. Lord! what a boat it is!" taking a last look at the picture, as they began to be in motion.

"Did you say that you had something to tell me, sir?"

"Yes, I have, presently. But here comes a friend, Captain Brigden; I shall only say, 'How d'ye do?' as we pass, however. I shall not stop. 'How d'ye do?' Brigden stares to see any-body with me but my wife. She, poor soul, is tied by the leg. She has a blister on one of her heels, as large as a three-shilling piece. If you look across the street, you will see Ad-miral Brand coming down and his brother. Shabby fellows, both of them! I am glad they are not on this side of the way. Sophy cannot bear them. They played me a pitiful trick once: got away some of my best men. I will tell you the whole story another time. There comes old Sir Archibald Drew and his grandson. Look, he sees us; he kisses his hand to you; he takes you for my wife. Ah! the peace has come too soon for that younker. Poor old Sir Archibald! How do you like Bath, Miss Elliot? It suits us very well. We are always meeting with some old friend or other; the streets full of them every morning; sure to have plenty of chat; and then we get away from them all, and shut ourselves into our lodgings, and draw in our chairs, and are as snug as if we were at Kellynch, ay, or as we used to be even at North Yarmouth and Deal. We do not like our lodgings here the worse, I can tell you, for putting us in mind of those we first had at North Yar-mouth. The wind blows through one of the cupboards just in the same way."

When they were got a little further, Anne ventured to press again for what he had to communicate. She had hoped when clear of Milsom Street to have her curiosity gratified; but she was still obliged to wait, for the Admiral had made up his mind not to begin till they had gained the greater space and quiet of Belmont; and as she was not really Mrs. Croft, she must let him have his own way. As soon as they were fairly ascending Belmont, he began:

"Well, now you shall hear something that will surprise you. But first of all, you must tell me the name of the young lady I am going to talk about. That young lady, you know, that we have all been so concerned for. The Miss Musgrove that all this has been happening to. Her Christian name: I always forget her Christian name."

Anne had been ashamed to appear to comprehend so soon as she really did; but now she could safely suggest the name of "Louisa."

"Ay, ay, Miss Louisa Musgrove, that is the name. I wish young ladies had not such a number of fine Christian names. I should never be out if they were all Sophys, or something of that sort. Well, this Miss Louisa, we all thought, you know, was to marry Frederick. He was courting her week after week. The only wonder was, what they could be waiting for, till the business at Lyme came; then, indeed, it was clear enough that they must wait till her brain was set to right. But even then there was something odd in their way of going on. Instead of staying at Lyme, he went off to Plymouth, and then he went off to see Edward. When we came back from Minehead he was gone down to Edward's, and there he has been ever since. We have seen nothing of him since November. Even Sophy could not understand it. But now, the matter has taken the strangest turn of all; for this young lady, this same Miss Musgrove, instead of being to marry Frederick, is to marry James Benwick. You know James Benwick?"

"A little. I am a little acquainted with Captain Benwick."

"Well, she is to marry him. Nay, most likely they are married already, for I do not know what they should wait for."

"I thought Captain Benwick a very pleasing young man," said Anne, "and I understand that he bears an excellent character."

"Oh! yes, yes, there is not a word to be said against James Benwick. He is only a commander, it is true, made last summer, and these are bad times for getting on, but he has not another fault that I know of. An excellent, good-hearted fellow, I assure you; a very active, zealous officer, too, which is more than you would think for, perhaps, for that soft sort of manner does not do him justice."

"Indeed, you are mistaken there, sir; I should never augur want of spirit from Captain Benwick's manners. I thought them particularly pleasing, and I will answer for it, they would generally please."

"Well, well, ladies are the best judges; but James Benwick is rather too piano for me; and though very likely it is all our partiality, Sophy and I cannot help thinking Frederick's manners better than his. There is something about Frederick more to our taste."

Anne was caught. She had only meant to oppose the too common idea of spirit and gentleness being incompatible with each other, not at all to represent Captain Benwick's manners as the very best that could possibly be; and, after a little hesitation, she was beginning to say, "I was not entering into any comparison of the two friends;" but the Admiral interrupted her with:

"And the thing is certainly true. It is not a mere bit of gossip. We have it from Frederick himself. His sister had a letter from him yesterday, in which he tells us of it, and he had just had it in a letter from Harville, written upon the spot, from Uppercross. I fancy they are all at Uppercross."

This was an opportunity which Anne could not resist; she said, therefore, "I hope, Admiral, I hope there is nothing in the style of Captain Wentworth's letter to make you and Mrs. Croft particularly uneasy. It did certainly seem, last autumn, as if there were an attachment between him and Louisa Musgrove; but I hope it may be understood to have worn out on each side equally, and without violence. I hope his letter does not breathe the spirit of an ill-used man."

"Not at all, not at all; there is not an oath or a murmur from beginning to end."

Anne looked down to hide her smile.

"No, no; Frederick is not a man to whine and complain; he has too much spirit for that. If the girl likes another man better, it is very fit she should have him."

"Certainly. But what I mean is, that I hope there is nothing in Captain Wentworth's manner of writing to make you suppose he thinks himself ill-used by his friend, which might appear, you know, without its being absolutely said. I should be very sorry that such a friendship as has subsisted between him and Captain Benwick should be destroyed, or even wounded by a circumstance of this sort."

"Yes, yes, I understand you. But there is nothing at all of that nature in the letter. He does not give the least fling at Benwick; does not so much as say, 'I wonder at it. I have a reason of my own for wondering at it.' No, you would not guess, from his way of writing, that he had ever thought of this Miss (what's her name?) for himself. He very handsomely hopes they will be happy together; and there is nothing very unforgiving in that, I think."

Anne did not receive the perfect conviction which the

Admiral meant to convey, but it would have been useless to press the enquiry further. She therefore satisfied herself with commonplace remarks or quiet attention, and the Admiral had it all his own way.

"Poor Frederick!" said he, at last. "Now he must begin all over again with somebody else. I think we must get him to Bath. Sophy must write, and beg him to come to Bath. Here are pretty girls enough, I am sure. It would be of no use to go to Uppercross again, for that other Miss Musgrove, I find, is bespoken by her cousin, the young parson. Do not you think, Miss Elliot, we had better try to get him to Bath?"

19

WHILE ADMIRAL CROFT was taking this walk with Anne, and expressing his wish of getting Captain Wentworth to Bath, Captain Wentworth was already on his way thither. Before Mrs. Croft had written, he was arrived, and the very next time Anne walked out, she saw him.

Mr. Elliot was attending his two cousins and Mrs. Clay. They were in Milsom Street. It began to rain, not much, but enough to make shelter desirable for women, and quite enough to make it very desirable for Miss Elliot to have the advantage of being conveyed home in Lady Dalrymple's carriage, which was seen waiting at a little distance: she, Anne, and Mrs. Clay, therefore, turned into Molland's, while Mr. Elliot stepped to Lady Dalrymple, to request her assistance. He soon joined them again, successful, of course; Lady Dalrymple would be most happy to take them home, and would call for them in a few minutes.

Her ladyship's carriage was a barouche, and did not hold more than four with any comfort. Miss Carteret was with her mother; consequently it was not reasonable to expect accommodation for all the three Camden Place ladies. There could be no doubt as to Miss Elliot. Whoever suffered inconvenience, she must suffer none, but it occupied a little time to settle the point of civility between the other two. The rain was a mere trifle, and Anne was most sincere in preferring a walk with Mr. Elliot. But the rain was also a mere trifle to Mrs. Clay; she would hardly allow it even to drop at all, and her boots were so thick! much thicker than Miss Anne's; and, in short, her civility rendered her quite as anxious to be left to walk with Mr. Elliot as Anne could be, and it was discussed between them with a generosity so polite and so determined, that the others were obliged to settle it for them; Miss Elliot maintaining that Mrs. Clay had a little cold already, and Mr. Elliot, deciding, on appeal, that his cousin Anne's boots were rather the thickest.

It was fixed, accordingly, that Mrs. Clay should be of the party in the carriage; and they had just reached this point, when Anne, as she sat near the window, descried, most decidedly and distinctly, Captain Wentworth walking down the street.

Her start was perceptible only to herself; but she instantly felt that she was the greatest simpleton in the world, the most unaccountable and absurd! For a few minutes she saw nothing before her: it was all confusion. She was lost, and when she had scolded back her senses, she found the others still waiting for the carriage, and Mr. Elliot (always obliging) just setting off for Union Street on a commission of Mrs. Clay's.

She now felt a great inclination to go to the outer door; she wanted to see if it rained. Why was she to suspect herself of another motive? Captain Wentworth must be out of sight.

She left her seat, she would go; one half of her should not be always so much wiser than the other half, or always suspecting the other of being worse than it was. She would see if it rained. She was sent back, however, in a moment, by the entrance of Captain Wentworth himself, among a party of gentlemen and ladies, evidently his acquaintances, and whom he must have joined a little below Milsom Street. He was more obviously struck and confused by the sight of her than she had ever observed before; he looked quite red. For the first time since their renewed acquaintance, she felt that she was betraying the least sensibility of the two. She had the advantage of him in the preparation of the last few moments. All the overpowering, blinding, bewildering, first effects of strong surprise were over with her. Still, however, she had enough to feel! It was agitation, pain, pleasure; a something between delight and misery.

He spoke to her, and then turned away. The character of his manner was embarrassment. She could not have called it either cold or friendly, or anything so certainly as embarrassed.

After a short interval, however, he came towards her, and spoke again. Mutual enquiries on common subjects passed: neither of them, probably, much the wiser for what they heard, and Anne continuing fully sensible of his being less at ease than formerly. They had, by dint of being so very much together, got to speak to each other with a considerable portion of apparent indifference and calmness; but he could not do it now. Time had changed him, or Louisa had changed him. There was consciousness of some sort or other. He looked very well, not as if he had been suffering in health or spirits, and he talked of Uppercross, of the Musgroves, nay, even of Louisa, and had even a momentary look of his own arch significance as he named her; but yet it was Captain Wentworth not comfortable, not easy, not able to feign that he was.

It did not surprise, but it grieved Anne to observe that Elizabeth would not know him. She saw that he saw Elizabeth, that Elizabeth saw him, that there was complete internal recognition on each side; she was convinced that he was ready to be acknowledged as an acquaintance, expecting it, and she had the pain of seeing her sister turn away with unalterable coldness.

Lady Dalrymple's carriage, for which Miss Elliot was growing very impatient, now drew up; the servant came to announce it. It was beginning to rain again, and altogether there was a delay, and a bustle, and a talking, which must make all the little crowd in the shop understand that Lady Dalrymple was calling to convey Miss Elliot. At last Miss Elliot and her friend, unattended but by the servant (for there was no cousin returned), were walking off; and Captain Wentworth, watching them, turned again to Anne, and by manner, rather than words, was offering his services to her.

"I am much obliged to you," was her answer, "but I am not going with them. The carriage would not accommodate so many. I walk: I prefer walking."

"But it rains."

"Oh! very little. Nothing that I regard."

After a moment's pause, he said: "Though I came only yesterday, I have equipped myself properly for Bath already, you see" (pointing to a new umbrella); "I wish you would make us of it, if you are determined to walk; though I think it would be more prudent to let me get you a chair."

She was very much obliged to him, but declined it all, repeating her conviction that the rain would come to nothing at present, and adding, "I am only waiting for Mr. Elliot. He will be here in a moment, I am sure."

She had hardly spoken the words when Mr. Elliot walked in. Captain Wentworth recollected him perfectly. There was no difference between him and the man who had stood on the steps at Lyme, admiring Anne as she passed, except in the air and look, and manner of the privileged relation and friend. He came in with eagerness, appeared to see and think only of her, apologised for his stay, was grieved to have kept her waiting, and anxious to get her away without further loss of time, and before the rain increased; and in another moment they walked off together, her arm under his, a gentle and embarrassed glance, and a "Good morning to you!" being all that she had time for, as she passed away.

As soon as they were out of sight, the ladies of Captain Wentworth's party began talking of them.

"Mr. Elliot does not dislike his cousin, I fancy?"

"Oh! no, that is clear enough. One can guess what will happen there. He is always with them; half lives in the family, I believe. What a very good-looking man!"

"Yes, and Miss Atkinson, who dined with him once at the Wallises, says he is the most agreeable man she ever was in company with."

"She is pretty, I think, Anne Elliot; very pretty when one comes to look at her. It is not the fashion to say so, but I confess I admire her more than her sister."

"Oh! so do I."

"And so do I. No comparison. But the men are all wild after Miss Elliot. Anne is too delicate for them."

Anne would have been particularly obliged to her cousin if he would have walked by her side all the way to Camden Place without saying a word. She had never found it so difficult to listen to him, though nothing could exceed his solicitude and care, and though his subjects were principally such as were wont to be always interesting: praise, warm, just and discriminating, of Lady Russell, and insinuations highly rational against Mrs. Clay. But just now she could think only of Captain Wentworth. She could not understand his present feelings, whether he were really suffering much from disappointment or not; and till that point were settled, she could not be quite herself.

She hoped to be wise and reasonable in time; but alas! alas! she must confess to herself that she was not wise yet.

Another circumstance very essential for her to know was, how long he meant to be in Bath; he had not mentioned it, or she could not recollect it. He might be only passing through. But it was more probable that he should be come to stay. In that case, so liable as everybody was to meet everybody in Bath, Lady Russell would in all likelihood see him somewhere. Would she recollect him? How would it all be?

She had already been obliged to tell Lady Russell that Louisa Musgrove was to marry Captain Benwick. It had cost her something to encounter Lady Russell's surprise; and now, if she were by any chance to be thrown into company with Captain Wentworth, her imperfect knowledge of the matter might add another shade of prejudice against him.

The following morning Anne was out with her friend, and for the first hour, in an incessant and fearful sort of watch for him in vain; but at last, in returning down Pulteney Street, she distinguished him on the right hand pavement at such a distance as to have him in view the greater part of the street. There were many other men about him, many groups walking the same way, but there was no mistaking him. She looked instinctively at Lady Russell, but not from any mad idea of her recognising him so soon as she did herself. No, it was not to be supposed that Lady Russell would perceive him till they were nearly opposite. She looked at her, however, from time to time, anxiously; and when the moment approached which must point him out, though not daring to look again (for her own countenance she knew was unfit to be seen), she was yet perfectly conscious of Lady Russell's eyes being turned exactly in the direction for him—of her being, in short, intently observing him. She could thoroughly comprehend the sort of fascination he must possess over Lady Russell's mind, the difficulty it must be for her to withdraw her eyes, the astonishment she must be feeling that eight or nine years should have passed over him, and in foreign climes and in active service too, without robbing him of one personal grace!

At last, Lady Russell drew back her head. "Now, how would she speak of him?"

"You will wonder," said she, "what has been fixing my eye so long; but I was looking after some window-curtains, which Lady Alicia and Mrs. Frankland were telling me of last night. They described the drawing-room window-curtains of one of the houses on this side of the way, and this part of the street, as being the handsomest and best hung of any in Bath, but could not recollect the exact number, and I have been trying to find out which it could be; but I confess I can see no curtains hereabouts that answer their description."

Anne sighed, and blushed, and smiled, in pity and disdain, either at her friend or herself. The part which provoked her most, was that in all this waste of foresight and caution, she should have lost the right moment for seeing whether he saw them.

A day or two passed without producing anything. The theatre or the rooms, where he was most likely to be, were not fashionable enough for the Elliots, whose evening amusements were solely in the elegant stupidity of private parties, in which they were getting more and more engaged; and Anne, wearied of such a state of stagnation, sick of knowing nothing, and fancying herself stronger because her strength was not tried, was quite impatient for the concert evening. It was a concert for the benefit of a person patronised by Lady Dalrymple. Of course they must attend. It was really expected to be a good one, and Captain Wentworth was very fond of music. If she could only have a few minutes' conversation with him again, she fancied she should be satisfied; and as to the power of addressing him, she felt all over courage if the opportunity occurred. Elizabeth had turned from him, Lady Russell overlooked him; her nerves were strengthened by these circumstances; she felt that she owed him attention.

She had once partly promised Mrs. Smith to spend the evening with her; but in a short hurried call she excused herself and put it off, with the more decided promise of a longer visit on the morrow. Mrs. Smith gave a most good-humoured acquiescence.

"By all means," said she; "only tell me all about it, when you do come. Who is your party?"

Anne named them all. Mrs. Smith made no reply; but when she was leaving her said, and with an expression half serious, half arch, "Well, I heartily wish your concert may answer; and do not fail me to-morrow if you can come; for I begin to have a foreboding that I may not have many more visits from you."

Anne was startled and confused; but after standing in a moment's suspense, was obliged, and not sorry to be obliged, to hurry away.

20

SIR WALTER, his two daughters, and Mrs. Clay, were the earliest of all their party at the rooms in the evening; and as Lady Dalrymple must be waited for, they took their station by one of the fires in the Octagon Room. But hardly were they so settled, when the door opened again, and Captain Wentworth walked in alone. Anne was the nearest to him, and making a little advance, she instantly spoke. He was preparing only to bow and pass on, but her gentle "How do you do?" brought him out of the straight line to stand near her, and make enquiries in return, in spite of the formidable father and sister in the background. Their being in the background was a support to Anne; she knew nothing of their looks, and felt equal to everything which she believed right to be done.

While they were speaking, a whispering between her father and Elizabeth caught her ear. She could not distinguish, but she must guess the subject; and on Captain Wentworth's making a distant bow, she comprehended that her father had judged so well as to give him that simple acknowledgment of acquaintance, and she was just in time by a side glance to see a slight curtsey from Elizabeth herself. This, though late, and reluctant, and ungracious, was yet better than nothing and her spirits improved.

After talking, however, of the weather, and Bath, and the concert, their conversation began to flag, and so little was said at last, that she was expecting him to go every moment, but he did not; he seemed in no hurry to leave her; and presently with renewed spirit, with a little smile, a little glow, he said:

"I have hardly seen you since our day at Lyme. I am afraid you must have suffered from the shock, and the more from its not overpowering you at the time."

She assured him that she had not.

"It was a frightful hour," said he, "a frightful day!" and he passed his hand across his eyes, as if the remembrance were still too painful, but in a moment, half smiling again, added, "The day has produced some effects, however; has had some consequences which must be considered as the very reverse of frightful. When you had the presence of mind to suggest that Benwick would be the properest person to fetch a surgeon, you could have little idea of his being eventually one of those most concerned in her recovery."

"Certainly I could have none. But it appears—I should hope it would be a very happy match. There are on both sides good principles and good temper."

"Yes," said he, looking not exactly forward; "but there, I think, ends the resemblance. With all my soul I wish them happy, and rejoice over every circumstance in favour of it. They have no difficulties to contend with at home, no opposition, no caprice, no delays. The Musgroves are behaving like themselves, most honourably and kindly, only anxious with true parental hearts to promote their daughter's comfort. All this is much, very much in favour of their happiness; more than perhaps—"

He stopped. A sudden recollection seemed to occur, and to give him some taste of that emotion which was reddening Anne's cheeks and fixing her eyes on the ground. After clearing his throat, however, he proceeded thus:

"I confess that I do think there is a disparity, too great a disparity, and in a point no less essential than mind. I regard Louisa Musgrove as a very amiable, sweet-tempered girl, and not deficient in understanding, but Benwick is something more. He is a clever man, a reading man; and I confess, that I do consider his attaching himself to her with some surprise. Had it been the effect of gratitude, had he learnt to love her, because he believed her to be preferring him, it would have been another thing. But I have no reason to suppose it so. It seems, on the contrary, to have been a perfectly spontaneous, untaught feeling on his side, and this surprises me. A man like him, in his situation! with a heart pierced, wounded, almost broken! Fanny Harville was a very superior creature, and his attachment to her was indeed attachment. A man does not recover from such a devotion of the heart to such a woman! He ought not; he does not."

Either from the consciousness, however, that his friend had recovered, or from some other consciousness, he went no further; and Anne, who, in spite of the agitated voice in which the latter part had been uttered, and in spite of all the various noises of the room, the almost ceaseless slam of the door, and ceaseless buzz of persons walking through, had distinguished every word, was struck, gratified, confused, and beginning to breathe very quick, and feel a hundred things in a moment. It was impossible for her to enter on such a subject; and yet, after a pause, feeling the necessity of speaking, and having not the smallest wish for a total change, she only deviated so far as to say:

"You were a good while at Lyme, I think?"

"About a fortnight. I could not leave it till Louisa's doing well was quite ascertained. I had been too deeply concerned in the mischief to be soon at peace. It had been my doing, solely mine. She would not have been obstinate if I had not been weak. The country round Lyme is very fine. I walked and rode a great deal, and the more I saw, the more I found to admire."

"I should very much like to see Lyme again," said Anne.

"Indeed! I should not have supposed that you could have found anything in Lyme to inspire such a feeling. The horror and distress you were involved in, the stretch of mind, the wear of spirits! I should have thought your last impressions of Lyme must have been strong disgust."

"The last few hours were certainly very painful," replied Anne; "but when pain is over, the remembrance of it often becomes a pleasure. One does not love a place the less for having suffered in it, unless it has been all suffering, nothing but suffering, which was by no means the case at Lyme. We were only in anxiety and distress during the last two hours, and previously there had been a great deal of enjoyment. So much novelty and beauty! I have travelled so little, that every fresh place would be interesting to me; but there is real beauty at Lyme, and in short," with a faint blush at some recollections, "altogether my impressions of the place are very agreeable."

As she ceased, the entrance door opened again, and the very party appeared for whom they were waiting. "Lady Dalrymple, Lady Dalrymple!" was the rejoicing sound; and with all the eagerness compatible with anxious elegance, Sir Walter and his two ladies stepped forward to meet her. Lady

Dalrymple and Miss Carteret, escorted by Mr. Elliot and Colonel Wallis, who had happened to arrive nearly at the same instant, advanced into the room. The others joined them, and it was a group in which Anne found herself also necessarily included. She was divided from Captain Wentworth. Their interesting, almost too interesting conversation, must be broken up for a time, but slight was the penance compared with the happiness which brought it on! She had learnt, in the last ten minutes, more of his feelings towards Louisa, more of all his feelings, than she dared to think of; and she gave herself up to the demands of the party, to the needful civilities of the moment, with exquisite, though agitated sensations. She was in good humour with all. She had received ideas which disposed her to be courteous and kind to all, and to pity every one, as being less happy than herself.

The delightful emotions were a little subdued, when on stepping back from the group, to be joined again by Captain Wentworth, she saw that he was gone. She was just in time to see him turn into the Concert Room. He was gone; he had disappeared, she felt a moment's regret. But "they should meet again. He would look for her, he would find her out long before the evening was over, and at present, perhaps, it was as well to be sunder. She was in need of a little interval for recollection."

Upon Lady Russell's appearance soon afterwards, the whole party was collected, and all that remained was to marshal themselves, and proceed into the Concert Room; and be of all the consequence in their power, draw as many eyes, excite as many whispers, and disturb as many people as they could.

Very, very happy were both Elizabeth and Anne Elliot as they walked in. Elizabeth arm-in-arm with Miss Carteret, and looking on the broad back of the dowager Viscountess Dalrymple before her, had nothing to wish for which did not seem within her reach; and Anne—but it would be an insult to the nature of Anne's felicity to draw any comparison between it and her sister's; the origin of one all selfish vanity, of the other all generous attachment.

Anne saw nothing, thought nothing of the brilliancy of the room. Her happiness was from within. Her eyes were bright, and her cheeks glowed; but she knew nothing about it. She was thinking only of the last half hour, and as they passed to their seats, her mind took a hasty range over it. His choice of subjects, his expressions, and still more his manner and look, had been such as she could see in only one light. His opinion of Louisa Musgrove's inferiority, an opinion which he had seemed solicitous to give, his wonder at Captain Benwick, his feelings as to a first, strong attachment; sentences begun which he could not finish, his half-averted eyes and more than half-expressive glance, all, all declared that he had a heart returning to her at last; that anger, resentment, avoidance, were no more; and that they were succeeded, not merely by friendship and regard, but by the tenderness of the past. Yes, some share of the tenderness of the past! She could not contemplate the change as implying less. He must love her.

These were thoughts, with their attendant visions, which occupied and flurried her too much to leave her any power of observation; and she passed along the room without having a glimpse of him, without even trying to discern him. When their places were determined on, and they were all properly arranged, she looked round to see if he should happen to be in the same part of the room, but he was not; her eye could not reach him; and the concert being just opening, she must consent for a time to be happy in a humbler way.

The party was divided and disposed of on two contiguous benches: Anne was among those on the foremost, and Mr. Elliot had manœuvred so well, with the assistance of his friend Colonel Wallis, as to have a seat by her. Miss Elliot, surrounded by her cousins, and the principal object of Colonel Wallis's gallantry, was quite contented.

Anne's mind was in a most favourable state for the entertainment of the evening; it was just occupation enough: she had feelings for the tender, spirits for the gay, attention for the scientific, and patience for the wearisome; and had never liked a concert better, at least during the first act. Towards the close of it, in the interval succeeding an Italian song, she explained the words of the song to Mr. Elliot. They had a concert bill between them.

"This," said she, "is nearly the sense, or rather the meaning of the words, for certainly the sense of an Italian love-song must not be talked of, but it is as nearly the meaning as I can give; for I do not pretend to understand the language. I am a very poor Italian scholar."

"Yes, yes, I see you are. I see you know nothing of the matter. You have only knowledge enough of the language to translate at sight these inverted, transposed, curtailed Italian lines, into clear, comprehensible, elegant English. You need not say anything more of your ignorance. Here is complete proof."

"I will not oppose such kind politeness; but I should be sorry to be examined by a real proficient."

"I have not had the pleasure of visiting in Camden Place so long," replied he, "without knowing something of Miss Anne Elliot; and I do regard her as one who is too modest for the world in general to be aware of half her accomplishments, and too highly accomplished for modesty to be natural in any other woman."

"For shame! For shame! This is too much of flattery. I forget what we are to have next," turning to the bill.

"Perhaps," said Mr. Elliot, speaking low, "I have had a longer acquaintance with your character than you are aware of."

"Indeed! How so? You can have been acquainted with it only since I came to Bath, excepting as you might hear me previously spoken of in my own family."

"I knew you by report long before you came to Bath. I had heard you described by those who knew you intimately. I have been acquainted with you by character many years. Your person, your disposition, accomplishments, manner; they were all described, they were all present to me."

Mr. Elliot was not disappointed in the interest he hoped to raise. No one can withstand the charm of such a mystery. To have been described long ago to a recent acquaintance, by nameless people, is irresistible; and Anne was all curiosity. She wondered, and questioned him eagerly; but in vain. He delighted in being asked, but he would not tell.

"No, no, some time or other, perhaps, but not now. He would mention no names now; but such, he could assure her, had been the fact. He had many years ago received such a description of Miss Anne Elliot as had inspired him with the highest idea of her merit, and excited the warmest curiosity to know her."

Anne could think of no one so likely to have spoken with partiality of her many years ago as the Mr. Wentworth of Monkford, Captain Wentworth's brother. He might have been in Mr. Elliot's company, but she had not courage to ask the question.

"The name of Anne Elliot," said he, "has long had an interesting sound to me. Very long has it possessed a charm over my fancy; and, if I dared, I would breathe my wishes that the name might never change."

Such, she believed, were his words; but scarcely had she received their sound, than her attention was caught by other sounds immediately behind her, which rendered everything else trivial. Her father and Lady Dalrymple were speaking.

"A well-looking man," said Sir Walter, "a very well-looking man."

"A very fine young man, indeed!" said Lady Dalrymple. "More air than one often sees in Bath. Irish, I dare say?"

"No, I just know his name. A bowing acquaintance. Wentworth, Captain Wentworth of the navy. His sister married my tenant in Somersetshire, the Croft, who rents Kellynch."

Before Sir Walter had reached this point, Anne's eyes had caught the right direction, and distinguished Captain Wentworth, standing among a cluster of men at a little distance. As her eyes fell on him, his seemed to be withdrawn from her. It had that appearance. It seemed as if she had been one moment too late; and as long as she dared observe, he did not look again; but the performance was recommencing, and she was forced to seem to restore her attention to the orchestra, and look straight forward.

When she could give another glance, he had moved away. He could not have come nearer to her if he would; she was so surrounded and shut in: but she would rather have caught his eye.

Mr. Elliot's speech, too, distressed her. She had no longer any inclination to talk to him. She wished him not so near her.

The first act was over. Now she hoped for some beneficial change; and, after a period of nothing-saying amongst the party, some of them did decide on going in quest of tea. Anne was one of the few who did not choose to move. She remained in her seat, and so did Lady Russell; but she had the pleasure of getting rid of Mr. Elliot; and she did not mean, whatever she might feel on Lady Russell's account, to shrink from conversation with Captain Wentworth, if he gave her the opportunity. She was persuaded by Lady Russell's countenance that she had seen him.

He did not come, however. Anne sometimes fancied she discerned him at a distance, but he never came. The anxious interval wore away unproductively. The others returned, the room filled again, benches were reclaimed and repossessed, and another hour of pleasure or of penance was to be sat out, another hour of music was to give delight or the gapes, as real or affected taste for it prevailed. To Anne it chiefly wore the prospect of an hour of agitation. She could not quit that room in peace without seeing Captain Wentworth once more, without the interchange of one friendly look.

In re-settling themselves there were now many changes, the result of which was favourable for her. Colonel Wallis declined sitting down again, and Mr. Elliot was invited by Elizabeth and Miss Carteret, in a manner not to be refused, to sit between them; and by some other removals, and a little scheming of her own, Anne was enabled to place herself much nearer the end of the bench than she had been before, much more within reach of a passer-by. She could not do so, without comparing herself with Miss Larolles, the inimitable Miss Larolles; but still she did it, and not with much happier effect; though by what seemed prosperity in the shape of an early abdication in her next neighbours, she found herself at the very end of the bench before the concert closed.

Such was her situation, with a vacant space at hand, when

Captain Wentworth was again in sight. She saw him not far off. He saw her too; yet he looked grave, and seemed irresolute, and only by very slow degrees came at last near enough to speak to her. She felt that something must be the matter. The change was indubitable. The difference between his present air and what it had been in the Octagon Room was strikingly great. Why was it? She thought of her father, of Lady Russell. Could there have been any unpleasant glances? He began by speaking of the concert gravely, more like the Captain Wentworth of Uppercross; owned himself disappointed, had expected better singing; and, in short, must confess that he should not be sorry when it was over. Anne replied, and spoke in defence of the performance so well, and yet in allowance for his feelings so pleasantly, that his countenance improved, and he replied again with almost a smile. They talked for a few minutes more; the improvement held; he even looked down towards the bench, as if he saw a place on it well worth occupying; when at that moment a touch on her shoulder obliged Anne to turn round. It came from Mr. Elliot. He begged her pardon, but she must be applied to, to explain Italian again. Miss Carteret was very anxious to have a general idea of what was next to be sung. Anne could not refuse; but never had she sacrificed to politeness with a more suffering spirit.

A few minutes, though as few as possible, were inevitably consumed; and when her own mistress again, when able to turn and look as she had done before, she found herself accosted by Captain Wentworth, in a reserved yet hurried sort of farewell. "He must wish her good night; he was going; he should get home as fast as he could."

"Is not this song worth staying for?" said Anne, suddenly struck by an idea which made her yet more anxious to be encouraging.

"No!" he replied, impressively, "there is nothing worth my staying for;" and he was gone directly.

Jealousy of Mr. Elliot! It was the only intelligible motive. Captain Wentworth jealous of her affection! Could she have believed it a week ago; three hours ago! For a moment the gratification was exquisite. But, alas! there were very different thoughts to succeed. How was such jealousy to be quieted? How was the truth to reach him? How, in all the peculiar disadvantages of their respective situations, would he ever learn her real sentiments? It was misery to think of Mr. Elliot's attentions. Their evil was incalculable.

21

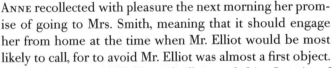

ANNE recollected with pleasure the next morning her promise of going to Mrs. Smith, meaning that it should engage her from home at the time when Mr. Elliot would be most likely to call, for to avoid Mr. Elliot was almost a first object.

She felt a great deal of goodwill towards him. In spite of the mischief of his attentions, she owed him gratitude and regard, perhaps compassion. She could not help thinking much of the extraordinary circumstances attending their acquaintance, of the right which he seemed to have to interest her, by everything in situation, by his own sentiments, by his early prepossession. It was altogether very extraordinary; flattering, but painful. There was much to regret. How she might have felt had there been no Captain Wentworth in the case, was not worth enquiry; for there was a Captain Wentworth; and be the conclusion of the present suspense good or bad, her affection would be his for ever. Their union, she believed, could not divide her more from other men than their final separation.

Prettier musings of high-wrought love and eternal constancy could never have passed along the streets of Bath than Anne was sporting with from Camden Place to Westgate Buildings. It was almost enough to spread purification and perfume all the way.

She was sure of a pleasant reception; and her friend seemed this morning particularly obliged to her for coming, seemed hardly to have expected her, though it had been an appointment.

An account of the concert was immediately claimed; and Anne's recollections of the concert were quite happy enough to animate her features and make her rejoice to talk of it. All that she could tell she told most gladly, but the all was little for one who had been there, and unsatisfactory for such an enquirer as Mrs. Smith, who had already heard, through the short cut of a laundress and a waiter, rather more of the general success and produce of the evening than Anne could relate, and who now asked in vain for several particulars of the company. Everybody of any consequence or notoriety in Bath was well known by name to Mrs. Smith.

"The little Durands were there, I conclude," said she, "with their mouths open to catch the music, like unfledged sparrows ready to be fed. They never miss a concert."

"Yes; I did not see them myself, but I heard Mr. Elliot say they were in the room."

"The Ibbotsons, were they there? and the two new beauties, with the tall Irish officer, who is talked of for one of them?"

"I do not know. I do not think they were."

"Old Lady Mary MacLean? I need not ask after her. She never misses, I know, and you must have seen her. She must have been in your own circle; for as you went with Lady

Dalrymple, you were in the seats of grandeur, round the orchestra, of course."

"No, that was what I dreaded. It would have been very unpleasant to me in every respect. But happily Lady Dalrymple always chooses to be farther off; and we were exceedingly well placed, that is, for hearing; I must not say for seeing, because I appear to have seen very little."

"Oh! you saw enough for your own amusement. I can understand. There is a sort of domestic enjoyment to be known even in a crowd, and this you had. You were a large party in yourselves, and you wanted nothing beyond."

"But I ought to have looked about me more," said Anne, conscious while she spoke that there had in fact been no want of looking about, that the object only had been deficient.

"No, no; you were better employed. You need not tell me that you had a pleasant evening. I see it in your eye. I perfectly see how the hours passed: that you had always something agreeable to listen to. In the intervals of the concert it was conversation."

Anne half smiled and said, "Do you see that in my eye?"

"Yes, I do. Your countenance perfectly informs me that you were in company last night with the person whom you think the most agreeable in the world, the person who interests you at this present time more than all the rest of the world put together."

A blush overspread Anne's cheeks. She could say nothing.

"And such being the case," continued Mrs. Smith, after a short pause, "I hope you believe that I do know how to value your kindness in coming to me this morning. It is really very good of you to come and sit with me, when you must have so many pleasanter demands upon your time."

Anne heard nothing of this. She was still in the astonishment and confusion excited by her friend's penetration, unable to imagine how any report of Captain Wentworth could have reached her. After another short silence:

"Pray," said Mrs. Smith, "is Mr. Elliot aware of your acquaintance with me? Does he know that I am in Bath?"

"Mr. Elliot!!" repeated Anne, looking up surprised. A moment's reflection showed her the mistake she had been under. She caught it instantaneously; and recovering courage with the feeling of safety, soon added, more composedly, "Are you acquainted with Mr. Elliot?"

"I have been a good deal acquainted with him," replied Mrs. Smith, gravely, "but it seems worn out now. It is a great while since we met."

"I was not at all aware of this. You never mentioned it before. Had I known it, I would have had the pleasure of talking to him about you."

"To confess the truth," said Mrs. Smith, assuming her usual air of cheerfulness, "that is exactly the pleasure I want you to have. I want you to talk about me to Mr. Elliot. I want your interest with him. He can be of essential service to me; and if you would have the goodness, my dear Miss Elliot, to make it an object to yourself, of course it is done."

"I should be extremely happy; I hope you cannot doubt my willingness to be of even the slightest use to you," replied Anne; "but I suspect that you are considering me as having a higher claim on Mr. Elliot, a greater right to influence him, than is really the case. I am sure you have, somehow or other, imbibed such a notion. You must consider me only as Mr. Elliot's relation. If in that light there is anything which you suppose his cousin might fairly ask of him, I beg you would not hesitate to employ me."

Mrs. Smith gave her a penetrating glance, and then, smiling, said:

"I have been a little premature, I perceive; I beg your pardon. I ought to have waited for official information. But now, my dear Miss Elliot, as an old friend, do give me a hint as to when I may speak. Next week? To be sure by next week I may be allowed to think it all settled, and build my own selfish schemes on Mr. Elliot's good fortune."

"No," replied Anne, "nor next week, nor next, nor next. I assure you that nothing of the sort you are thinking of will be settled any week. I am not going to marry Mr. Elliot. I should like to know why you imagine I am?"

Mrs. Smith looked at her again, looked earnestly, smiled, shook her head, and exclaimed:

"Now, how I do wish I understood you! How I do wish I knew what you were at! I have a great idea that you do not design to be cruel, when the right moment comes. Till it does come, you know, we women never mean to have anybody. It is a thing of course among us, that every man is refused, till he offers. But why should you be cruel? Let me plead for my—present friend I cannot call him, but for my former friend. Where can you look for a more suitable match? Where could you expect a more gentlemanlike, agreeable man? Let me recommend Mr. Elliot. I am sure you hear nothing but good of him from Colonel Wallis; and who can know him better than Colonel Wallis?"

"My dear Mrs. Smith, Mr. Elliot's wife has not been dead much above half a year. He ought not to be supposed to be paying his addresses to anyone."

"Oh, if these are your only objections," cried Mrs. Smith, archly, "Mr. Elliot is safe, and I shall give myself no more trouble about him. Do not forget me when you are married, that's all. Let him know me to be a friend of yours, and then he will think little of the trouble required, which it is very natural for him now, with so many affairs and engagements of his own, to avoid and get rid of as he can; very natural, perhaps. Ninety-nine out of a hundred would do the same. Of course, he cannot be aware of the importance to me. Well, my dear Miss Elliot, I hope and trust you will be very happy. Mr. Elliot has sense to understand the value of such a woman. Your peace will not be shipwrecked as mine has been. You are safe in all worldly matters, and safe in his character. He will not be led astray; he will not be misled by others to his ruin."

"No," said Anne, "I can readily believe all that of my cousin. He seems to have a calm decided temper, not at all open to dangerous impressions. I consider him with great respect. I have no reason, from anything that has fallen within my observation, to do otherwise. But I have not known him long; and he is not a man, I think, to be known intimately soon. Will not this manner of speaking of him, Mrs. Smith, convince you that he is nothing to me? Surely this must be calm enough. And, upon my word, he is nothing to me. Should he ever propose to me (which I have very little reason to imagine he has any thought of doing), I shall not accept him. I assure you I shall not. I assure you, Mr. Elliot had not the share, which you have been supposing, in whatever pleasure the concert of last night might afford: not Mr. Elliot; it is not Mr. Elliot that—"

She stopped, regretting, with a deep blush, that she had implied so much; but less would hardly have been sufficient. Mrs. Smith would hardly have believed so soon in Mr. Elliot's failure, but from the perception of there being a somebody else. As it was, she instantly submitted, and with all the semblance of seeing nothing beyond; and Anne, eager to escape further notice, was impatient to know why Mrs. Smith should have fancied she was to marry Mr. Elliot; where she could have received the idea, or from whom she could have heard it.

"Do tell me how it first came into your head?"

"It first came into my head," replied Mrs. Smith, "upon finding how much you were together, and feeling it to be the most profitable thing in the world to be wished for by everybody belonging to either of you; and you may depend upon it, that all your acquaintances have disposed of you in the same way. But I never heard it spoken of till two days ago."

"And has it, indeed, been spoken of?"

"Did you observe the woman who opened the door to you when you called yesterday?"

"No. Was not it Mrs. Speed, as usual, or the maid? I observed no one in particular."

"It was my friend Mrs. Rooke; Nurse Rooke; who, by-the-bye, had a great curiosity to see you, and was delighted to be in the way to let you in. She came away from Marlborough Buildings only on Sunday; and she it was who told me you were to marry Mr. Elliot. She had had it from Mrs. Wallis herself, which did not seem bad authority. She sat an hour with me on Monday evening, and gave me the whole history."

"The whole history!" repeated Anne, laughing. "She could not make a very long history, I think, of one such little article of unfounded news."

Mrs. Smith said nothing.

"But," continued Anne, presently, "though there is no truth in my having this claim on Mr. Elliot, I should be extremely happy to be of use to you, in any way that I could. Shall I mention to him your being in Bath? Shall I take any message?"

"No, I thank you; no, certainly not. In the warmth of the moment, and under a mistaken impression, I might, perhaps, have endeavoured to interest you in some circumstances; but not now. No, I thank you, I have nothing to trouble you with."

"I think you spoke of having known Mr. Elliot many years?"

"I did."

"Not before he married, I suppose?"

"Yes; he was not married when I knew him first." ·

"And—were you much acquainted?"

"Intimately."

"Indeed! Then do tell me what he was at that time of life. I have a great curiosity to know what Mr. Elliot was as a very young man. Was he at all such as he appears now?"

"I have not seen Mr. Elliot these three years," was Mrs. Smith's answer, given so gravely that it was impossible to pursue the subject further; and Anne felt that she had gained nothing but an increase of curiosity. They were both silent: Mrs. Smith very thoughtful. At last—

"I beg your pardon, my dear Miss Elliot," she cried in her natural tone of cordiality, "I beg your pardon for the short answers I have been giving you, but I have been uncertain what I ought to do. I have been doubting and considering as to what I ought to tell you. There were many things to be taken into the account. One hates to be officious, to be giving bad impressions, making mischief. Even the smooth surface of a family union seems worth preserving, though there may be nothing durable beneath. However, I have determined; I think I am right; I think you ought to be made acquainted with Mr. Elliot's real character. Though I fully believe that at present you have not the smallest intention of accepting him, there is no saying what may happen. You might, some time or other, be differently affected towards him. Hear the truth, therefore, now, while you are unprejudiced. Mr. Elliot is a man without heart or conscience; a designing, wary, cold-blooded being, who thinks only of himself; who, for his own interest or ease, would be guilty of any cruelty, or any treachery, that could be perpetrated without risk of his general character. He has no feeling for others. Those whom he has been the chief cause of leading into ruin, he can neglect and desert without the smallest compunction. He is totally beyond the reach of any sentiment of justice or compassion. Oh! he is black at heart; hollow and black!"

Anne's astonished air, and exclamation of wonder, made her pause, and in a calmer manner, she added:

"My expressions startle you. You must allow for an injured, angry woman. But I will try to command myself. I will not abuse him. I will only tell you what I have found him. Facts shall speak. He was the intimate friend of my dear husband, who trusted and loved him, and thought him as good as himself. The intimacy had been formed before our marriage. I found them most intimate friends; and I, too, became excessively pleased with Mr. Elliot, and entertained the highest opinion of him. At nineteen, you know, one does not think very seriously; but Mr. Elliot appeared to me quite as good as others, and much more agreeable than most others, and we were almost always together. We were principally in town, living in very good style. He was then the inferior in circumstances; he was then the poor one; he had chambers in the Temple, and it was as much as he could do to support the appearance of a gentleman. He had always a home with us whenever he chose it; he was always welcome; he was like a brother. My poor Charles, who had the finest, most generous spirit in the world, would have divided his last farthing with him; I know that his purse was open to him; I know that he often assisted him."

"This must have been about that very period of Mr. Elliot's life," said Anne, "which has always excited my particular curiosity. It must have been about the same time that he became known to my father and sister. I never knew him myself, I only heard of him; but there was a something in his conduct then, with regard to my father and sister, and afterwards in the circumstances of his marriage, which I never could quite reconcile with present times. It seemed to announce a different sort of man."

"I know it all, I know it all," cried Mrs. Smith. "He had been introduced to Sir Walter and your sister before I was acquainted with him, but I heard him speak of them for ever. I know he was invited and encouraged, and I know he did not choose to go. I can satisfy you, perhaps, on points which you would little expect; and as to his marriage, I knew all about it at the time. I was privy to all the fors and againsts; I was the friend to whom he confided his hopes and plans; and though I did not know his wife previously, her inferior situation in society, indeed, rendered that impossible, yet I knew her all her life afterwards, or at least till within the last two years of her life, and can answer any question you wish to put."

"Nay," said Anne, "I have no particular enquiry to make about her. I have always understood they were not a happy couple. But I should like to know why, at that time of his life, he should slight my father's acquaintance as he did. My father was certainly disposed to take very kind and proper notice of him. Why did Mr. Elliot draw back?"

"Mr. Elliot," replied Mrs. Smith, "at that period of his life had one object in view: to make his fortune, and by a rather quicker process than the law. He was determined to make it by marriage. He was determined, at least, not to mar it by an imprudent marriage; and I know it was his belief (whether justly or not, of course I cannot decide), that your father and sister, in their civilities and invitations, were designing a match between the heir and the young lady, and it was impossible that such a match should have answered his ideas of wealth and independence. That was his motive for drawing back, I can assure you. He told me the whole story. He had no concealments with me. It was curious, that having just left you behind me in Bath, my first and principal acquaintance on marrying should be your cousin; and that, through him, I should be continually hearing of your father and sister. He described one Miss Elliot, and I thought very affectionately of the other."

"Perhaps," cried Anne, struck by a sudden idea, "you sometimes spoke of me to Mr. Elliot?"

"To be sure I did; very often. I used to boast of my own Anne Elliot, and vouch for your being a very different creature from——"

She checked herself just in time.

"This accounts for something which Mr. Elliot said last night," cried Anne. "This explains it. I found he had been used to hear of me. I could not comprehend how. What wild imaginations one forms where dear self is concerned! How sure to be mistaken! But I beg your pardon; I have interrupted you. Mr. Elliot married then completely for money? The circumstance, probably, which first opened your eyes to his character?"

Mrs. Smith hesitated a little here. "Oh! those things are too common. When one lives in the world, a man or woman's marrying for money is too common to strike one as it ought. I was very young, and associated only with the young, and we were a thoughtless, gay set, without any strict rules of conduct. We lived for enjoyment. I think differently now; time and sickness and sorrow have given me other notions; but at that period, I must own I saw nothing reprehensible in what Mr. Elliot was doing 'To do the best for himself' passed as a duty."

"But was not she a very low woman?"

"Yes; which I objected to, but he would not regard. Money, money, was all that he wanted. Her father was a grazier, her grandfather had been a butcher, but that was all nothing. She was a fine woman, had had a decent education, was brought forward by some cousins, thrown by chance into Mr. Elliot's company, and fell in love with him; and not a difficulty or a scruple was there on his side with respect to her birth. All his caution was spent in being secured of the real amount of her fortune, before he committed himself. Depend upon it, whatever esteem Mr. Elliot may have for his own situation in life now, as a young man he had not the smallest value for it. His chance of the Kellynch estate was something, but all the honour of the family he held as cheap as dirt. I have often heard him declare, that if baronetcies were saleable, anybody should have his for fifty pounds, arms and motto, name and livery included; but I will not pretend to repeat half that I used to hear him say on that subject. It would not be fair; and yet you ought to have proof, for what is all this but assertion, and you shall have proof."

"Indeed, my dear Mrs. Smith, I want none," cried Anne. "You have asserted nothing contradictory to what Mr. Elliot appeared to be some years ago. This is all in confirmation, rather, of what we used to hear and believe. I am more curious to know why he should be so different now."

"But for my satisfaction, if you will have the goodness to ring for Mary; stay: I am sure you will have the still greater goodness of going yourself into my bedroom, and bringing me the small inlaid box which you will find on the upper shelf of the closet."

Anne seeing her friend to be earnestly bent on it, did as she was desired. The box was brought and placed before her, and Mrs. Smith, sighing over it as she unlocked it, said:

"This is full of papers belonging to him, to my husband; a small portion only of what I had to look over when I lost him. The letter I am looking for was one written by Mr. Elliot to him before our marriage, and happened to be saved; why, one can hardly imagine. But he was careless and unmethodical, like other men, about those things; and when I came to examine his papers, I found it with others, still more trivial, from different people scattered here and there, while many letters and memorandums of real importance had been destroyed. Here it is; I would not burn it, because being even then very little satisfied with Mr. Elliot, I was determined to preserve every document of former intimacy. I have now another motive for being glad that I can produce it."

This was the letter, directed to "Charles Smith, Esq., Tunbridge Wells," and dated from London, as far back as July, 1803:—

DEAR SMITH,—

I have received yours. Your kindness almost overpowers me. I wish nature had made such hearts as yours more common, but I have lived three-and-twenty years in the world, and have seen none like it. At present, believe me, I have no need of your services, being in cash again. Give me joy: I have got rid of Sir Walter and Miss. They are gone back to Kellynch, and almost made me swear to visit them this summer; but my first visit to Kellynch will be with a surveyor, to tell me how to bring it with best advantage to the hammer. The baronet, nevertheless, is not unlikely to marry again; he is quite fool enough. If he does, however, they will leave me in peace, which may be a decent equivalent for the re-version. He is worse than last year.

I wish I had any name but Elliot. I am sick of it. The name of Walter I can drop, thank God! and I desire you will never insult me with my second W. again, meaning, for the rest of my life, to be only yours truly,—

WM. ELLIOT.

Such a letter could not be read without putting Anne in a glow; and Mrs. Smith, observing the high colour in her face, said:

"The language, I know, is highly disrespectful. Though I have forgot the exact terms, I have a perfect impression of the general meaning. But it shows you the man. Mark his professions to my poor husband. Can anything be stronger?"

Anne could not immediately get over the shock and mor-tification of finding such words applied to her father. She was obliged to recollect that her seeing the letter was a vi-olation of the laws of honour, that no one ought to be judged or to be known by such testimonies, that no private correspondence could bear the eye of others, before she could recover calmness enough to return the letter which she had been meditating over, and say:

"Thank you. This is full proof undoubtedly: proof of everything you were saying. But why be acquainted with us now?"

"I can explain this too," cried Mrs. Smith, smiling.

"Can you really?"

"Yes. I have shown you Mr. Elliot as he was a dozen years ago, and I will show him as he is now. I cannot produce written proof again, but I can give as authentic oral testimony as you can desire, of what he is now wanting, and what he is now doing. He is no hypocrite now. He truly wants to marry you. His present attentions to your family are very sincere: quite from the heart. I will give you my authority: his friend Colonel Wallis."

"Colonel Wallis! are you acquainted with him?"

"No. It does not come to me in quite so direct a line as that; it takes a bend or two, but nothing of consequence. The stream is as good as at first; the little rubbish it collects in the turnings is easily moved away. Mr. Elliot talks unreservedly to Colonel Wallis of his views on you, which said Colonel Wallis, I imagine to be, in himself a sensible, careful, discerning sort of character; but Colonel Wallis has a very pretty silly wife, to whom he tells things which he had better not, and he repeats it all to her. She in the overflowing spirits of her recovery, repeats it all to her nurse; and the nurse knowing my acquaintance with you, very naturally brings it all to me. On Monday evening, my good friend Mrs. Rooke let me thus much into the secrets of Marlborough Buildings. When I talked of a whole history, therefore, you see I was not romancing so much as you supposed."

"My dear Mrs. Smith, your authority is deficient. This will not do. Mr. Elliot's having any views on me will not in the

least account for the efforts he made towards a reconciliation with my father. That was all prior to my coming to Bath.
I found them on the most friendly terms when I arrived."

"I know you did; I know it all perfectly, but—"

"Indeed, Mrs. Smith, we must not expect to get real information in such a line. Facts or opinions which are to pass
through the hands of so many, to be misconceived by folly
in one, and ignorance in another, can hardly have much
truth left."

"Only give me a hearing. You will soon be able to judge
of the general credit due, by listening to some particulars
which you can yourself immediately contradict or confirm.
Nobody supposes that you were his first inducement. He
had seen you, indeed, before he came to Bath, and admired
you, but without knowing it to be you. So says my historian,
at least. Is this true? Did he see you last summer or autumn
'somewhere down in the west,' to use her own words, without knowing it to be you?"

"He certainly did. So far it is very true. At Lyme. I happened to be at Lyme."

"Well," continued Mrs. Smith, triumphantly, "grant my
friend the credit due to the establishment of the first point
asserted. He saw you then at Lyme, and liked you so well
as to be exceedingly pleased to meet with you again in Camden Place, as Miss Anne Elliot, and from that moment, I have
no doubt, had a double motive in his visits there. But there
was another, and an earlier, which I will now explain. If there
is anything in my story which you know to be either false
or improbable, stop me. My account states, that your sister's
friend, the lady now staying with you, whom I have heard
you mention, came to Bath with Miss Elliot and Sir Walter
as long ago as September (in short when they first came
themselves), and has been staying there ever since; that she

is a clever, insinuating, handsome woman, poor and plausible, and altogether such in situation and manner, as to give a general idea, among Sir Walter's acquaintances, of her meaning to be Lady Elliot, and as general a surprise that Miss Elliot should be, apparently, blind to the danger."

Here Mrs. Smith paused a moment; but Anne had not a word to say, and she continued:

"This was the light in which it appeared to those who knew the family long before you returned to it; and Colonel Wallis had his eye upon your father enough to be sensible of it, though he did not then visit in Camden Place; but his regard for Mr. Elliot gave him an interest in watching all that was going on there, and when Mr. Elliot came to Bath for a day or two, as he happened to do a little before Christmas, Colonel Wallis made him acquainted with the appearance of things, and the reports beginning to prevail. Now you are to understand, that time had worked a very material change in Mr. Elliot's opinions as to the value of a baronetcy. Upon all points of blood and connection he is a completely altered man. Having long had as much money as he could spend, nothing to wish for on the side of avarice or indulgence, he has been gradually learning to pin his happiness upon the consequence he is heir to. I thought it coming on before our acquaintance ceased, but it is now a confirmed feeling. He cannot bear the idea of not being Sir William. You may guess, therefore, that the news he heard from his friend could not be very agreeable, and you may guess what it produced; the resolution of coming back to Bath as soon as possible, and of fixing himself there for a time, with the view of renewing his former acquaintance, and recovering such a footing in the family as might give him the means of ascertaining the degree of his danger, and of circumventing the lady if he found it material. This was agreed upon between the two friends as the only thing to be done; and Colonel Wallis was to assist in every way that he could. He was to be introduced, and Mrs. Wallis was to be introduced, and everybody was to be introduced. Mr. Elliot came back accordingly; and on application was forgiven, as you know, and re-admitted into the family; and there it was his constant object, and his only object (till your arrival added another motive), to watch Sir Walter and Mrs. Clay. He omitted no opportunity of being with them, threw himself in their way, called at all hours; but I need not be particular on this subject. You can imagine what an artful man would do; and with this guide, perhaps, may recollect what you have seen him do."

"Yes," said Anne, "you tell me nothing which does not accord with what I have known, or could imagine. There is always something offensive in the details of cunning. The manœuvres of selfishness and duplicity must ever be revolting, but I have heard nothing which really surprises me. I know those who would be shocked by such a representation of Mr. Elliot, who would have difficulty in believing it, but I have never been satisfied. I have always wanted some other motive for his conduct than appeared. I should like to know his present opinion, as to the probability of the event he has been in dread of; whether he considers the danger to be lessening or not."

"Lessening, I understand," replied Mrs. Smith. "He thinks Mrs. Clay afraid of him, aware that he sees through her, and not daring to proceed as she might do in his absence. But since he must be absent some time or other, I do not perceive how he can ever be secure while she holds her present influence. Mrs. Wallis has an amusing idea, as nurse tells me, that it is to be put into the marriage articles when you and Mr. Elliot marry, that your father is not to marry Mrs. Clay.

A scheme worthy of Mrs. Wallis's understanding, by all accounts; but my sensible Nurse Rooke sees the absurdity of it. 'Why, to be sure, ma'am,' said she, 'it would not prevent his marrying anybody else.' And, indeed, to own the truth, I do not think nurse, in her heart, is a very strenuous opposer of Sir Walter's making a second match. She must be allowed to be a favourer of matrimony you know; and (since self will intrude) who can say that she may not have some flying visions of attending the next Lady Elliot, through Mrs. Wallis's recommendation?"

"I am very glad to know all this," said Anne, after a little thoughtfulness. "It will be more painful to me in some respects to be in company with him, but I shall know better what to do. My line of conduct will be more direct. Mr. Elliot is evidently a disingenuous, artificial, worldly man, who has had never any better principle to guide him than selfishness."

But Mr. Elliot was not yet done with. Mrs. Smith had been carried away from her first direction, and Anne had forgotten, in the interest of her own family concerns, how much had been originally implied against him; but her attention was now called to the explanation of those first hints, and she listened to a recital which, if it did not perfectly justify the unqualified bitterness of Mrs. Smith, proved him to have been very unfeeling in his conduct towards her; very deficient both in justice and compassion.

She learned that (the intimacy between them continuing unimpaired by Mr. Elliot's marriage) they had been as before always together, and Mr. Elliot had led his friend into expenses much beyond his fortune. Mrs. Smith did not want to take the blame to herself, and was most tender of throwing any on her husband; but Anne could collect that their income had never been equal to their style of living, and that from the first there had been a great deal of general and joint extravagance. From his wife's account of him she could discern Mr. Smith to have been a man of warm feelings, easy temper, careless habits, and not strong understanding; much more amiable than his friend, and very unlike him, led by him, and probably despised by him. Mr. Elliot, raised by his marriage to great affluence, and disposed to every gratification of pleasure and vanity which could be commanded without involving himself (for with all his self-indulgence he had become a prudent man), and beginning to be rich, just as his friend ought to have found himself to be poor, seemed to have had no concern at all for that friend's probable finances, but, on the contrary, had been prompting and encouraging expenses which could end only in ruin: and the Smiths accordingly had been ruined.

The husband had died just in time to be spared the full knowledge of it. They had previously known embarrassments enough to try the friendship of their friends, and to prove that Mr. Elliot's had better not be tried; but it was not till his death that the wretched state of his affairs was fully known. With a confidence in Mr. Elliot's regard, more creditable to his feelings than his judgment, Mr. Smith had appointed him the executor of his will; but Mr. Elliot would not act, and the difficulties and distresses which this refusal had heaped on her, in addition to the inevitable sufferings of her situation, had been such as could not be related without anguish of spirit, or listened to without corresponding indignation.

Anne was shown some letters of his on the occasion, answers to urgent applications from Mrs. Smith, which all breathed the same stern resolution of not engaging in a fruitless trouble, and, under a cold civility, the same hard-hearted indifference to any of the evils it might bring on her. It was a dreadful picture of ingratitude and inhumanity; and Anne felt, at some moments, that no flagrant open crime could have been worse. She had a great deal to listen to; all the particulars of past sad scenes, all the minutiæ of distress upon distress, which in former conversations had been merely hinted at, were dwelt on now with a natural indulgence. Anne could perfectly comprehend the exquisite relief, and was only the more inclined to wonder at the composure of her friend's usual state of mind.

There was one circumstance in the history of her grievances of particular irritation. She had good reason to believe that some property of her husband in the West Indies, which had been for many years under a sort of sequestration for the payment of its own incumbrances, might be recoverable by proper measures; and this property, though not large, would be enough to make her comparatively rich. But there was nobody to stir in it. Mr. Elliot would do nothing, and she could do nothing herself, equally disabled from personal exertion by her state of bodily weakness, and from employing others by her want of money. She had no natural connections to assist her even with their counsel, and she could not afford to purchase the assistance of the law. This was a cruel aggravation of actually straightened means. To feel that she ought to be in better circumstances, that a little trouble in the right place might do it, and to fear that delay might be even weakening her claims was hard to bear.

It was on this point that she had hoped to engage Anne's good offices with Mr. Elliot. She had previously, in the anticipation of their marriage, been very apprehensive of losing her friend by it; but on being assured that he could have made no attempt of that nature, since he did not even know her to be in Bath, it immediately occurred that something might be done in her favour by the influence of the woman he loved, and she had been hastily preparing to interest Anne's feelings as far as the observances due to Mr. Elliot's character would allow, when Anne's refutation of the supposed engagement changed the face of everything; and while it took from her the new-formed hope of succeeding in the object of her first anxiety, left her at least the comfort of telling the whole story her own way.

After listening to this full description of Mr. Elliot, Anne could not but express some surprise at Mrs. Smith's having spoken of him so favourably in the beginning of their conversation. "She had seemed to recommend and praise him!"

"My dear," was Mrs. Smith's reply, "there was nothing else to be done. I considered your marrying him as certain, though he might not yet have made the offer, and I could no more speak the truth of him, than if he had been your husband. My heart bled for you as I talked of happiness; and yet he is sensible, he is agreeable, and with such a woman as you, it was not absolutely hopeless. He was very unkind to his first wife. They were wretched together. But she was too ignorant and giddy for respect, and he had never loved her. I was willing to hope that you must fare better."

Anne could just acknowledge within herself such a possibility of having been induced to marry him, as made her shudder at the idea of the misery which must have followed. It was just possible that she might have been persuaded by Lady Russell! And under such a supposition, which would have been most miserable, when time had disclosed all, too late?

It was very desirable that Lady Russell should be no longer deceived; and one of the concluding arrangements of this important conference, which carried them through the greater part of the morning, was, that Anne had full liberty to communicate to her friend everything relative to Mrs. Smith, in which his conduct was involved.

22

ANNE went home to think over all that she had heard. In one point, her feelings were relieved by this knowledge of Mr. Elliot. There was no longer anything of tenderness due to him. He stood as opposed to Captain Wentworth, in all his own unwelcome obtrusiveness; and the evil of his attentions last night, the irremediable mischief he might have done, was considered with sensations unqualified, unperplexed. Pity for him was all over. But this was the only point of relief. In every other respect, in looking around her, or penetrating forward, she saw more to distrust and to apprehend. She was concerned for the disappointment and pain Lady Russell would be feeling; for the mortifications which must be hanging over her father and sister, and had all the distress of foreseeing many evils without knowing how to avert any one of them. She was most thankful for her own knowledge of him. She had never considered herself as entitled to reward for not slighting an old friend like Mrs. Smith, but here was a reward, indeed, springing from it! Mrs.

Smith had been able to tell her what no one else could have done. Could the knowledge have been extended through her family? But this was a vain idea. She must talk to Lady Russell, tell her, consult with her, and having done her best, wait the event with as much composure as possible; and after all, her greatest want of composure would be in that quarter of the mind which could not be opened to Lady Russell; in that flow of anxieties and fears which must be all to herself.

She found on reaching home, that she had, as she intended, escaped seeing Mr. Elliot; that he had called and paid them a long morning visit; but hardly had she congratulated herself, and felt safe, when she heard that he was coming again in the evening.

"I had not the smallest intention of asking him," said Elizabeth, with affected carelessness, "but he gave so many hints; so Mrs. Clay says, at least."

"Indeed, I do say it. I never saw anybody in my life spell harder for an invitation. Poor man! I was really in pain for him; for your hard-hearted sister, Miss Anne, seems bent on cruelty."

"Oh!" cried Elizabeth, "I have been rather too much used to the game to be soon overcome by a gentleman's hints. However, when I found how excessively he was regretting that he should miss my father this morning, I gave way immediately, for I would never really omit an opportunity of bringing him and Sir Walter together. They appear to so much advantage in company with each other. Each behaving so pleasantly. Mr. Elliot looking up with so much respect."

"Quite delightful!" cried Mrs. Clay, not daring, however, to turn her eyes towards Anne. "Exactly like father and son! Dear Miss Elliot, may I not say father and son?"

"Oh! I lay no embargo on anybody's words. If you will

have such ideas! But, upon my word, I am scarcely sensible of his attentions being beyond those of other men."

"My dear Miss Elliot!" exclaimed Mrs. Clay, lifting up her hands and eyes, and sinking all the rest of her astonishment in a convenient silence.

"Well, my dear Penelope, you need not be so alarmed about him. I did invite him, you know. I sent him away with smiles. When I found he was really going to his friends at Thornberry Park for the whole day to-morrow, I had compassion on him."

Anne admired the good acting of the friend, in being able to show such pleasure, as she did, in the expectation and in the actual arrival of the very person whose presence must really be interfering with her prime object. It was impossible but that Mrs. Clay must hate the sight of Mr. Elliot; and yet she could assume a most obliging, placid look, and appear quite satisfied with the curtailed license of devoting herself only half as much to Sir Walter as she would have done otherwise.

To Anne herself it was most distressing to see Mr. Elliot enter the room; and quite painful to have him approach and speak to her. She had been used before to feel that he could not be always quite sincere, but now she saw insincerity in everything. His attentive deference to her father, contrasted with his former language, was odious; and when she thought of his cruel conduct towards Mrs. Smith, she could hardly bear the sight of his present smiles and mildness, or the sound of his artificial good sentiments.

She meant to avoid any such alteration of manners as might provoke a remonstrance on his side. It was a great object with her to escape all enquiry or éclat; but it was her intention to be as decidedly cool to him as might be compatible with their relationship; and to retract, as quietly as she could, the few steps of unnecessary intimacy she had been gradually led along. She was accordingly more guarded, and more cool, than she had been the night before.

He wanted to animate her curiosity again as to how and where he could have heard her formerly praised; wanted very much to be gratified by more solicitation; but the charm was broken: he found that the heat and animation of a public room was necessary to kindle his modest cousin's vanity; he found, at least, that it was not to be done now, by any of those attempts which he could hazard among the too-commanding claims of the others. He little surmised that it was a subject acting now exactly against his interest, bringing immediately to her thoughts all those parts of his conduct which were least excusable.

She had some satisfaction in finding that he was really going out of Bath the next morning, going early, and that he would be gone the greater part of two days. He was invited again to Camden Place the very evening of his return; but from Thursday to Saturday evening his absence was certain. It was bad enough that a Mrs. Clay should be always before her; but that a deeper hypocrite should be added to their party, seemed the destruction of everything like peace and comfort. It was so humiliating to reflect on the constant deception practised on her father and Elizabeth; to consider the various sources of mortification preparing for them! Mrs. Clay's selfishness was not so complicated nor so revolting as his; and Anne would have compounded for the marriage at once, with all its evils, to be clear of Mr. Elliot's subtleties in endeavouring to prevent it.

On Friday morning she meant to go very early to Lady Russell, and accomplish the necessary communication; and she would have gone directly after breakfast, but that Mrs.

Clay was also going out on some obliging purpose of saving her sister trouble, which determined her to wait till she might be safe from such a companion. She saw Mrs. Clay fairly off, therefore, before she began to talk of spending the morning in Rivers Street.

"Very well," said Elizabeth, "I have nothing to send but my love. Oh! you may as well take back that tiresome book she would lend me, and pretend I have read it through. I really cannot be plaguing myself for ever with all the new poems and states of the nation that come out. Lady Russell quite bores one with her new publications. You need not tell her so, but I thought her dress hideous the other night. I used to think she had some taste in dress, but I was ashamed of her at the concert. Something so formal and *arrangé* in her air! and she sits so upright! My best love, of course."

"And mine," added Sir Walter. "Kindest regards. And you may say, that I mean to call upon her soon. Make a civil message; but I shall only leave my card. Morning visits are never fair by women at her time of life, who make themselves up so little. If she would only wear rouge she would not be afraid of being seen; but last time I called, I observed the blinds were let down immediately."

While her father spoke, there was a knock at the door. Who could it be? Anne, remembering the preconcerted visits, at all hours, of Mr. Elliot, would have expected him, but for his known engagement seven miles off. After the usual period of suspense, the usual sounds of approach were heard, and "Mr. and Mrs. Charles Musgrove" were ushered into the room.

Surprise was the strongest emotion raised by their appearance; but Anne was really glad to see them; and the others were not so sorry but that they could put on a decent air of welcome; and as soon as it became clear that these, their nearest relations, were not arrived with any views of accommodation in that house, Sir Walter and Elizabeth were able to rise in cordiality, and do the honours of it very well. They were come to Bath for a few days with Mrs. Musgrove, and were at the White Hart. So much was pretty soon understood; but till Sir Walter and Elizabeth were walking Mary into the other drawing-room, and regaling themselves with her admiration, Anne could not draw upon Charles's brain for a regular history of their coming, or an explanation of some smiling hints of particular business, which had been ostentatiously dropped by Mary, as well as of some apparent confusion as to whom their party consisted of.

She then found that it consisted of Mrs. Musgrove, Henrietta, and Captain Harville, beside their two selves. He gave her a very plain, intelligible account of the whole; a narration in which she saw a great deal of most characteristic proceeding. The scheme had received its first impulse by Captain Harville's wanting to come to Bath on business. He had begun to talk of it a week ago; and by way of doing something, as shooting was over, Charles had proposed coming with him, and Mrs. Harville had seemed to like the idea of it very much, as an advantage to her husband; but Mary could not bear to be left, and had made herself so unhappy about it, that for a day or two everything seemed to be in suspense, or at an end. But then, it had been taken up by his father and mother. His mother had some old friends in Bath whom she wanted to see; it was thought a good opportunity for Henrietta to come and buy wedding-clothes for herself and her sister; and, in short, it ended in being his mother's party, that everything might be comfortable and easy to Captain Harville; and he and Mary were included in it by way of general convenience. They had arrived late the night before. Mrs. Harville, her children, and Captain Benwick, remained with Mr. Musgrove and Louisa at Uppercross.

Anne's only surprise was, that affairs should be in forwardness enough for Henrietta's wedding-clothes to be talked of. She had imagined such difficulties of fortune to exist there as must prevent the marriage from being near at hand; but she learned from Charles that, very recently (since Mary's last letter to herself), Charles Hayter had been applied to by a friend to hold a living for a youth who could not possibly claim it under many years; and that on the strength of this present income, with almost a certainty of something more permanent long before the term in question, the two families had consented to the young people's wishes, and that their marriage was likely to take place in a few months, quite as soon as Louisa's. "And a very good living it was," Charles added: "only five-and-twenty miles from Uppercross, and in a very fine country: fine part of Dorsetshire. In the centre of some of the best preserves in the kingdom, surrounded by three great proprietors, each more careful and jealous than the other; and to two of the three at least, Charles Hayter might get a special recommendation. Not that he will value it as he ought," he observed: "Charles is too cool about sporting. That's the worst of him."

"I am extremely glad, indeed," cried Anne; "particularly glad that this should happen; and that of two sisters who both deserve equally well, and who have always been such good friends, the pleasant prospects of one should not be dimming those of the other — that they should be so equal in their prosperity and comfort. I hope your father and mother are quite happy with regard to both."

"Oh yes! My father would be as well pleased if the gentlemen were richer, but he has no other fault to find. Money, you know, coming down with money—two daughters at once—it cannot be a very agreeable operation, and it streightens him as to many things. However, I do not mean to say they have not a right to it. It is very fit they should have daughters' shares; and I am sure he has always been a very kind, liberal father to me. Mary does not above half like Henrietta's match. She never did, you know. But she does not do him justice, nor think enough about Winthrop. I cannot make her attend to the value of the property. It is a very fair match as times go; and I have liked Charles Hayter all my life, and I shall not leave off now."

"Such excellent parents as Mr. and Mrs. Musgrove," exclaimed Anne, "should be happy in their children's marriages. They do everything to confer happiness, I am sure. What a blessing to young people to be in such hands! Your father and mother seem totally free from all those ambitious feelings which have led to so much misconduct and misery, both in young and old. I hope you think Louisa perfectly recovered now?"

He answered rather hesitatingly, "Yes, I believe I do; very much recovered; but she is altered; there is no running or jumping about, no laughing or dancing; it is quite different. If one happens only to shut the door a little hard, she starts and wriggles like a young dab-chick in the water; and Benwick sits at her elbow, reading verses, or whispering to her, all day long."

Anne could not help laughing. "That cannot be much to your taste, I know," said she; "but I do believe him to be an excellent young man."

"To be sure he is: nobody doubts it; and I hope you do not think I am so illiberal as to want every man to have the same objects and pleasures as myself. I have a great value for Benwick; and when one can but get him to talk, he has plenty to say. His reading has done him no harm, for he has fought as well as read. He is a brave fellow. I got more acquainted with him last Monday than ever I did before. We had a famous set-to at rat-hunting all the morning in my father's great barns; and he played his part so well that I have liked him the better ever since."

Here they were interrupted by the absolute necessity of Charles's following the others to admire mirrors and china: but Anne had heard enough to understand the present state of Uppercross, and rejoice in its happiness; and though she sighed as she rejoiced, her sigh had none of the ill-will of envy in it. She would certainly have risen to their blessings if she could, but she did not want to lessen theirs.

The visit passed off altogether in high good humour. Mary was in excellent spirits, enjoying the gaiety and the change, and so well satisfied with the journey in her mother-in-law's carriage with four horses, and with her own complete independence of Camden Place, that she was exactly in a temper to admire everything as she ought, and enter most readily into all the superiorities of the house, as they were detailed to her. She had no demands on her father or sister, and her consequence was just enough increased by their handsome drawing-rooms.

Elizabeth was, for a short time, suffering a good deal. She felt that Mrs. Musgrove and all her party ought to be asked to dine with them; but she could not bear to have the difference of style, the reduction of servants, which a dinner must betray, witnessed by those who had been always so inferior to the Elliots of Kellynch. It was a struggle between propriety and vanity; but vanity got the better, and then Elizabeth was happy again. These were her internal persuasions: "Old-fashioned notions; country hospitality; we do not profess to give dinners; few people in Bath do; Lady Alicia never does; did not even ask her own sister's family, though they were here a month; and I daresay it would be very inconvenient to Mrs. Musgrove; put her quite out of her way. I am sure she would rather not come; she cannot feel easy with us. I will ask them all for an evening; that will be much better; that will be a novelty and a treat. They have not seen two such drawing-rooms before. They will be delighted to come to-morrow evening. It shall be a regular party, small, but most elegant." And this satisfied Elizabeth; and when the invitation was given to the two present, and promised for the absent, Mary was as completely satisfied. She was particularly asked to meet Mr. Elliot, and be introduced to Lady Dalrymple and Miss Carteret, who were fortunately already engaged to come; and she could not have received a more gratifying attention. Miss Elliot was to have the honour of calling on Mrs. Musgrove in the course of the morning; and Anne walked off with Charles and Mary, to go and see her and Henrietta directly.

Her plan of sitting with Lady Russell must give way for the present. They all three called in Rivers Street for a couple of minutes; but Anne convinced herself that a day's delay of the intended communication could be of no consequence, and hastened forward to the White Hart, to see again the friends and companions of the last autumn, with an eagerness of good-will which many associations contributed to form.

They found Mrs. Musgrove and her daughter within, and by themselves, and Anne had the kindest welcome from each. Henrietta was exactly in that state of recently-improved views, of fresh-formed happiness, which made her full of regard and interest for everybody she had ever liked before at all; and Mrs. Musgrove's real affection had been

won by her usefulness when they were in distress. It was a
heartiness, and a warmth, and a sincerity which Anne delighted in the more, from the sad want of such blessings at
home. She was entreated to give them as much of her time
as possible, invited for every day and all day long, or rather
claimed as a part of the family; and, in return, she naturally
fell into all her wonted ways of attention and assistance, and
on Charles's leaving them together, was listening to Mrs.
Musgrove's history of Louisa, and to Henrietta's of herself,
giving opinions on business, and recommendations to shops;
with intervals of every help which Mary required, from al-
tering her ribbon to settling her accounts; from finding her
keys, and assorting her trinkets, to trying to convince her
that she was not ill-used by anybody; which Mary, well
amused as she generally was, in her station at a window
overlooking the entrance to the Pump Room, could not but
have her moments of imagining.

A morning of thorough confusion was to be expected. A
large party in an hotel ensured a quick-changing, unsettled
scene. One five minutes brought a note, the next a parcel;
and Anne had not been there half an hour, when their
dining-room, spacious as it was, seemed more than half
filled; a party of steady old friends were seated round Mrs.
Musgrove, and Charles came back with Captains Harville
and Wentworth. The appearance of the latter could not be
more than the surprise of the moment. It was impossible for
her to have forgotten to feel that this arrival of their common friends must be soon bringing them together again.
Their last meeting had been most important in opening his
feelings: she had derived from it a delightful conviction; but
she feared from his looks, that the same unfortunate persuasion, which had hastened him away from the concert

room, still governed. He did not seem to want to be near enough for conversation.

She tried to be calm, and leave things to take their course, and tried to dwell much on this argument of rational dependence:—"Surely, if there be constant attachment on each side, our hearts must understand each other ere long. We are not boy and girl, to be captiously irritable, misled by every moment's inadvertence, and wantonly playing with our own happiness." And yet, a few minutes afterwards, she felt as if their being in company with each other, under their present circumstances, could only be exposing them to inadvertencies and misconstructions of the most mischievous kind.

"Anne," cried Mary, still at her window, "there is Mrs. Clay, I am sure, standing under the colonnade, and a gentleman with her. I saw them turn the corner from Bath Street just now. They seem deep in talk. Who is it? Come, and tell me. Good heavens! I recollect. It is Mr. Elliot himself."

"No," cried Anne, quickly, "it cannot be Mr. Elliot, I assure you. He was to leave Bath at nine this morning, and does not come back till to-morrow."

As she spoke, she felt that Captain Wentworth was looking at her, the consciousness of which vexed and embarrassed her, and made her regret that she had said so much, simple as it was.

Mary, resenting that she should be supposed not to know her own cousin, began talking very warmly about the family features, and protesting still more positively that it was Mr. Elliot, calling again upon Anne to come and look herself, but Anne did not mean to stir, and tried to be cool and unconcerned. Her distress returned however, on perceiving smiles and intelligent glances pass between two or three of the lady visitors, as if they believed themselves quite in the secret. It was evident that the report concerning her had spread, and a short pause succeeded, which seemed to ensure that it would now spread further.

"Do come, Anne," cried Mary, "come and look yourself. You will be too late if you do not make haste. They are parting: they are shaking hands. He is turning away. Not know Mr. Elliot, indeed! You seem to have forgot all about Lyme."

To pacify Mary, and perhaps screen her own embarrassment, Anne did move quietly to the window. She was just in time to ascertain that it really was Mr. Elliot, which she had never believed, before he disappeared on one side, as Mrs. Clay walked quickly off on the other; and checking the surprise which she could not but feel at such an appearance of friendly conference between two persons of totally opposite interests, she calmly said, "Yes, it is Mr. Elliot, certainly. He has changed his hour of going, I suppose, that is all, or I may be mistaken, I might not attend;" and walked back to her chair, recomposed, and with the comfortable hope of having acquitted herself well.

The visitors took their leave; and Charles, having civilly seen them off, and then made a face at them, and abused them for coming, began with: "Well, mother, I have done something for you that you will like. I have been to the theatre, and secured a box for to-morrow night. A'n't I a good boy? I know you love a play; and there is room for us all. It holds nine. I have engaged Captain Wentworth. Anne will not be sorry to join us, I am sure. We all like a play. Have not I done well, mother?"

Mrs. Musgrove was good humouredly beginning to express her perfect readiness for the play, if Henrietta and all the others like it, when Mary eagerly interrupted her by exclaiming:

"Good heavens! Charles, how can you think of such a thing? Take a box for to-morrow night! Have you forgot that we are engaged to Camden Place to-morrow night? and that we were most particularly asked to meet Lady Dalrymple and her daughter, and Mr. Elliot, all the principal family connections, on purpose to be introduced to them? How can you be so forgetful?"

"Phoo! phoo!" replied Charles, "what's an evening party? Never worth remembering. Your father might have asked us to dinner, I think, if he had wanted to see us. You may do as you like, but I shall go to the play."

"Oh! Charles, I declare it will be too abominable if you do, when you promised to go."

"No, I did not promise. I only smirked and bowed, and said the word 'happy.' There was no promise."

"But you must go, Charles. It would be unpardonable to fail. We were asked on purpose to be introduced. There was always such a great connection between the Dalrymples and ourselves. Nothing ever happened on either side that was not announced immediately. We are quite near relations, you know; and Mr. Elliot too, whom you ought so particularly to be acquainted with! Every attention is due to Mr. Elliot. Consider, my father's heir: the future representative of the family."

"Don't talk to me about heirs and representatives," cried Charles. "I am not one of those who neglect the reigning power to bow to the rising sun. If I would not go for the sake of your father, I should think it scandalous to go for the sake of his heir. What is Mr. Elliot to me?" The careless expression was life to Anne, who saw that Captain Wentworth was all attention, looking and listening with his whole soul; and that the last words brought his enquiring eyes from Charles to herself.

Charles and Mary still talked on in the same style; he, half serious and half jesting, maintaining the scheme for the play, and she, invariably serious, most warmly opposing it, and not omitting to make it known that, however determined to go to Camden Place herself, she should not think herself very well used, if they went to the play without her. Mrs. Musgrove interposed.

"We had better put it off. Charles, you had much better go back and change the box for Tuesday. It would be a pity to be divided, and we should be losing Miss Anne too, if there is a party at her father's; and I am sure neither Henrietta nor I should care at all for the play if Miss Anne could not be with us."

Anne felt truly obliged to her for such kindness; and quite as much so for the opportunity it gave her of decidedly saying:

"If it depended only on my inclination, ma'am, the party at home (excepting on Mary's account) would not be the smallest impediment. I have no pleasure in the sort of meeting, and should be too happy to change it for a play, and with you. But it had better not be attempted, perhaps." She had spoken it; but she trembled when it was done, conscious that her words were listened to, and daring not even to try to observe their effect.

It was soon generally agreed that Tuesday should be the day; Charles only reserving the advantage of still teasing his wife, by persisting that he would go to the play to-morrow, if nobody else would.

Captain Wentworth left his seat, and walked to the fireplace; probably for the sake of walking away from it soon afterwards, and taking a station, with less barefaced design, by Anne.

"You have not been long enough in Bath," said he, "to enjoy the evening parties of the place."

"Oh! no. The usual character of them has nothing for me. I am no card-player."

"You were not formerly, I know. You did not used to like cards; but time makes many changes."

"I am not yet so much changed," cried Anne, and stopped, fearing she hardly knew what misconstruction. After waiting a few moments he said, and as if it were the result of immediate feeling, "It is a period indeed! Eight years and a half is a period!"

Whether he would have proceeded further was left to Anne's imagination to ponder over in a calmer hour; for while still hearing the sounds he had uttered she was startled to other subjects by Henrietta, eager to make use of the present leisure for getting out, and calling on her companions to lose no time, lest somebody else should come in.

They were obliged to move. Anne talked of being perfectly ready, and tried to look it; but she felt that could Henrietta have known the regret and reluctance of her heart in quitting that chair, in preparing to quit the room, she would have found, in all her own sensations for her cousin, in the very security of his affection, wherewith to pity her.

Their preparations, however, were stopped short. Alarming sounds were heard; other visitors approached and the door was thrown open for Sir Walter and Miss Elliot, whose entrance seemed to give a general chill. Anne felt an instant oppression, and wherever she looked saw symptoms of the same. The comfort, the freedom, the gaiety of the room was over, hushed into cold composure, determined silence, or insipid talk, to meet the heartless elegance of her father and sister. How mortifying to feel that it was so!

Her jealous eye was satisfied in one particular. Captain Wentworth was acknowledged again by each, by Elizabeth more graciously than before. She even addressed him once, and looked at him more than once. Elizabeth was, in fact, revolving a great measure. The sequel explained it. After the waste of a few minutes in saying the proper nothings, she began to give the invitation which was to comprise all the remaining dues of the Musgroves. "To-morrow evening, to meet a few friends: no formal party." It was all said very gracefully, and the cards with which she had provided herself, the "Miss Elliot at home," were laid on the table, with a courteous, comprehensive smile to all, and one smile and one card more decidedly for Captain Wentworth. The truth was, that Elizabeth had been long enough in Bath to understand the importance of a man of such an air and appearance as his. The past was nothing. The present was that Captain Wentworth would move about well in her drawing-room. The card was pointedly given, and Sir Walter and Elizabeth arose and disappeared.

The interruption had been short though severe, and ease and animation returned to most of those they left as the door shut them out, but not to Anne. She could think only of the invitation she had with such astonishment witnessed, and of the manner in which it had been received: a manner of doubtful meaning, of surprise rather than gratification, of polite acknowledgment rather than acceptance. She knew him: she saw disdain in his eyes, and could not venture to believe that he had determined to accept such an offering as an atonement for all the insolence of the past. Her spirits sank. He held the card in his hand after they were gone, as if deeply considering it.

"Only think of Elizabeth's including everybody!" whispered Mary, very audibly. "I do not wonder Captain Wentworth is delighted! You see he cannot put the card out of his hand."

Anne caught his eye, saw his cheeks glow, and his mouth form itself into a momentary expression of contempt, and turned away, that she might neither see nor hear more to vex her.

The party separated. The gentlemen had their own pursuits, the ladies proceeded on their own business, and they met no more while Anne belonged to them. She was earnestly begged to return and dine, and give them all the rest of the day, but her spirits had been so long exerted that at present she felt unequal to more, and fit only for home, where she might be sure of being as silent as she chose.

Promising to be with them the whole of the following morning, therefore, she closed the fatigues of the present by a toilsome walk to Camden Place, there to spend the evening chiefly in listening to the busy arrangements of Elizabeth and Mrs. Clay for the morrow's party, the frequent enumeration of the persons invited, and the continually improving detail of all the embellishments which were to make it the most completely elegant of its kind in Bath, while harassing herself in secret with the never-ending question of whether Captain Wentworth would come or not? They were reckoning him as certain, but with her it was a gnawing solicitude never appeased for five minutes together. She generally thought he would come, because she generally thought he ought; but it was a case which she could not so shape into any positive act of duty or discretion, as inevitably to defy the suggestions of very opposite feelings.

She only roused herself from the broodings of this restless agitation, to let Mrs. Clay know that she had been seen

with Mr. Elliot three hours after his being supposed to be out of Bath, for, having watched in vain for some intimation of the interview from the lady herself, she determined to mention it, and it seemed to her that there was guilt in Mrs. Clay's face as she listened. It was transient: cleared away in an instant; but Anne could imagine she read there the consciousness of having, by some complication of mutual trick, or some overbearing authority of his, been obliged to attend (perhaps for half an hour) to his lectures and restrictions on her designs on Sir Walter. She exclaimed, however, with a very tolerable imitation of nature:

"Oh, dear! very true. Only think, Miss Elliot, to my great surprise I met with Mr. Elliot in Bath Street. I was never more astonished. He turned back and walked with me to the Pump Yard. He had been prevented setting off for Thornberry, but I really forget by what; for I was in a hurry, and could not much attend, and I can only answer for his being determined not to be delayed in his return. He wanted to know how early he might be admitted to-morrow. He was full of 'to-morrow,' and it is very evident that I have been full of it too, ever since I entered the house and learned the extension of your plan and all that had happened, or my seeing him could never have gone so entirely out of my head."

23

ONE DAY ONLY HAD PASSED since Anne's conversation with Mrs. Smith; but a keener interest had succeeded, and she was now so little touched by Mr. Elliot's conduct, except by its effects in one quarter, that it became a matter of course the next morning still to defer her explanatory visit in Rivers Street. She had promised to be with the Musgroves from breakfast to dinner. Her faith was plighted, and Mr. Elliot's character, like the Sultaness Scheherazade's head, must live another day.

She could not keep her appointment punctually, however; the weather was unfavourable, and she had grieved over the rain on her friend's account, and felt it very much on her own, before she was able to attempt the walk. When she reached the White Hart, and made her way to the proper apartment, she found herself neither arriving quite in time, nor the first to arrive. The party before her were, Mrs. Musgrove talking to Mrs. Croft, and Captain Harville to Captain Wentworth; and she immediately heard that Mary and Henrietta, too impatient to wait, had gone out the moment it had cleared, but would be back again soon, and that the strictest injunctions had been left with Mrs. Musgrove to keep her there till they returned. She had only to submit, sit down, be outwardly composed, and feel herself plunged at once in all the agitations which she had merely laid her account of tasting a little before the morning closed. There was no delay, no waste of time. She was deep in the happiness of such misery, or the misery of such happiness, instantly. Two minutes after her entering the room, Captain Wentworth said:

"We will write the letter we were talking of, Harville, now, if you will give me materials."

Materials were all at hand, on a separate table; he went to it, and nearly turning his back on them all, was engrossed by writing.

Mrs. Musgrove was giving Mrs. Croft the history of her eldest daughter's engagement, and just in that inconvenient tone of voice which was perfectly audible while it pretended to be a whisper. Anne felt that she did not belong to the conversation, and yet, as Captain Harville seemed thoughtful and not disposed to talk, she could not avoid hearing many undesirable particulars; such as, "how Mr. Musgrove and my brother Hayter had met again and again to talk it over; what my brother Hayter had said one day, and what Mr. Musgrove had proposed the next, and what had occurred to my sister Hayter, and what the young people had wished, and what I said at first I never could consent to, but was afterwards persuaded to think might do very well," and a great deal in the same style of open-hearted communication: minutiæ which, even with every advantage of taste and delicacy good Mrs. Musgrove could not give, could be properly interesting only to the principals. Mrs. Croft was attending with great good-humour, and whenever she spoke at all it was very sensibly. Anne hoped the gentlemen might each be too much self-occupied to hear.

"And so, ma'am, all these things considered," said Mrs. Musgrove, in her powerful whisper, "though we could have wished it different, yet, altogether, we did not think it fair to stand out any longer, for Charles Hayter was quite wild about it, and Henrietta was pretty near as bad; and so we thought they had better marry at once, and make the best of it, as many others have done before them. At any rate, said I, it will be better than a long engagement."

"That is precisely what I was going to observe," cried Mrs. Croft. "I would rather have young people settle on a small income at once, and have to struggle with a few difficulties together, than be involved in a long engagement. I always think that no mutual——"

"Oh! dear Mrs. Croft," cried Mrs. Musgrove, unable to let her finish her speech, "there is nothing I so abominate for young people as a long engagement. It is what I always protested against for my children. It is all very well, I used to say, for young people to be engaged, if there is a certainty of their being able to marry in six months, or even in twelve; but a long engagement——!"

"Yes, dear ma'am," said Mrs. Croft, "or an uncertain engagement, an engagement which may be long. To begin without knowing that at such a time there will be the means of marrying, I hold to be very unsafe and unwise, and what I think all parents should prevent as far as they can."

Anne found an unexpected interest here. She felt its application to herself, felt it in a nervous thrill all over her; and at the same moment that her eyes instinctively glanced towards the distant table, Captain Wentworth's pen ceased to move, his head was raised pausing, listening, and he turned round the next instant to give a look, one quick, conscious look at her.

The two ladies continued to talk, to re-urge the same admitted truths, and enforce them with such examples of the ill effect of a contrary practice as had fallen within their observation, but Anne heard nothing distinctly; it was only a buzz of words in her ear, her mind was in confusion.

Captain Harville, who had in truth been hearing none of it, now left his seat and moved to a window, and Anne seeming to watch him, though it was from thorough absence of mind, became gradually sensible that he was inviting her to join him where he stood. He looked at her with a smile, and a little motion of the head, which expressed, "Come to me, I have something to say;" and the unaffected, easy kindness of manner which denoted the feelings of an older acquaintance than he really was, strongly enforced the invitation. She roused herself and went to him. The window at which he stood was at the other end of the room from where the two ladies were sitting, and though nearer to Captain Wentworth's table, not very near. As she joined him, Captain Harville's countenance re-assumed the serious, thoughtful expression, which seemed its natural character.

"Look here," said he, unfolding a parcel in his hand, and displaying a small miniature painting; "do you know who that is?"

"Certainly; Captain Benwick."

"Yes, and you may guess who it is for. But" (in a deep tone), "it was not done for her. Miss Elliot, do you remember our walking together at Lyme, and grieving for him? I little thought then—but no matter. This was drawn at the Cape. He met with a clever young German artist at the Cape in compliance with a promise to my poor sister, sat to him, and was bringing it home for her; and I have now the charge of getting it properly set for another! It was a commission to me! But who else was there to employ? I hope I can allow for him. I am not sorry, indeed, to make it over to another. He undertakes it;" (looking towards Captain Wentworth) "he is writing about it now." And with a quivering lip he wound up the whole by adding, "Poor Fanny! she would not have forgotten him so soon."

"No," replied Anne, in a low feeling voice, "that I can easily believe."

"It was not in her nature. She doted on him."

"It would not be the nature of any woman who truly loved."

Captain Harville smiled, as much as to say, "Do you claim that for your sex?" and she answered the question, smiling also, "Yes. We certainly do not forget you so soon as you forget us. It is, perhaps, our fate rather than our merit. We cannot help ourselves. We live at home, quiet, confined, and our feelings prey upon us. You are forced on exertion. You have always a profession, pursuits, business of some sort or other, to take you back into the world immediately, and continual occupation and change soon weaken impressions."

"Granting your assertion that the world does all this so soon for men (which, however, I do not think I shall grant), it does not apply to Benwick. He has not been forced upon any exertion. The peace turned him on shore at the very moment, and he has been living with us, in our little family circle, ever since."

"True," said Anne, "very true; I did not recollect; but what shall we say now, Captain Harville? If the change be not from outward circumstances, it must be from within; it must be nature, man's nature, which has done the business for Captain Benwick."

"No, no, it is not man's nature. I will not allow it to be more man's nature than woman's to be inconstant and forget those they do love, or have loved. I believe the reverse. I believe in a true analogy between our bodily frames and our mental; and that as our bodies are the strongest, so are our feelings; capable of bearing most rough usage, and riding out the heaviest weather."

"Your feelings may be the strongest," replied Anne, "but the same spirit of analogy will authorise me to assert that ours are the most tender. Man is more robust than woman, but he is not longer lived; which exactly explains my view of the nature of their attachments. Nay, it would be too hard upon you, if it were otherwise. You have difficulties, and privations, and dangers enough to struggle with. You are always labouring and toiling, exposed to every risk and hardship. Your home, country, friends, all quitted. Neither time, nor health, nor life, to be called your own. It would be too hard, indeed" (with a faltering voice), "if woman's feelings were to be added to all this."

"We shall never agree upon this question," Captain Harville was beginning to say, when a slight noise called their attention to Captain Wentworth's hitherto perfectly quiet division of the room. It was nothing more than that his pen had fallen down; but Anne was startled at finding him nearer than she had supposed, and half inclined to suspect that the pen had only fallen because he had been occupied by them, striving to catch sounds, which yet she did not think he could have caught.

"Have you finished your letter?" said Captain Harville.

"Not quite, a few lines more. I shall have done in five minutes."

"There is no hurry on my side. I am only ready whenever you are. I am in very good anchorage here" (smiling at

Anne), "well supplied and want for nothing. No hurry for a signal at all. Well, Miss Elliot" (lowering his voice), "as I was saying, we shall never agree, I suppose, upon this point. No man and woman would, probably. But let me observe that all histories are against you — all stories, prose and verse. If I had such a memory as Benwick, I could bring you fifty quotations in a moment on my side of the argument, and I do not think I ever opened a book in my life which had not something to say upon woman's inconstancy. Songs and proverbs all talk of woman's fickleness. But, perhaps, you will say, these were all written by men."

"Perhaps I shall. Yes, yes, if you please, no reference to examples in books. Men have had every advantage of us in telling their own story. Education has been theirs in so much higher a degree; the pen has been in their hands. I will not allow books to prove anything."

"But how shall we prove anything?"

"We never shall. We never can expect to prove anything upon such a point. It is a difference of opinion which does not admit of proof. We each begin, probably, with a little bias towards our own sex; and upon that bias build every circumstance in favour of it which has occurred within our own circle; many of which circumstances (perhaps those very cases which strike us the most) may be precisely such as cannot be brought forward without betraying a confidence, or in some respect, saying what should not be said."

"Ah!" cried Captain Harville, in a tone of strong feeling, "if I could but make you comprehend what a man suffers when he takes a last look at his wife and children, and watches the boat that he has sent them off in, as long as it is in sight, and then turns away and says, 'God knows whether we ever meet again!' And then, if I could convey to you the glow of his soul when he does see them again; when, coming back after a twelvemonth's absence, perhaps, and obliged to put into another port, he calculates how soon it be possible to get them there, pretending to deceive himself, and saying, 'They cannot be here till such a day,' but all the while hoping for them twelve hours sooner, and seeing them arrive at last, as if Heaven had given them wings, by many hours sooner still! If I could explain to you all this, and all that a man can bear and do, and glories to do, for the sake of these treasures of his existence! I speak, you know, only of such men as have hearts!" pressing his own with emotion.

"Oh!" cried Anne, eagerly, "I hope to do justice to all that is felt by you, and by those who resemble you. God forbid that I should under-value the warm and faithful feelings of any of my fellow creatures! I should deserve utter contempt if I dared to suppose that true attachment and constancy were known only by woman. No, I believe you capable of everything great and good in your married lives. I believe you equal to every important exertion, and to every domestic forbearance, so long as—if I may be allowed the expression, so long as you have an object. I mean while the woman you love lives, and lives for you. All the privilege I claim for my own sex (it is not a very enviable one: you need not covet it), is that of loving longest, when existence or when hope is gone!"

She could not immediately have uttered another sentence; her heart was too full, her breath too much oppressed.

"You are a good soul," cried Captain Harville, putting his hand on her arm, quite affectionately. "There is no quarrelling with you. And when I think of Benwick, my tongue is tied."

Their attention was called towards the others. Mrs. Croft was taking leave.

"Here, Frederick, you and I part company, I believe," said

she. "I am going home, and you have an engagement with your friend. To-night we may have the pleasure of all meeting again at your party" (turning to Anne). "We had your sister's card yesterday, and I understood Frederick had a card too, though I did not see it; and you are disengaged, Frederick, are you not, as well as ourselves?"

Captain Wentworth was folding up a letter in great haste, and either could not or would not answer fully.

"Yes," said he, "very true; here we separate, but Harville and I shall soon be after you; that is, Harville, if you are ready, I am in half a minute. I know you will not be sorry to be off. I shall be at your service in half a minute."

Mrs. Croft left them, and Captain Wentworth, having sealed his letter with great rapidity, was indeed ready, and had even a hurried, agitated air, which showed impatience to be gone. Anne knew not how to understand it. She had the kindest "Good morning, God bless you!" from Captain Harville, but from him not a word, nor a look! He had passed out of the room without a look!

She had only time, however, to move closer to the table where he had been writing, when footsteps were heard returning; the door opened, it was himself. He begged their pardon, but he had forgotten his gloves, and instantly crossing the room to the writing table, and standing with his back towards Mrs. Musgrove, he drew out a letter from under the scattered paper, placed it before Anne with eyes of glowing entreaty fixed on her for a time, and hastily collecting his gloves, was again out of the room, almost before Mrs. Musgrove was aware of his being in it: the work of an instant!

The revolution which one instant had made in Anne was almost beyond expression. The letter, with a direction hardly legible, to "Miss A. E——," was evidently the one which he had been folding so hastily. While supposed to be writing only to Captain Benwick he had been also addressing her!

On the contents of that letter depended all which this world could do for her. Anything was possible, anything might be defied rather than suspense. Mrs. Musgrove had little arrangements of her own at her own table; to their protection she must trust, and, sinking into the chair which he had occupied, succeeding to the very spot where he had leaned and written, her eyes devoured the following words:

I can listen no longer in silence. I must speak to you by such means as are within my reach. You pierce my soul. I am half agony, half hope. Tell me not that I am too late, that such precious feelings are gone for ever. I offer myself to you again with a heart even more your own than when you almost broke it, eight years and a half ago. Dare not say that man forgets sooner than woman, that his love has an earlier death. I have loved none but you. Unjust I may have been, weak and resentful I have been, but never inconstant. You alone have brought me to Bath. For you alone, I think and plan. Have you not seen this? Can you fail to have understood my wishes? I had not waited even these ten days, could I have read your feelings, as I think you must have penetrated mine. I can hardly write. I am every instant hearing something which overpowers me. You sink your voice, but I can distinguish the tones of that voice when they would be lost on others. Too good, too excellent creature! You do us justice, indeed. You do believe that there is true attachment and constancy among men. Believe it to be most fervent, most undeviating, in

F. W.

I must go, uncertain of my fate; but I shall return hither, or follow your party, as soon as possible. A word, a look, will be enough to decide whether I enter your father's house this evening or never.

Such a letter was not to be soon recovered from. Half an hour's solitude and reflection might have tranquillised her; but the ten minutes only which now passed before she was interrupted, with all the restraints of her situation, could do nothing towards tranquillity. Every moment rather brought fresh agitation. It was an overpowering happiness. And before she was beyond the first stage of full sensation, Charles, Mary, and Henrietta, all came in.

The absolute necessity of seeming like herself produced then an immediate struggle; but after a while she could do no more. She began not to understand a word they said, and was obliged to plead indisposition and excuse herself. They could then see that she looked very ill, were shocked and concerned, and would not stir without her for the world. This was dreadful. Would they only have gone away, and left her in the quiet possession of that room it would have been her cure; but to have them all standing or waiting around her was distracting, and in desperation, she said she would go home.

"By all means, my dear," cried Mrs. Musgrove, "go home directly, and take care of yourself, that you may be fit for the evening. I wish Sarah was here to doctor you, but I am no doctor myself. Charles, ring and order a chair. She must not walk."

But the chair would never do. Worse than all! To lose the possibility of speaking two words to Captain Wentworth in the course of her quiet, solitary progress up the town (and she felt almost certain of meeting him) could not be borne.

The chair was earnestly protested against, and Mrs. Musgrove, who thought only of one sort of illness, having assured herself with some anxiety, that there had been no fall in the case; that Anne had not at any time lately slipped down, and got a blow on her head; that she was perfectly convinced of having had no fall; could part with her cheerfully, and depend on finding her better at night.

Anxious to omit no precaution, Anne struggled, and said:

"I am afraid, ma'am, that it is not perfectly understood. Pray be so good as to mention to the other gentlemen that we hope to see your whole party this evening. I am afraid there has been some mistake; and I wish you particularly to assure Captain Harville and Captain Wentworth, that we hope to see them both."

"Oh; my dear, it is quite understood, I give you my word. Captain Harville has no thought but of going."

"Do you think so? But I am afraid; and I should be so very sorry. Will you promise me to mention it when you see them again? You will see them both again this morning, I dare say. Do promise me."

"To be sure I will, if you wish it. Charles, if you see Captain Harville anywhere, remember to give Miss Anne's message. But, indeed, my dear, you need not be uneasy. Captain Harville holds himself quite engaged, I'll answer for it; and Captain Wentworth the same, I dare say."

Anne could do no more; but her heart prophesied some mischance to damp the perfection of her felicity. It could not be very lasting, however. Even if he did not come to Camden Place himself, it would be in her power to send an intelligible sentence by Captain Harville. Another momentary vexation occurred. Charles, in his real concern and good nature, would go home with her; there was no preventing him. This was almost cruel. But she could not be long ungrateful; he was sacrificing an engagement at a gunsmith's to be of use to her, and she set off with him, with no feeling but gratitude apparent.

They were in Union Street, when a quicker step behind, a something of familiar sound, gave her two moments' preparation for the sight of Captain Wentworth. He joined them; but, as if irresolute whether to join or to pass on, said nothing, only looked. Anne could command herself enough to receive that look, and not repulsively. The cheeks which had been pale now glowed, and the movements which had hesitated were decided. He walked by her side. Presently, struck by a sudden thought, Charles said:

"Captain Wentworth, which way are you going? Only to Gay Street, or farther up the town?"

"I hardly know," replied Captain Wentworth, surprised.

"Are you going as high as Belmont? Are you going near Camden Place? Because, if you are, I shall have no scruple in asking you to take my place, and give Anne your arm to her father's door. She is rather done for this morning, and must not go so far without help, and I ought to be at that fellow's in the Market Place. He promised me the sight of a capital gun he is just going to send off; said he would keep it unpacked to the last possible moment, that I might see it; and if I do not turn back now, I have no chance. By his description, a good deal like the second sized double-barrel of mine, which you shot with one day round Winthrop."

There could not be an objection. There could be only a most proper alacrity, a most obliging compliance for public view; and smiles reined in and spirits dancing in private rapture. In half a minute Charles was at the bottom of Union Street again, and the other two proceeding together: and soon words enough had passed between them to decide their direction towards the comparatively quiet and retired gravel walk, where the power of conversation would make the present hour a blessing indeed, and prepare it for all the immortality which the happiest recollections of their own future lives could bestow. There they exchanged again those feelings and those promises which had once before seemed to secure everything, but which had been followed by so many, many years of division and estrangement. There they returned again into the past, more exquisitely happy, perhaps, in their reunion, than when it had been first projected; more tender, more tried, more fixed in a knowledge of each other's character, truth, and attachment; more equal to act, more justified in acting. And there, as they slowly paced the gradual ascent, heedless of every group around them, seeing neither sauntering politicians, bustling housekeepers, flirting girls, nor nursery-maids and children, they could indulge in those retrospections and acknowledgments, and especially in those explanations of what had directly preceded the present moment, which were so poignant and so ceaseless in interest. All the little variations of the last week were gone through; and of yesterday and to-day there could scarcely be an end.

She had not mistaken him. Jealousy of Mr. Elliot had been the retarding weight, the doubt, the torment. That had begun to operate in the very hour of first meeting her in Bath; that had returned, after a short suspension, to ruin the concert; and that had influenced him in everything he had said and done, or omitted to say and do, in the last four-and-twenty hours. It had been gradually yielding to the better hopes which her looks, or words, or actions occasionally encouraged; it had been vanquished at last by those sentiments and those tones which had reached him while she talked with Captain Harville; and under the irresistible governance of which he had seized a sheet of paper, and poured out his feelings.

Of what he had then written nothing was to be retracted or qualified. He persisted in having loved none but her. She had never been supplanted. He never even believed himself to see her equal. Thus much, indeed, he was obliged to acknowledge: that he had been constant unconsciously, nay unintentionally; that he had meant to forget her, and believed it to be done. He had imagined himself indifferent, when he had only been angry; and he had been unjust to her merits, because he had been a sufferer from them. Her character was now fixed on his mind as perfection itself, maintaining the loveliest medium of fortitude and gentleness; but he was obliged to acknowledge that only at Uppercross had he learnt to do her justice, and only at Lyme had he begun to understand himself. At Lyme he had received lessons of more than one sort. The passing admiration of Mr. Elliot had at least roused him, and the scenes on the Cobb and at Captain Harville's had fixed her superiority.

In his preceding attempts to attach himself to Louisa Musgrove (the attempts of angry pride), he protested that he had for ever felt it to be impossible; that he had not cared, could not care, for Louisa; though till that day, till the leisure for reflection which followed it, he had not understood the perfect excellence of the mind with which Louisa's could so ill bear a comparison, or the perfect unrivalled hold it possessed over his own. There, he had learnt to distinguish between the steadiness of principle and the obstinacy of self-will, between the darings of heedlessness and the resolution of a collected mind. There he had seen everything to exalt in his estimation the woman he had lost; and there

begun to deplore the pride, the folly, the madness of resentment, which had kept him from trying to regain her
when thrown in his way.

From that period his penance had become severe. He had
no sooner been free from the horror and remorse attending
the first few days of Louisa's accident, no sooner begun to
feel himself alive again, than he had begun to feel himself,
though alive, not at liberty.

"I found," said he, "that I was considered by Harville
an engaged man! That neither Harville nor his wife entertained a doubt of our mutual attachment. I was startled and
shocked. To a degree, I could contradict this instantly; but,
when I began to reflect that others might have felt the
same—her own family, nay, perhaps herself—I was no longer
at my own disposal. I was hers in honour if she wished it. I
had been unguarded. I had not thought seriously on this
subject before. I had not considered that my excessive intimacy must have its danger of ill consequence in many
ways; and that I had no right to be trying whether I could
attach myself to either of the girls, at the risk of raising even
an unpleasant report, were there no other ill effects. I had
been grossly wrong, and must abide the consequences."

He found too late, in short, that he had entangled himself; and that precisely as he became fully satisfied of his
not caring for Louisa at all he must regard himself as bound
to her, if her sentiments for him were what the Harvilles
supposed. It determined him to leave Lyme, and await her
complete recovery elsewhere. He would gladly weaken, by
any fair means, whatever feelings or speculations concerning him might exist; and he went, therefore, to his brother's,
meaning after a while to return to Kellynch, and act as circumstances might require.

"I was six weeks with Edward," said he, "and saw him

happy. I could have no other pleasure. I deserved none. He enquired after you very particularly; asked even if you were personally altered, little suspecting that to my eye you could never alter."

Anne smiled, and let it pass. It was too pleasing a blunder for a reproach. It is something for a woman to be assured, in her eight-and-twentieth year, that she has not lost one charm of earlier youth: but the value of such homage was inexpressibly increased to Anne, by comparing it with former words, and feeling it to be the result, not the cause, of a revival of his warm attachment.

He had remained in Shropshire, lamenting the blindness of his own pride, and the blunders of his own calculations, till at once released from Louisa by the astonishing and felicitous intelligence of her engagement with Benwick.

"Here," said he, "ended the worst of my state; for now I could at least put myself in the way of happiness; I could exert myself; I could do something. But to be waiting so long in inaction, and waiting only for evil, had been dreadful. Within the first five minutes I said, 'I will be at Bath on Wednesday,' and I was. Was it unpardonable to think it worth my while to come? and to arrive with some degree of hope? You were single. It was possible that you might retain the feelings of the past, as I did: and one encouragement happened to be mine. I could never doubt that you would be loved and sought by others, but I knew to a certainty that you had refused one man, at least, of better pretensions than myself; and I could not help often saying, 'Was this for me?'"

Their first meeting in Milsom Street afforded much to be said, but the concert still more. That evening seemed to be made up of exquisite moments. The moment of her stepping forward in the Octagon Room to speak to him: the moment of Mr. Elliot's appearing and tearing her away, and one or two subsequent moments, marked by returning hope or increasing despondency, were dwelt on with energy.

"To see you," cried he, "in the midst of those who could not be my well-wishers; to see your cousin close by you, conversing and smiling, and feel all the horrible eligibilities and proprieties of the match! To consider it as the certain wish of every being who could hope to influence you! Even if your own feelings were reluctant or indifferent, to consider what powerful supports would be his! Was it not enough to make the fool of me which I appeared? How could I look on without agony? Was not the very sight of the friend who sat behind you, was not the recollection of what had been, the knowledge of her influence, the indelible, immovable impression of what persuasion had once done—was it not all against me?"

"You should have distinguished," replied Anne. "You should not have suspected me now; the case so different, and my age so different. If I was wrong in yielding to persuasion once, remember that it was to persuasion exerted on the side of safety, not of risk. When I yielded, I thought it was to duty, but no duty could be called in aid here. In marrying a man indifferent to me, all risk would have been incurred, and all duty violated."

"Perhaps I ought to have reasoned thus," he replied, "but I could not. I could not derive benefit from the late knowledge I had acquired of your character. I could not bring it into play; it was overwhelmed, buried, lost in those earlier feelings which I had been smarting under year after year. I could think of you only as one who had yielded, who had given me up, who had been influenced by anyone rather than by me. I saw you with the very person who had guided you in that year of misery. I had no reason to believe her of less authority now. The force of habit was to be added."

"I should have thought," said Anne, "that my manner to yourself might have spared you much or all of this."

"No, no! Your manner might be only the ease which your engagement to another man would give. I left you in this belief; and yet, I was determined to see you again. My spirits rallied with the morning, and I felt that I had still a motive for remaining here."

At last Anne was at home again, and happier than any one in that house could have conceived. All the surprise and suspense, and every other painful part of the morning dissipated by this conversation, she re-entered the house so happy as to be obliged to find an alloy in some momentary apprehensions of its being impossible to last. An interval of meditation, serious and grateful, was the best corrective of everything dangerous in such high-wrought felicity; and she went to her room, and grew steadfast and fearless in the thankfulness of her enjoyment.

The evening come, the drawing-rooms were lighted up, the company assembled. It was but a card-party, it was but a mixture of those who had never met before, and those who met too often: a common place business, too numerous for intimacy, too small for variety; but Anne had never found an evening shorter. Glowing and lovely in sensibility and happiness, and more generally admired than she thought about or cared for, she had cheerful or forbearing feelings for every creature around her. Mr. Elliot was there; she avoided, but she could pity him. The Wallises, she had amusement in understanding them. Lady Dalrymple and Miss Carteret—they would soon be innoxious cousins to her. She cared not for Mrs. Clay, and had nothing to blush for in the public manners of her father and sister. With the Musgroves there was the happy chat of perfect ease; with Captain Harville, the kind-hearted intercourse of brother and sister; with Lady Russell, attempts at conversation, which a delicious consciousness cut short; with Admiral and Mrs. Croft, everything of peculiar cordiality and fervent interest, which the same consciousness sought to conceal; and with Captain Wentworth, some moments of communication continually occurring, and always the hope of more, and always the knowledge of his being there.

It was in one of these short meetings, each apparently occupied in admiring a fine display of greenhouse plants, that she said:

"I have been thinking over the past, and trying impartially to judge of the right and wrong, I mean with regard to myself; and I must believe that I was right, much as I suffered from it, that I was perfectly right in being guided by the friend whom you will love better than you do now. To me, she was in the place of a parent. Do not mistake me, however. I am not saying that she did not err in her advice. It was, perhaps, one of those cases in which advice is good or bad only as the event decides; and for myself, I certainly never should, in any circumstance of tolerable similarity, give such advice. But I mean, that I was right in submitting to her, and that if I had done otherwise, I should have suffered more in continuing the engagement than I did even in giving it up, because I should have suffered in my conscience. I have now, as far as such a sentiment is allowable in human nature, nothing to reproach myself with; and if I mistake not, a strong sense of duty is no bad part of a woman's portion."

He looked at her, looked at Lady Russell, and looking again at her, replied, as if in cool deliberation:

"Not yet, but there are hopes of her being forgiven in time. I trust to being in charity with her soon. But I too have been thinking over the past, and a question has suggested itself, whether there may not have been one person more my enemy even than that lady? My own self. Tell me if, when I returned to England, in the year eight, with a few thousand pounds, and was posted into the *Laconia*, if I had then written to you, would you have answered my letter? Would you, in short, have renewed the engagement then?"

"Would I?" was all her answer; but the accent was decisive enough.

"Good God!" he cried, "you would! It is not that I did not think of it, or desire it, as what could alone crown all my other success; but I was proud, too proud to ask again. I did not understand you. I shut my eyes, and would not understand you, or do you justice. This is a recollection which ought to make me forgive everyone sooner than myself. Six years of separation and suffering might have been spared. It is a sort of pain, too, which is new to me. I have been used to the gratification of believing myself to earn every blessing that I enjoyed. I have valued myself on honourable toils and just rewards. Like other great men under reverses," he added, with a smile, "I must endeavour to subdue my mind to my fortune. I must learn to brook being happier than I deserve."

24

WHO CAN BE IN DOUBT of what followed? When any two young people take it into their heads to marry, they are pretty sure by perseverance to carry their point, be they ever so poor, or ever so imprudent, or ever so little likely to be necessary to each other's ultimate comfort. This may be bad morality to conclude with, but I believe it to be truth; and if such parties succeed, how should a Captain Wentworth and an Anne Elliot, with the advantage of maturity of mind, consciousness of right, and one independent fortune between them, fail of bearing down every opposition? They might, in fact, have borne down a great deal more than they met with, for there was little to distress them beyond the want of graciousness and warmth. Sir Walter made no objection, and Elizabeth did nothing worse than look cold and unconcerned. Captain Wentworth, with five-and-twenty thousand pounds, and as high in his profession as merit and activity could place him, was no longer nobody. He was now esteemed quite worthy to address the daughter of a foolish, spendthrift baronet, who had not had principle or sense enough to maintain himself in the situation in which Providence had placed him, and who could give his daughter at present but a small part of the share of ten thousand pounds which must be hers hereafter.

Sir Walter, indeed, though he had no affection for Anne, had no vanity flattered, to make him really happy on the occasion, was very far from thinking it a bad match for her. On the contrary, when he saw more of Captain Wentworth, saw him repeatedly by daylight, and eyed him well, he was very much struck by his personal claims, and felt that his superiority of appearance might not be unfairly balanced against her superiority of rank; and all this, assisted by his well-sounding name, enabled Sir Walter, at last, to prepare his pen, with a very good grace, for the insertion of the marriage in the volume of honour.

The only one among them whose opposition of feeling could excite any serious anxiety was Lady Russell. Anne knew that Lady Russell must be suffering some pain in understanding and relinquishing Mr. Elliot, and be making some struggles to become truly acquainted with, and do justice to Captain Wentworth. This, however, was what Lady Russell had now to do. She must learn to feel that she had been mistaken with regard to both; that she had been unfairly influenced by appearances in each; that because Captain Wentworth's manners had not suited her own ideas she had been too quick in suspecting them to indicate a character of dangerous impetuosity; and that because Mr. Elliot's manners had precisely pleased her in their propriety and correctness, their general politeness and suavity, she had been too quick in receiving them as the certain result of the most correct opinions and well-regulated mind. There was nothing less for Lady Russell to do than to admit that she had been pretty completely wrong, and to take up a new set of opinions and of hopes.

There is a quickness of perception in some, a nicety in the discernment of character, a natural penetration, in short, which no experience in others can equal, and Lady Russell had been less gifted in this part of understanding than her young friend. But she was a very good woman, and if her second object was to be sensible and well-judging, her first was to see Anne happy. She loved Anne better than she loved her own abilities; and, when the awkwardness of the beginning was over, found little hardship in attaching herself as a mother to the man who was securing the happiness of her other child.

Of all the family, Mary was probably the one most immediately gratified by the circumstance. It was creditable to have a sister married, and she might flatter herself with having been greatly instrumental to the connection, by keeping Anne with her in the autumn; and as her own sister must be better than her husband's sisters, it was very agreeable that Captain Wentworth should be a richer man than either Captain Benwick or Charles Hayter. She had something to suffer, perhaps, when they came into contact again, in seeing Anne restored to the rights of seniority, and the mistress of a very pretty landaulette; but she had a future to look forward to of powerful consolation. Anne had no Uppercross Hall before her, no landed estate, no headship of a family; and if they could but keep Captain Wentworth from being made a baronet, she would not change situations with Anne.

It would be well for the eldest sister if she were equally satisfied with her situation, for a change is not very probable there. She had soon the mortification of seeing Mr. Elliot withdraw, and no one of proper condition has since presented himself to raise even the unfounded hopes which sunk with him.

The news of his cousin Anne's engagement burst on Mr. Elliot most unexpectedly. It deranged his best plan of domestic happiness, his best hope of keeping Sir Walter single by the watchfulness which a son-in-law's rights would have given. But, though discomfited and disappointed, he could still do something for his own interest and his own enjoyment. He soon quitted Bath; and on Mrs. Clay's quitting it soon afterwards, and being next heard of as established under his protection in London, it was evident how double a game he had been playing, and how determined he was to save himself from being cut out by one artful woman, at least.

Mrs. Clay's affections had overpowered her interest, and she had sacrificed, for the young man's sake, the possibility of scheming longer for Sir Walter. She has abilities, however, as well as affections; and it is now a doubtful point whether his cunning, or hers, may finally carry the day; whether, after preventing her from being the wife of Sir Walter, he may not be wheedled and caressed at last into making her the wife of Sir William.

It cannot be doubted that Sir Walter and Elizabeth were shocked and mortified by the loss of their companion, and the discovery of their deception in her. They had their great cousins, to be sure, to resort to for comfort; but they must long feel that to flatter and follow others, without being flattered and followed in turn, is but a state of half enjoyment.

Anne, satisfied at a very early period of Lady Russell's meaning to love Captain Wentworth as she ought, had no other alloy to the happiness of her prospects than what arose from the consciousness of having no relations to bestow on him which a man of sense could value. There she felt her own inferiority keenly. The disproportion in their fortune was nothing; it did not give her a moment's regret; but to have no family to receive and estimate him properly, nothing of respectability, of harmony, of goodwill, to offer in return for all the worth and all the prompt welcome which met her in his brothers and sisters, was a source of as lively pain as her mind could well be sensible of under circumstances of otherwise strong felicity. She had but two friends in the world to add to his list, Lady Russell and Mrs. Smith. To those, however, he was very well disposed to attach himself. Lady Russell, in spite of all her former transgressions, he could now value from his heart. While he was not obliged to say that he believed her to have been right in originally dividing them, he was ready to say almost everything else in her favour, and as for Mrs. Smith, she had claims of various kinds to recommend her quickly and permanently.

Her recent good offices by Anne had been enough in themselves, and their marriage, instead of depriving her of one friend, secured her two. She was their earliest visitor in their settled life, and Captain Wentworth, by putting her in the way of recovering her husband's property in the West Indies, by writing for her, acting for her, and seeing her through all the petty difficulties of the case with the activity and exertion of a fearless man and a determined friend, fully requited the services which she had rendered, or ever meant to render, to his wife.

Mrs. Smith's enjoyments were not spoiled by this improvement of income, with some improvement of health, and the acquisition of such friends to be often with, for her cheerfulness and mental alacrity did not fail her; and while these prime supplies of good remained, she might have bid defiance even to greater accessions of worldly prosperity. She might have been absolutely rich and perfectly healthy, and yet be happy. Her spring of felicity was in the glow of her spirits, as her friend Anne's was in the warmth of her heart. Anne was tenderness itself, and she had the full worth of it in Captain Wentworth's affection. His profession was all that could ever make her friends wish that tenderness less, the dread of a future war all that could dim her sunshine. She gloried in being a sailor's wife, but she must pay the tax of quick alarm for belonging to that profession which is, if possible, more distinguished in its domestic virtues than in its national importance.

FINIS

TALLY HALL PRESS CLASSICS
are typeset in Berthold Bodoni Old Face,
designed in 1983 by Günter Gerhard Lange
after the classic typefaces of
Giambattista Bodoni (1740–1813),
the Italian father of the Modern style.

Characterized by vertical stress, flat serifs,
and strong contrast between thick and thin strokes,
Bodoni's faces were considered radical in their time.
Many present-day versions are cold and mechanical,
but Lange's produces a clarity, warmth, and dignity
ideally suited to the wide range of literature
published by Tally Hall Press.

Berthold Bodoni Old Face is accompanied as display by
Walbaum, designed in 1934 by the Monotype Design Sta
after Justus Erich Walbaum's 1803 face, and
Copperplate, designed in 1901 by Frederic W. Goudy.

Tally Hall Press classics are
designed, typeset, and produced by
Impressions Book and Journal Services, Inc.,
Madison, Wisconsin, and Ann Arbor, Michigan.

Designed by William Kasdorf